"What kind of perso

"I don't really know that," Hunt said. "Do I?"

"You know a whole lot more about me than I do about you." Yancy threw that at him, tight and quivering with emotions, three years worth of fear and uncertainty and unanswered questions. "I live my life in the public eye. You live yours in the shadows. You're a—a—"

"Ghost?" A single word, spoken softly in the darkness.

Her chest constricted with the pain of remembering. She gave a helpless whimper of a laugh and turned away from him.

"Why did I keep Laila with me, and not hand her off to some stranger?" She paused, then took a careful breath and answered truthfully. "At first, I guess it was because she seemed so...lost. So scared. The way she looked at me...as if she trusted me."

"I told her she could."

How different his voice sounded. Did she only imagine it was emotion she heard? Or was she projecting her own inner turmoil onto him? Surely the Hunt Grainger she knew would never allow himself to be caught in such an unguarded moment.

But then, I really don't know him at all.

* * *

Stay tuned for the next book in Kathleen Creighton's Scandals of Sierra Malone miniseries.

If you're on Twitter, tell us what you think of Harlequin Romantic Suspense! #harlequinromsuspense

Dear Reader,

It's been a while since I last asked you to journey with me to beautiful June Canyon, California, where reclusive eccentric billionaire "Sierra" Sam Malone is attempting to atone for a lifetime of scandalous and reckless behavior. It was not my intention to stay away so long. After all, there are stories yet to be told, at least two more heirs for Sam to meet, two more granddaughters who may, possibly, come to forgive him. Maybe even learn to love him.

What is it someone supposedly has said? Life is what happens to you while you're busy making other plans?

Sometimes unexpected events can turn your life in a whole new direction, and it's not always easy to find your footing on this new and often rocky path. In a way, that's what happens to Yancy Malone and Hunt Grainger, as something neither of them could have foreseen turns their lives upside down, and sends them on a journey neither of them could have imagined. In the course of this journey they must experience tragedy and danger, duty and sacrifice, heartache and loss, before they can finally come to a place where both can accept, forgive... and love.

This is Yancy and Hunt's love story, true. But it's the story of another sort of love, too. The story of how "the soldier's secret" brings unexpected light and joy to an old man's heart.

Journey with me now, back to June Canyon...

Kathleen

GUARDING THE
SOLDIER'S SECRET

Kathleen Creighton

HARLEQUIN® ROMANTIC SUSPENSE

Recycling programs
for this product may
not exist in your area.

ISBN-13: 978-0-373-28199-2

Guarding the Soldier's Secret

Printed in U.S.A.

Kathleen Creighton has roots deep in the California soil but has relocated to South Carolina. As a child, she enjoyed listening to old-timers' tales, and her fascination with the past only deepened as she grew older. Today, she is interested in everything—art, music, gardening, zoology, anthropology and history—but people are at the top of her list. She also has a lifelong passion for writing, and now combines all her loves in romance novels.

This book is for my children.
I am never so proud of you as
when life knocks you down,
and you somehow manage to
pick yourselves up and go on,
stronger than ever.

*too hot. The mother dog liked it, too, because she
'd see what was outside but nobody could see her
er puppies.*

was a good place. A safe place.

*On that day, Laila went one last time to say good-
t to the puppies. She knew it was time to go in-
for supper and to learn the lessons her mother
teaching her. Someday she would go to school—
mother had told her so—and she must be ready so
other children wouldn't think she was stupid. But it
so much fun to hold the puppies under her chin and
them tickle her neck with their little wet noses and
r the cute grunting sounds puppies make, while the
her dog watched, not minding at all. Laila's mother
already called her once, but...oh, just a few more
utes, she told herself, and then she would go.*

*he heard a new sound and caught a breath and held
she could listen. Yes—it was a truck coming along
dirt road, coming to their house! Not very many
ple came this way, especially not in a truck. Laila's
rt gave a little* bump. *Maybe it was Akaa Hunt! It
' been such a long time since he had come to visit.
Carefully she put the puppy she was holding back be-
its mother. She was about to crawl out of her hid-
place when something stopped her.*

*The mother dog was growling. It was a scary sound,
Laila had never heard her make before. The yel-
hair on the back of the mother dog's neck was stick-
up, and her teeth were showing. They were very big
h. Slowly Laila backed up and shrank into the shad-
, and the mother dog stopped growling and licked
muzzle and whimpered softly, almost, Laila thought,
f she was saying* I'm sorry.

Now Laila couldn't see the truck because it had

Introduction

From the Memoirs of Sierra Sam Malone:

*The day the railroad bulls beat me to a pulp and
threw me off the train in the middle of a California desert, I wouldn't have bet a wooden nickel
on my chances of living to see another sunrise.
Who would have thought I'd live to become one
of the richest men in the country and make movies
and hobnob with the biggest and brightest stars in
Hollywood. Hobnob, hell, I bought and sold 'em.*

Married one, too.

*Barbara Chase wasn't the first beautiful woman
fool enough to marry me, but after she left her baby
girl with a sitter and her clothes on a Malibu beach
and walked into the sunset, I swore she'd be the
last. The way I'd treated my first wife, Elizabeth,
causing her to want no part of me in her life or our*

son's, and now Barbara taking the way out she did, made it pretty clear to me I was not fit husband material. Or father material, either, for that matter. Which is why I sent my baby daughter off to be raised by Barbara's folks in Nebraska.

Which turned out to be another mistake, but that's another story.

So, I had sworn off love, after Barbara, though not off women. No...never off women. Of those there was always a plentiful supply, easily available and more than willing to please me. Mine for the taking. And I took without conscience or regrets.

When Katherine came to me with a sensible business proposition, I thought it seemed like a good idea at the time. Power and prestige, in exchange for the thing that mattered the least to me—money. The funny thing was, we were a good match, Kate and I, and we lasted longer than either of us expected.

But when tragedy struck, we lacked the one thing that might have seen us through the storm. And that was love.

Prologue

Somewhere in eastern Afghanistan
Three years previous

Laila loved puppies. She was sure there wa in the whole world cuter than puppies. E baby goats. And lambs, of course. She like lambs sucked on her fingers when they we and hadn't figured out there wasn't any n them to drink.

Laila's mother said she liked puppies, t the house. She said the puppies and thei to stay outside, but she made them a nice of her old tshaaderis, behind the storage part of the neighbor's wall had fallen dow sort of cave. It was just big enough for La inside when she wanted to visit the puppi and warm in there, but it was also cool *stopped in front of the house. She wanted to go and find out who had come to visit, but when she started to crawl out of her hiding place, the mother dog put her paw on Laila's leg and growled even more loudly than before. Laila didn't want to see those big teeth again, so she crept back farther into the shadows. She stayed very still and quiet, and the mother dog and even the puppies were quiet, too.*

Then she heard a new sound. It wasn't like anything she had ever heard, but it made her more frightened than she'd ever been in her life before. It was high and sharp and terrible, and it made her feel cold inside, like she was going to throw up. It came again and again and again, and Laila put her hands over her ears to shut out the noise.

The worst thing was it sounded like her mother's voice. But how could that be? Why would her mother make such a terrible sound?

She whimpered, "Ammi, Ammi!" and curled up in a ball and huddled close to the mother dog and the puppies. The mother dog growled softly, way down in her throat. Laila shivered and shivered and couldn't stop, and after a while she heard the truck doors slam and the truck drive away.

Laila waited for her mother to come and tell her it was time for lessons and supper. But her mother didn't come.

Laila didn't want to be a baby, but she couldn't help it. She cried and whimpered, "Ammi… Ammi…"

The mother dog whined and licked the tears from her face, and after a long, long time, Laila slept.

PART I

Afghanistan

Chapter 1

The room was dark, but the darkness was not absolute. By staring with wide-open eyes, Yancy could make out shapes against the whitewashed mud-brick walls: the foot of her narrow cot with the slight mound of her feet beneath the blanket; the pile in the far corner that was her personal gear; the table opposite the door and the water jug from last night's supper.

Nothing appeared out of place. Nothing appeared to be amiss.

But something had awakened her.

Tense and alert, she listened for the faint rustle of clothing, the barely discernible sounds of breath and heartbeat. She heard nothing but her own. And yet she was absolutely certain she was not alone in that room.

Then…a lightning flurry of movement…a sudden sense of bulk and heat…and before she could draw breath to scream, a hand clamped over her mouth. Adrenaline flooded her body and coiled through her muscles, but even as she recognized the futility of struggle, a stirring of breath warmed the shell of her ear, carrying with it the softest of whispers.

"Yankee…it's me. It's me."

The adrenaline froze in her veins. There was a rushing of wind in her ears. She felt an easing of the pressure of the hand covering her mouth and turned her face to escape it before drawing a shallow breath, making an effort to keep her voice light and steady even though she knew *he* could feel her body's shaking.

"I'd assumed you were dead," she said.

His laughter was all but soundless and held no trace of amusement. "I must be a ghost, then."

She didn't reply, and his weight and heat shifted away from her, leaving her feeling not relieved, but chilled and vulnerable.

His voice came from the darkness, low, musical, slightly sultry. "You used to call me that—Ghost. Remember?"

Remember? Oh, how she wished she did not. But her senses hadn't forgotten. Defying her will, they stirred with familiar responses.

She cleared her throat and this time answered him. "Of course I remember."

A sense of unreality had settled over her, and with it a blessed numbness. She hitched herself into a sitting position and drew up her knees under the blankets, rested her elbows on them and combed back her hair with her fingers. Deliberately, she yawned and spoke to the shadows into which he'd withdrawn.

"So…what are you doing here?" *And how long will you stay…this time?*

She could keep her voice devoid of emotion in spite

of the shakes, confident she would sound merely curious. She was Yancy Katherine Malone, after all. She'd stood before cameras and reported live while bullets and rocks and bottles flew and bombs and mortars exploded around her and the air she breathed was filled with the screams of the injured and the shouts of the enraged and the stench of burning flags and tanks and human flesh. She was known for being cool under fire.

This was a piece of cake.

It should have been.

This time his laughter brought a vision to her mind, so clear it seemed more real than memory: a mouth upturned at the corners in a smile so at odds with the fierce golden glare of the eyes that went with it. *Lion's eyes.*

"You didn't used to have to ask," he said.

Oh, I remember the night you came as you so often did, coming into my bed with a rush of air, your body cold against my back but warming quickly with my heat. Already wide-awake and shivery, I smiled in the darkness and murmured a sleepy "Who's that?"

"Who do you think?" A chuckle and a rasp of beard in the curve of my neck.

I turned in your arms, feigning surprise. "Oh—it's you."

You said in a growl from deep in your chest, "You were expecting...someone else?"

I laughed, and your mouth silenced my reply.

I remember thinking, So it's been a month? Four weeks without a word from you?

But you are here now, and I've learned not to wonder or ask why.

I've learned to be thankful for the moment...this moment. And to remind myself again that it is never wise to fall in love with a ghost.

* * *

"Nice deflection," Yancy said, but even as the words left her mouth she realized this was different from all the other times he'd come and gone and shown up again without word or warning.

He was different. He sounded different. Almost…wary. Even uncertain, impossible as that would seem to most who knew him as Hunt Grainger, man of steel, Special Ops warrior, a man high on adrenaline and in love with the life of risk and danger he'd lived for so long. A man without fear, not even—perhaps least of all—of death.

Superhuman.

That was how she'd seen him first. More machine— a killing machine—than man.

The worst thing about battle is the sound. You'd think it would be the images, wouldn't you? Or even the smells, that nose-burning, throat-clogging mix of smoke and explosives and blood and dust and fear. And it's true that even now a whiff of one or the other of those will bring the images back in full horror and living color. But the sound is simply intolerable. I still watch raw footage with the sound muted, to save myself another round of those recurring nightmares.

That day I remember curling into fetal position with my hands over my ears, praying my flak jacket and helmet would stop the bullets, that the mud-brick walls wouldn't bury us alive, and if that was too much to ask, at least that I would die quickly and without too much pain. Even in that hideous din, I remember hearing Will, the cameraman, swearing, and someone else, I don't know who, muttering something in rhythmic cadence that might have been the Hail Mary.

I heard—no, felt—the percussion of machine-gun

fire, so close it was a physical assault on my eardrums, and between bursts there were shouts, unintelligible at first, but then... Oh, my God, yes, it was—it was English!

I heard the scrape of boots, felt the thud of heavy feet on the hard-packed earth beneath me, and the blessed shout: "You all okay in here?"

I dared open my eyes and saw the room fill with what seemed almost to be alien beings. Superbeings, certainly, more machine than men, laden as they were with their gear and weapons and helmets and body armor. One knelt beside me, and I saw his eyes, brilliant, amber gold in color, and so intense it seemed I could feel their heat.

"Are you hurt?" he shouted, and I shook my head.

"Can you walk?"

I nodded.

"Then let's get the hell outa here."

Somehow I was on my feet. "The truck—" I think I shouted.

"Forget the truck. We've got a chopper. This way— move!"

As if I had a choice, with this man-machine's arm around my waist, half carrying me. But I could see Will and the other members of my crew being similarly hustled through the rooms of the bombed-out house—mostly rubble now—and gave myself up to being rescued and focused my attention on trying not to step on anything that might have been body parts.

Once clear of the house, we ran across open ground with all the speed we television newspeople were capable of, bent almost double as if that would make us less vulnerable to bullets and mortar shells. My rescuer kept me tucked under his arm, practically under his body, shielding me with his own armor.

I could hear the thump-thump-thump of rotors, and

then my rescuer's hands grasped my waist and hoisted me bodily into the helicopter. Within seconds we were all aboard—rescue squad, news crew and most of our gear—and the chopper lunged into the air. As it banked and swept away from the battle zone, heading back toward the base, blessed quiet—comparatively speaking— settled over us. Above the creak and rustle of armor-clad warriors settling themselves and their weapons in for the journey, I could hear my own heart beating, out of sync with the thump of the chopper blades.

When I could breathe evenly enough to speak without gasping, I looked over at my personal savior. I found him watching me, eyes half-closed in his blackened face, the fire in them banked for the moment.

"Thanks," I said, knowing how profoundly inadequate it was.

A smile transformed him instantly from machine into man. "Just doin' our job, ma'am," he drawled.

"What's your name, soldier?" I asked, remembering my own job, belatedly.

Still smiling, he shook his head. "Soldier's enough."

That was the first hint she'd had of how human he was; later, she'd found he could even be vulnerable. Though… she'd never seen him afraid, not once in all the years he'd flitted in and out of her life like a shadow.

But he's afraid now.

She was almost certain of it. What could have happened to him in the year since she'd last seen him… touched him…felt his touch? Possibilities flashed through her mind, scenarios formless as wisps of smoke.

She strained her ears, listening in the silence of that room, silence that stretched beyond the mud-brick walls and small shuttered window into the cold Afghan night.

There were no sounds of battle tonight, no voices raised in fear or anger, song or prayer, not even the cry of a night bird or barking of an abandoned dog. Again she listened for the rustling of clothing, the whisper of quickened breathing. And again, all she heard was her own heartbeat.

Anger came like a small hot whirlwind. She sucked it in and held it close as she threw back the heavy woven wool blankets, thankful once again for the years of experience that had taught her to sleep fully clothed in these remote outposts.

"What do you want?" The question came in a tumble of uneven breath as she stabbed the darkness with her feet, searching for her boots. "Damn you, at least tell me why you're here. I think you owe me that much."

The answer barely disturbed the silence. "You're right. I do." There was a quick, soft exhalation and then: "I need your help."

And for Yancy, where there had been heat, now there was cold, a new chill that penetrated to the pit of her stomach. On a sharp gasp she asked, "What's wrong? Are you hurt?"

"No. Nothing like that."

"For God's sake, Hunt." Still shaky, she pulled her coat from the foot of the cot and swung it around her shoulders. It wasn't until she stood up that she realized how unreliable her legs were. She groped for the battery-powered lantern and swore under her breath when she kicked it in the near-darkness.

"No," her visitor said harshly. "No light."

Unformed notions swirled like swamp fog through her mind. *Oh, God, he's been wounded...horribly disfigured...doesn't want me to see...*

As if he'd read her thought, his voice held a touch of

irony. "I need to open the door... Don't want the light to show outside. Okay? Just...wait..."

She caught back questions and stood hugging her coat around her, trying not to shiver as she stared at the place where she remembered the outside door was. She listened to faint sounds, felt the movement of air as the door opened all but invisibly against the blackness of the night. After a moment, she heard the door close. The shadows in the room rearranged themselves.

Hunt spoke, barely a whisper. "You can put the light on now, if you need to."

Yancy fumbled again for the lantern and this time found it and switched it on. Light flooded the room, a visual assault after such darkness.

She turned quickly, heart pounding, not knowing what to expect, afraid of what she would see. And went utterly still with shock. Whatever she'd expected, it wasn't this.

Where the shadow had been that was Hunt Grainger, now there were two figures. A tall man wearing traditional Afghan clothing and a full beard, thick and dark. With him was a small Afghan child—a boy, judging from the way he was dressed, and no more than four or five years old.

"Not quite what you expected, I guess." Hunt's voice was still soft, but again with that hint of wry humor as he gave words to her thoughts.

"Not...quite," she managed to murmur, still staring at the child clinging to Hunt's leg with the fierce determination of a drowning cat. "Who is he?"

"*She*. It's safer if..." There was a pause before he continued. "Her name's Laila."

Yancy lifted her eyes to look at him, understanding beginning to dawn. *Could it possibly be...? How does he know what I...?* Uneasiness tightened her chest.

"Why— How...?" She stopped, knowing it was useless to try to rush him.

"Her mother's dead." The statement came in a flat undertone. He tipped his turbaned head toward the child. "And if she stays in this country she might as well be. She needs to get out, and I know you can make that happen."

Her small gasp of laughter was an automatic and, she knew, futile diversion. "Why would you think—"

He cut her off without raising his voice. "Yankee, I *know*. Okay? I know what you do, who you work for— besides WNN. I know your organization has the machine in place, the people—and I don't mean them." He jerked his head toward the door behind him, indicating the rest of the house and the rooms where the other members of the news crew were quartered. "You have the means to do this. You know how. You've done it before."

Yancy hesitated a moment longer, then nodded. A cloak of calm came around her, and the ground steadied under her feet. She didn't know how or why Hunt Grainger knew about INCBRO, but the fact that he did wasn't a complete surprise. Hunt and the others like him seemed to know things no one else did.

"She's a child bride, then?"

Hunt made a scoffing sound. "If that's what you call it. They bartered a five-year-old child to a tribal leader, in exchange, I suppose, for a promise of protection."

"They?" She had squatted down, balanced on one knee, and was gazing again at the child, who still had her face buried in Hunt's long *chapan*.

She thought, *My God, a bride? She's so small...*

"Her family." His voice had an edge of steel. "Of course."

Yancy glanced up at him, but all she could see of his

face in the dim light and behind the dark curtain of beard was the glitter of his eyes. *So familiar, and yet I've never seen him look like this...*

Swallowing the knot of rage and sickness that had lodged in her throat, she spoke quietly. "Does she speak any English?"

"A little. Probably understands more than she speaks. *When* she speaks. Right now she's not saying much of anything."

She straightened up, letting out a breath. "Hunt, I don't know what you know about the organization—INCBRO. We're more about trying to intercede diplomatically— you know, educate and persuade family members, get them to understand they can do better for their daughters by letting them go to school instead of marrying them off as children. If they don't have the money to do that, we try to help them. We don't usually take a child out of the culture and environment they're accustomed to. We don't just…pick them up and carry them off—not that we don't wish we could, sometimes…"

"But you've done just that, in certain cases. As a last resort? When the girl's life was at stake. Haven't you?"

"Well, I—"

"Her mother's name was Zahra."

She heard an edge of flint in his voice—and something else she couldn't name. It stirred conflicting emotions and swirled them together in her mind like a wicked little dust devil—fear, compassion…a hint of jealousy— making her heart stutter and her breath catch. But for only a moment. The thoughts and emotions settled like leaves when the wind has passed.

"So you knew her?"

"Yes. I knew her." His hand rested on the child's turbaned head, so gentle in contrast to the cold rage in his eyes. "I thought I'd found a safe place for them, but they—" He broke off with a meaningful glance at the child and stepped away from her, turning his back to her before he continued speaking to Yancy in a low murmur. "The male members of her family killed her— killed Zahra. How they found them I don't know. Thank God *this* one managed to hide. Look, I don't have time for details. I just know if she stays here they'll find her again sooner or later. In fact, the longer I stay here the more danger she's in—and you, too. I know your crew is about to wrap up—pulling out tomorrow, right?"

She nodded and again didn't bother to ask him how he knew.

"Okay. So take her with you. Get her on that underground railroad you help run. You're the only one who can get her out of Afghanistan. You can keep her safe." He pulled in a breath. "If you need money—"

"Not a problem. INCBRO is very well funded," Yancy said tightly.

He nodded and for a moment seemed to hesitate—that unfamiliar uncertainty again. Then he turned abruptly, went down on one knee and took the child by the shoulders. He spoke quietly to her in Pashto, a language Yancy was still struggling to learn. The little girl made a whimpering sound and reached for him, but he held her firmly away, still talking to her.

Then, in an abrupt change to English, he said slowly and clearly, "Laila, this woman is my friend. I told you about her, remember? She's going to take good care of you. She'll keep you safe. Okay?"

Laila kept her head bowed but silently nodded and, after a moment, lifted small clenched fists to scrub tears from her cheeks.

"That's my girl," Hunt said in a husky growl. "I'll

come and see you, soon as I can, I promise." Unexpectedly, he drew the child into his arms and held her close. Yancy's heart did a slow flip-flop. "But for now, I want you to go with Yancy. Can you do that?"

After a long pause, Laila nodded. Hunt released the child, rose to his feet and turned her toward Yancy. The little girl bravely lifted her eyes.

A smile of reassurance froze on Yancy's lips. She sucked in an audible breath. *Lion's eyes...golden eyes, tear-glazed but bright as flame...*

Her own gaze flew to Hunt, who had paused at the door to look back at her.

"Yes," he said gently, "she's mine. Does it matter?"

Yancy shook her head, barely aware she did so.

"Put out the light, will you?"

Numbly, she reached for the lantern. As the room plunged into darkness she felt a chill breeze and knew he was gone.

In the silence that fell then, a small cold hand crept into hers.

Chapter 2

Yancy tightened her grip on her daughter's hand as they wove their way together through the sluggish river of shoppers, stepping around parked cars and top-heavy pushcarts and the knots of women who were pausing to examine displays of brightly woven fabrics, piles of fresh-baked bread or bins of cheap plastic trinkets.

"Look, Mom, Mickey Mouse," Laila said, pointing, and Yancy smiled and squeezed her hand.

"Just like home."

Her daughter lifted her golden eyes, eyes now sparkling with the smile that was hidden beneath the drape of her scarf. "Well, not *exactly*."

Yancy laughed, feeling lighter in heart than she had since she'd made the decision to bring Laila with her on this trip to Afghanistan. She'd have preferred to wait until her adopted daughter was older before taking her to visit the country of her birth, but with the allied troops preparing to pull out for good, she knew there was no way to predict what the future might hold for the war-ravaged country. It might be a case of now or never.

Still, Laila was only eight years old. It had been three years since the traumatic events that had made it necessary to get the child out of Afghanistan for the sake of nothing less than her life.

Yancy hadn't tried to erase her daughter's memories of that terrible time—quite the opposite, in fact. Thinking it would be therapeutic for her to talk about it, she'd downloaded YouTube videos, which they'd watched together, Yancy answering Laila's questions, talking about the ways her life was different now. She'd even probed gently, never sure how much Laila had witnessed or remembered about her mother's murder. But Laila had never spoken of that day, and whether that was because she couldn't, or wouldn't, Yancy had no way of knowing.

Their first day in Kabul, Laila had clung close to Yancy's side, shrinking closer still at her first glimpse of the mysterious blue *burqas* that sprinkled the crowds even here in the modern capital city. Last night Yancy had asked her about that, wanting to know why Laila was frightened when they'd already talked about the fact that some women in Afghanistan covered themselves completely when they went out in public.

But Laila had only shrugged and mumbled, "I'm not scared. I just don't like them. I think they're…creepy."

Today, though, she seemed to be enjoying the crowds, the bustle and noise, the tapestry of different costumes: men and boys in everything from jeans, T-shirts and Western-style jackets to the traditional loose white trousers and tunics and long *chabas* embroidered with intricate patterns; the turbans or flat Afghan hats, or karakul hats like the one the president wore; women and girls in conservative Western-style dresses or flowing robes and draped head scarves, and, of course, the *burqas*. Every direction they looked was a new feast for the eyes.

A feast for all the senses. Though the sky overhead was the same crisp blue she recalled from previous trips to Afghanistan, here in the bazaar the air was dense with dust and exhaust, the familiar smells of spices and baking bread and overripe fruit and the musky scents of people. The noise of traffic and exotic music and voices raised in chatter or barter or a snatch of song made a tapestry of sound.

I've missed this, Yancy thought.

"What are those?" Laila pointed.

"Hmm...looks like dates," Yancy said.

"Can we get some?"

"You don't like dates, remember?"

"Yes, but I've never tasted *these* dates."

"Uh-huh." Recognizing that her child had been bitten by the shopping bug, Yancy diplomatically steered her to another display, where large flat metal bowls held an array of grains and beans and nuts. "How about we get some of these, instead? You like pistachios, don't you?"

Laila's answer was a happy gasp. She tugged at Yancy's hand like an excited puppy while Yancy bartered with the women hovering over the display. She counted out the money, then gave the drawstring shopping bag they'd brought with them—no paper or plastic here— to Laila to hold while the shopkeeper dumped a scoopful of nuts into it.

Laila said, *"Tashakkur!"* the way Yancy had taught

her, in a strong, clear voice, and the woman beamed her approval and added another handful of nuts to the bag.

They walked on, stopping to examine trinkets, discussing what gifts they should buy for Laila's school friends back home in Virginia. Yancy fingered beautiful scarves, debating which one to buy for her clothes-horse sister, Miranda.

The sun climbed higher and so did the temperature, and the crowds began to thin. Yancy noticed Laila's enthusiasm seemed to be waning, as well. Her footsteps lagged as she looked around her, craning her neck, clearly searching for something and disappointed she hadn't found it.

"Are you getting tired, sweetie?"

"No…" Laila lifted her shoulders in what was half sigh and half shrug. "I was just hoping…"

Yancy's stomach lurched. Surely, she couldn't be hoping to see *him.*

Impossible, anyway. He's dead. He must be. And how can she even remember?

"I thought there would be animals."

"Animals?" Yancy said blankly.

Laila was watching the toe of her sandal make designs in the dusty ground. She heaved another heart-tugging sigh. "Yes, like sheep or goats. Or donkeys. I like them. They had them at the market where I used to live." She lifted her gaze—and her chin—in a way that was almost a challenge. "I know because I *remember* them."

Yancy put her arm around her daughter's shoulders and pulled her close in a one-arm hug. "This is Kabul, honey. It's a very big city—like New York or Los Angeles. Probably there wouldn't be many sheep or goats or donkeys here in the middle of the city. But I promise we'll make sure and find some tomorrow when we go out in the country—okay?"

"Okay…" Clearly, her daughter was only somewhat appeased.

Changing the subject, Yancy said, "Hey, are you hungry? I know I am. How about we go back to the hotel and see if they have any ice cream."

"Pistachio?" Laila's golden eyes sparkled up at her with that wicked humor that never failed to wrench at Yancy's heart and bring back memories of a time she hoped someday to forget.

She's so like him. How am I ever going to be able to forget, with her as my constant reminder?

With one arm resting lightly across Laila's shoulders, Yancy lifted her head to survey their surroundings, hoping to determine the best and shortest route back to the main street where, presumably, they could flag down a taxi. But she found she couldn't see much because of the press of people that surrounded them.

Which was odd, because a moment ago she could have sworn there were only a few straggling shoppers here, dawdling about among the stalls. Now she and Laila appeared to be completely walled in by a crowd of people.

No, not a crowd. A group of men. Tall, bearded men, all dressed in traditional Afghan costume.

As the bolt of awareness shot through Yancy's brain, it triggered a wild montage of the warnings, cautions and instructions she'd heard time and time again when preparing to venture into volatile and unpredictable regions of the world. More than once she'd covered the story when a colleague had been abducted—or worse— and there had even been some close calls that were hers alone, the memories of which were all too vivid. She'd never really been frightened then—at least not that she could remember. But it was different now. Now there was Laila.

She tensed and strengthened her hold on her daughter's hand, at the same time nervously checking to make certain no stray locks of her own dark red hair had strayed from beneath her scarf. Keeping her eyes averted, she quickened her step.

Without any overtly threatening moves or gestures, the knot of men moved with her, keeping pace.

Yancy's mind raced, searching for explanations but capable only of shooting off questions. *Who are they? Taliban? What's happening? Why are they doing this? What do they want with me? Are we about to be kidnapped? What have I done?*

Or...is it Laila they're after?

Her heart banged against her ribs. Her scalp sizzled; she could actually feel her hair lift and stir against the silk fabric of her scarf. She could almost hear Hunt's voice... *They'll find her again, sooner or later...*

Oddly, the thought had a calming effect.

Laila? They can't take her. They will have to kill me first.

She drew in a long breath and let it out slowly. *Think. You have one advantage: you're a woman. They won't be expecting resistance from a woman. Plus, they won't want to touch you, a strange female, if they can avoid it. You know the moves—they won't expect that, either. Strike fast, strike hard, break loose.*

Then both of us run like hell.

They'd reached the outskirts of the bazaar. Beyond the human barricade that surrounded her, Yancy could hear cars moving slowly, tires crunching on the hard-baked ground. She could hear laughter, music coming from a car radio, the impatient beep of a horn. She wondered if one of those cars was meant for *them*. She imagined a sudden shriek of brakes, hard hands shoving her into a waiting vehicle, Laila screaming...

Or, infinitely worse, Laila being wrenched from her grasp. *Then* the slamming of car doors, a gunned motor and silence.

Twenty yards or so behind the odd clot of Afghan males in the otherwise free-flowing stream of midday traffic, Hunt Grainger maintained a relaxed and steady pace. Keeping anger in check along with surging adrenaline, he followed the phalanx's every movement, gauging the situation, biding his time, waiting for the moment.

And still hoping this was going to turn out to be nothing more ominous than a tight-knit group of male shoppers oblivious to the two insignificant females in their path. Still hoping it wouldn't be necessary to make himself known. He'd intended to do so eventually, of course, but at a time and place of his own choosing.

No, not this way. Not now.

The adrenaline was easier to deal with than the anger. He knew how to bank adrenaline, keep it focused and ready for the job at hand. He'd already assessed the odds of roughly ten to one, which didn't trouble him particularly—he'd handled worse. Although admittedly not with a woman and child in the immediate proximity of the operation. That might complicate things.

Damn Yancy, anyway!

What was she thinking, bringing the girl back to Afghanistan? Hadn't he made it clear to her how dangerous it was? If Zahra's family found out...

That was the troubling thing. They obviously *had* found out. *How? How could they know?*

Although, he supposed, if *he'd* known, it was possible someone else could, as well. A world-famous network war correspondent couldn't exactly keep a low profile.

The agency he'd hired to keep an eye on the two while he was out of reach had kept him informed of their travel plans, and he'd been watching them almost from the moment they'd arrived in the country. Admittedly that wasn't so much because he feared for their safety. Not then.

Truth was, he'd simply wanted to see them again. Both of them. Nothing wrong with that, he'd argued with himself as he'd lain wide-awake and sleepless in anticipation of their arrival. Laila was his daughter, after all.

And Yancy... Hell, he wasn't sure what Yancy was to him. Never had known.

What he did know was, it would be better for everyone if he could have stayed away, let them go on believing he was dead.

He'd told himself he'd look—that was all. Watch them from afar. Then let them go, never knowing.

It's better that way. For now.

That was the plan. One of them, anyway. Maybe he would have been able to keep to it, maybe not. Now it looked as if he wasn't going to have the luxury of choice.

His senses snapped to full alert when he noted what appeared to be a disturbance in the tight knot of men surrounding Yancy and Laila. The knot appeared to be unraveling. He quickened his pace, and several things happened in lightning-quick succession: One man seemed to stumble, then fall back against his comrades. This sent several to the ground in a tumble of flowing garments that might have been comical under different circumstances. Then two female figures, woman and child, broke free of the melee. They came straight toward him, running as if from the devil himself.

The woman's face was a mask of grim determination; the child's was blank with confusion. Hunt started forward, then halted when he saw the woman's eyes focus, home in on his face. He saw her eyes go wide, first with fear, then with stunned recognition. He saw her stumble slightly, her body flinch and her face drain of all color.

Unexpected pain sliced through him.

Dammit, Yancy. Not like this—this isn't the way I'd have chosen to break it to you.

An image came into his mind, one of those lightning flashes that stays on, seared into the memory like a brand.

...I'm strolling the boardwalk on the base with a couple of guys from my team, fresh off a successful mission with some leftover adrenaline to dispose of. Every soldier has his own way of dealing with it—that jacked-up reckless feeling you get sometimes when you've done your job and come back in one piece. Everything seems sharp and clear and simple. Life and death. You win or you lose. And that day we won. Life was good.

Times like that, some guys head straight for their laptops for a face-to-face with their families. A few go to the chapel, I guess. Me, I get a yearning for a little piece of home, so I hit the boardwalk and the same fast-food places I used to hang out in when I was a kid, growing up in the Midwest.

So my guys and I are debating the relative merits of subs, pizza and tacos, or whether we should go to Friday's and have all three. And that's when I see her. Them, actually—the news crew we'd picked up out of that fire-fight earlier in the day. They're gathered around a table drinking something tall and cold, all scrubbed and shiny like they've just come from the showers. They still have that dazed look civilians get when they've had a closer look than they ever wanted at what war's really like.

She's impossible to miss, with that red hair of hers, the wind blowing it around like dark flames. I guess I'm looking at her pretty hard and maybe she feels that, because she looks up just then, straight at me, and I see her eyes go big and wide with that look that says she's recognized me, too. I feel a kick underneath my ribs, which I chalk up to that leftover adrenaline, and I give her a nod. Maybe I smile at her, too.

I've worked my way through about half a foot-long meatball sub, joking with the guys across the table, when I hear, "Hey, soldier." And here she is, sitting down beside me.

The guys, of course, they give me the eye, elbow each other and get up and move to another table.

She says, "I don't mean to interrupt..."

I chew and swallow and reach for my napkin, wipe sauce off my face and clear my throat good. My heart's doing the happy-dance and there's nothing I can do about that, but I keep my voice polite and nothing more. "What can I do for you, ma'am?"

She winces and says, "Ma'am? Really?" and makes a face.

"It's a term of respect—like sir," *I tell her. Something makes me add, "From where I'm sitting, you definitely do* not *qualify as* sir."

She laughs, and I feel a sizzling inside my skin, and I know I'm going where I've got no business going. I'm feeling hot and hard and I blame that on the adrenaline, too.

"I don't know if I even said thank you," she says. "For saving my—all...of our lives."

She's looking at me with big brown eyes, and it occurs to me her eyes seem to match her hair, which doesn't make sense, because her hair is definitely auburn, and her eyes are definitely brown.

"You did," I say.

She nods. "And you said you were just doing your job." She's studying me, and there's this kind of a frown making lines between her eyebrows, like she can't figure me out. Then she turns her face away, but I can see it tighten up and change color anyway. "That's what it was to you, maybe. But to me it was a whole lot more. It was my life, you know?" She swipes her fingers across one cheek, clears her throat and adds, "And I want you to know I'm very grateful."

I want to touch her, and I pick up my sandwich so I can't. I take a bite, chew it, nod to the sandwich and say, "Glad I could help."

I feel her staring at me again. Softly she says, "I wish I understood what makes someone like you tick." I turn my head to look at her, and for a long time that's what we do—look at each other. Or maybe it only seems like a long time. Then she sort of smiles and says, "I don't suppose you'd consider—"

That wakes me up. "Not gonna happen," I tell her.

Her smile goes a little sideways. "I was going to say, 'I don't suppose you'd consider having dinner with me.'"

"No, you weren't."

She doesn't miss a beat, but leans closer and says, "What if I was?"

There's a long silence while I listen to the voices in my head telling me things I already know, all the reasons I want but can't have. Then, probably because I'm used to shaking hands with danger, I lean in closer to her and whisper, "It'd still be no."

She sits back and the contact between us snaps like a rubber band pulled too tight—it stings a little. She tilts her head and asks, "Why?"

I laugh—I mean, she has to ask?

"You're the media," I say, "and my job depends on secrecy."

"I'd never compromise that. You know us media folks always protect our sources."

I shake my head. "Sorry. Too big a risk."

"I thought that's what you do—take risks."

"Not stupid ones."

She thinks about that. Then after a moment, she nods, gets up and starts to walk away. While I'm silently cussing—myself, her, maybe fate—she comes back, leans down close to my ear and whispers, "If you change your mind, I'd still like to hear your story. Your terms, your rules. My quarters are in the Quonset next to the media's. You can find me there."

After she leaves I look at the sub I'm still holding in my hands, and I realize I've lost my appetite—for food, anyway. Right then the only thing I'm hungry for is a woman with auburn hair and matching eyes.

His trip down memory lane lasted for the space of the few seconds it took them to get to him. He reached out for Yancy, who staggered and almost fell into his arms, the child sandwiched between the two adults. He caught and steadied her while her eyes searched his face in shocked disbelief. Her mouth opened, but before she could fire off the questions he knew must be piled up inside her, he said in a low, guttural voice, "Go—run. Keep going. Don't stop for anything."

He had to hand it to her—no questions, no hesitation. She just nodded and took Laila's hand in a firm grip.

Hunt shoved the two of them behind him and turned

his attention to the would-be abductors, who by this time were sorting themselves out and shouting at each other in fury and outrage. A couple of them seemed to think they might give chase but changed their minds when they saw what was blocking their path. A tall man wearing the elaborately wound turban and embroidered vest of a Pashtun tribal elder would give the average urban Afghan male pause even if he wasn't portraying an attitude of authority, strength and menace. Hunt excelled at all three. In a matter of moments the men had dispersed and vanished into the crowds, both pedestrian and vehicular.

Hunt waited until he was certain the threat had passed, then turned to follow the woman and child, who had already vanished from sight. He walked rapidly but didn't run. He knew he'd find them again.

"Mommy? Who was that man? Who were those *other* men? Why were they following us? What did they want? Why did we run away?"

Yancy could only shake her head as she leaned against a mud-brick wall and fought to catch her breath. As she waited for her pounding heart to calm itself, her numbed brain struggled to absorb the reality that once again the assumption of Hunt Grainger's demise had been premature.

She tried to figure out how that made her feel.

I don't know how I feel!

There isn't time to feel. Not now. I have to get Laila to safety. Someplace safe...

Dear God, where? I don't even know where we are.

Laila was having no trouble finding breath for her usual stream of questions. Questions Yancy couldn't answer, not then. How would she answer...ever?

Mommy, who was that man?

He's your father, sweetie. The father that dropped you in my lap and disappeared from both our lives.

Who were those other men? What did they want?

I think they wanted to take you away from me...maybe kill me in order to do it.

Why?

Why? That's a good question. How do I answer that? How do I make you understand ignorance and evil?

Yancy held up a hand to stem the flow of words, then reached out to pull her daughter close to her side while she cast intent looks in every direction. She could see no sign of pursuit or anyone that looked threatening, but the fear lingered. She could feel Laila's body quivering as the child clutched her tightly and pressed her face against her side. She could feel her moist heat, smell terror and sweat, and for a moment rage clouded her vision.

Then, once again, she commanded herself to *think.*

I have to get us back to the hotel. She'll be safe there.

Thank goodness she still had her purse, the strap looped snugly across her chest from one shoulder to the opposite hip. She dug in it frantically, located her cell phone and turned it on. While she waited for it to locate a signal, she looked around, hoping to find a street sign or, failing that, some sort of landmark that might help a taxi find their location.

"Look, Mom—donkey," Laila said in a faint but hopeful voice.

Yancy watched the small dusty animal toiling up the rocky, rutted street—just a path, really—with a load of water jugs balanced on his scrawny back. A boy no more than eleven or twelve years old, dressed in baggy trousers and a T-shirt several sizes too big for him, trudged along beside the donkey and switched idly at its rump with a small stick. Several yards beyond the pair, a man plodded steadily uphill bearing a pole across his shoulders, a plastic water container suspended from each end. Several children ran by, their bare feet seemingly impervious to the rocky ground as they leaped nimbly across the ditch that ran down the middle of the street carrying sludge and raw sewage. And she realized she did know where they were, at least generally.

This was the old slummy part of Kabul, where mud-brick houses clung to the side of the mountain practically one on top of the other, most without electricity or running water. Where people lived in appalling poverty, and all the water needed for cooking and bathing had to be carried up from the community wells down below. Several years ago Yancy had done a feature on the conditions here. It was disheartening to see that nothing much had changed.

With unsteady fingers poised to punch in the number for her network's Kabul bureau, she hesitated. Of course, they'd send someone to pick them up if she asked, even though she was on leave, not assignment, and hadn't told anyone at the network of her travel plans. But if possible, she wanted to continue to fly under the radar, for so many reasons. This was a personal pilgrimage, for her and for Laila. Or it had been, until…

Until we were almost abducted in the middle of a Kabul bazaar, for who-knows-what reason.

Until a man I thought was dead stepped in to help us escape.

Or did I only imagine that part? Could he possibly be real?

But Laila had seen him, too.

"Mommy, I'm thirsty." Laila was tugging at her skirt.

"I know, baby. I'm thirsty, too." Shading her eyes with her free hand, she surveyed the jumble of houses and winding dirt paths through which they'd just come. Water would only be found at the bottom of the hill, as would paved streets and access to taxis. They couldn't stay where they were, obviously, but what if their would-be abductors were down there, as well, looking for them?

Inspiration struck as she remembered the shopping bag with the things they'd bought at the bazaar, including the scarves she'd picked up as gifts for Miranda.

Jamming her cell phone back into her purse, she opened the bag and pulled out the two most brightly colored and beautifully patterned scarves, one in rose and gold, the other in blue and green. She pulled off the much more sedate and modest gray one she was wearing and draped the rose-and-gold one over her head and shoulders, arranging it so it covered her hair and half of her face. Ignoring the glances of passersby, she exchanged Laila's white scarf for the prettier blue-and-green one, while Laila gazed at her with solemn eyes and said not a word, not even to ask a question.

Yancy straightened and took Laila's hand, shifted her purse onto her hip and said, "Okay, sweetie, let's go find some water, shall we?"

She wanted more than water. She wanted a huge glass of wine. Or maybe a slug of whiskey. She wanted to sink down with her back against the mud-brick wall and fall completely to pieces.

Not now. Not until Laila's safe. I have to get her to safety. Somehow.

She started down the dusty street, holding her head high and putting as much confidence in her step as she could summon while her heart pounded and cold sweat trickled between her shoulder blades. They'd gone no more than twenty yards or so before a tall, imposing figure stepped out of a narrow, branching alleyway to block their path.

Chapter 3

"This way—I've got a car." His voice low and terse. "They're probably still looking for you."

Yancy stood rock-still, conscious only of her burning eyes, pounding heart and the small moist hand in hers. She whispered, "Hunt?"

Deadpan, he said, "Yeah, Yankee, no ghost. It's really me. Come on—hurry up." He waited for them to slip past him into the narrow passageway, then followed, urging them to go faster, fast enough that Laila, with her shorter legs, had to trot to keep up.

Yancy's Irish temper sparked to life and built to a slow simmer. Not the best timing for it, she realized, but it did help burn off the fog of shock. Before her anger could reach full boil, she halted, so abruptly Hunt had to side-step nimbly to keep from bumping into her. She heard him swearing under his breath.

"What are you stopping for? Move, *move*."

Yancy tightened her grip on her purse strap. "That's not going to happen. Not another step. Not until you tell me what's going on."

From the shadows between his turban and beard, his eyes seemed to glow like those of a wild animal. "Can't you just trust me?" She stared at him without answering. He hissed out a breath. "Dammit, Yancy, this isn't the time. I'll answer your questions when I've got you to safety."

"Okay, sure, that's fine." Holding herself straight and firm, tall as she was, she still had to look up to meet *his* eyes. "Darn right you will. But there's someone else here I'm sure has questions. Maybe they *can't* wait. Did you even think about *her*? Did you stop to think you might be scaring her?"

She saw him hesitate, saw his gaze flick to Laila and something she couldn't identify flash across his eyes, though his features remained impassive. He dropped to one knee, took Laila by the arms and turned her to face him in a way she'd seen him do once before.

In a gentle voice she'd also heard him use once before, he said, "Hey, do you remember me?" Laila stared stoically back at him, rigid as a post. "Do you know who I am?"

Moments passed, filled with heartbeats and silence. Yancy held her breath until it hardened in her chest. Then Laila whispered a single word, in Pashto. *"Akaa..."*

There was a soft hiss of breath. He threw an unreadable glance at Yancy before turning his attention back to Laila. "That's right. Akaa Hunt, remember? I need you to come with me now—will you do that?"

He reached for her hand, but she shrank back against Yancy, shaking her head, whimpering, "No...no..."

Hunt drew back and draped the rejected hand across

a drawn-up knee. His voice was, if possible, even more gentle. "No? Why not?"

Yancy put her hand on Laila's shoulder and gave it a reassuring squeeze. She nearly choked on the words. "It's okay, baby. He's...our friend."

Laila turned swimming golden eyes toward Yancy and asked in a small voice, "Is he going to take me away, Mommy?" A tear made its way slowly down her cheek. "I don't want to leave you. Please don't make me go."

Again, pain sliced through Hunt's chest. He had to look away and his hand clenched into a fist while Yancy gathered *his daughter* close and murmured reassurances.

My daughter.

But I deserved that, I suppose.

Not that knowing it lessened the weight in the pit of his stomach to any noticeable degree.

He stood up and briefly laid his hand on Laila's scarf-draped head. "I'm not taking you away from your mom. You're both coming with me. Right...*Mom*?" He braced himself and met Yancy's eyes, prepared for the blazing anger he saw there, knowing he deserved that, too.

No apologies, Yankee. I did what was necessary. Couldn't be helped.

Laila looked to Yancy for confirmation, back at Hunt with her chin at a particular tilt, one he remembered well. "Okay, I'll go," she announced. "But I'm very tired of walking. My feet are tired. And I'm thirsty."

"No problem," Hunt said with a shrug. "I can carry you."

She bristled, as he'd known she would, and her chin rose up another notch. "Don't be silly. I'm way too big to carry. I'm eight years old. I'm not a baby."

Yancy automatically murmured, "Laila..."

Hunt spoke over her. "You're right—you're not. So,

we'd better get a move on, okay? It's not much farther. Sooner we get going, the sooner we'll be there."

"My mom said we were going to have ice cream. Do *you* have ice cream?"

He glanced at Yancy, who shrugged and looked away, hiding her expression behind a swath of scarf. He gave the kid—his kid—a sideways look. "I imagine that could be arranged."

"Pistachio?"

Pistachio? He and Yancy exchanged another look. His said, *What the hell?*

Hers, along with another shrug, said, *Don't look at me. She's got your DNA.*

He snorted and gave Laila his best glare. "How 'bout we save the negotiations for later? Right now, we're gonna play Follow The Leader, and I'm the leader—you got that?"

After a moment, she nodded, though he could tell from the gleam in her eyes she wasn't all that impressed with his claim to authority. Growling under his breath, he turned and led the way down the curving alley, trusting Yancy to bring the girl and keep up with him.

Mommy. My mom said...

It played over and over in his head. He was having trouble wrapping his head around that. Not the *fact* of it—he'd known about the adoption, of course. Maybe hearing her *say* the words... *No*—it was the way he *felt* when he heard her say the words. *That* was what he couldn't reconcile himself with.

Hunt Grainger—the Hunt Grainger he'd made himself into—couldn't afford the luxury of *feeling*. For so many years—he'd lost track of how many—he'd put away any feelings that threatened to get in his way, put them in a safe he'd long since lost the combination to.

He'd had a job to do, a job with lives at stake. Sometimes more than just lives. Sometimes the future of nations depended on his staying focused, going into impossible situations and getting the job done. Not only would feelings get in the way of him getting the job done, but they could be downright dangerous.

"No apologies. I do what I have to do."

I remember saying those words the night I finally went to her Quonset.

To tell you the truth, I don't know what drove me to knock on her door. It was a couple of weeks after my team pulled hers out of a firefight, the day she'd invited me to drop by and tell my story. Like the last time, we'd come in off a mission, only this one hadn't gone the way we'd planned. We hadn't lost anyone on the team, but there'd been civilian casualties. Children. Women. I had no intention of telling anybody about any of that, but I was carrying pictures in my head that weren't going to be erased by a sub sandwich, even if it was accompanied by a cold beer. Or several. Maybe I thought the company of a beautiful redheaded woman would do something to make me forget the image of a little girl clinging to her dead mother and crying, "Ammi, Ammi..." over and over.

But that wasn't the first time I'd had to deal with such things, and I knew it wouldn't be the last. So maybe what I was really looking for was an excuse to do what I'd been wanting to do all along.

Watching Hunt Grainger face off with his own daughter did a lot to restore Yancy's spirits. Oh, she was still half in shock, still angry, for so many reasons, and she still had more questions than she could put in coherent form, even though asking questions was how she made her living. But he was right—those were for another time. At the moment she was finding a certain measure of satisfaction in the look of utter helplessness she'd seen on Hunt's face when he was haggling with Laila. Who would have guessed the man she still thought of as more superhero than man, more machine than human, could be brought to earth by an eight-year-old girl?

But she'd seen that look of utter bewilderment on his face before. Only once. And it was probably what had made her sleep with him. At least the first time…

It's still sharp and clear in my memory, even after so long. I'm in my quarters, working on the copy for next day's report. I've always written my own. It's one of my trademarks as a correspondent. I don't know if he knocked; if he did I was deep into the work and didn't hear it. Then he is simply there, standing inside the door, standing straight and tall, almost at attention.

"Well, hello, soldier," I say as I hit Save on my laptop and close it.

He says, "My name's Hunt." My heart begins to beat faster, and I fight to maintain my poise.

"Does this mean you've decided to talk to me?" I ask with professional calm, holding on to a smile as he saunters toward me. He frowns and shakes his head. "Then why," I say, "are you here?"

"Damned if I know," he replies, and the look on his face makes me catch my breath. For the first and the only time, I see pain there, and sadness, and confusion. I don't know what to make of it.

Later I thought I'd mistaken the look completely; it seemed so out of character for him and never came again.

"Can...I help you?" I ask him, my smile faltering as he comes closer...so close. Though I'm not afraid, and I don't know why.

"I don't know," he says. "Maybe."

He touches me then, one hand on the side of my face... my neck. His eyes are like fire. I feel them burning me as he lowers his face closer to mine, and I hold my breath but don't move away.

Closer...closer, his mouth comes to mine, almost but not quite touching, hovering there, giving me time to stop what's coming. My held breath fills my chest and throat, almost choking me. My heartbeat rocks me. His breath on my lips is like a powerful drug, clouding my brain. I put my hand up to his where it lies against my cheek, but not to pull it away.

When his lips touch mine at last, it's as if a torch has been laid to dry tinder. There is no stopping it. And no going back.

The alley they were following opened onto a wider dirt street, this one crowded and noisy with pedestrians, mostly men, some pushing handcarts or leading donkeys. There were bicycles maneuvering through the crowd, and several cars were parked alongside the street, huddling as close as they could to the mud-brick buildings.

Hunt motioned for Yancy and Laila to stay back while he stepped into the street. Yancy watched as he surveyed it for several minutes in both directions, eyes touching on every pedestrian, every vehicle, every detail with the intensity of a trained sniper. Apparently satisfied nothing there represented any immediate danger to them, he gestured for Yancy and Laila to join him.

As she followed Hunt through the throngs of people,

Yancy kept her head bowed, clutched her scarf beneath her chin and held tightly to her daughter's hand. She couldn't help but think how they must appear: Afghan man with his wife and child meekly following behind. The thought made her vaguely queasy.

They hadn't gone far—Laila hadn't begun complaining again about her tired feet—when Hunt paused beside a dusty Mercedes of indeterminate color and vintage. He produced a set of keys from the folds of his tunic, unlocked the car and opened the back door.

"Get in and keep down," he said tersely. "Don't get up until I tell you."

Yancy had never been good at taking orders, but because she was mindful of Laila's own contrary nature, and in the interests of leading by example, she chose to do as Hunt told her. She stayed down, hunched over Laila to keep her from popping up to look, as well, while he got in the front, started the motor and inched the car into the flow of traffic. But as soon as the smoothness of the road and the change of traffic noise from pedestrian to vehicular told her they were on a busy city street, she sat up and looked around. After a moment, she said, "Where are we going?"

Hunt snorted. His eagle's glare met hers in the rearview mirror. "Thought I told you to stay down."

"This isn't the way to our hotel," Yancy pointed out, ignoring that. "Where are you taking us?"

Lashes shuttered his gaze as he shifted it back to the street ahead. "To my place."

Yancy considered that for a moment, while her heartbeat ticked a notch faster. She glanced at Laila, who had apparently tuned them out and was peering through the window with avid interest. She hitched herself forward and leaned her arms on the back of the front seat. "Is this a rescue," she inquired in a low voice, but with a light, almost musical tone, "or another abduction?"

Although her view of the side of his face was mostly beard, she noted the subtle change in its shape and caught the flash of teeth as he smiled. His eyes clashed briefly with hers in the mirror. "I'm taking you someplace I know she'll be safe."

Safe.

Laila knew she wasn't supposed to be listening, but she heard that word and knew they were talking about her, about wanting her to be safe, which was really funny because she didn't feel safe at all right now. She felt jumbled and mixed up and kind of scared, maybe a little bit happy—the part about Akaa Hunt being here—but mostly she wanted to close her eyes and ears and make the dreams go away.

At least, she'd always thought they were dreams.

I used to have them a lot, when I was little and first came to live with my new mom. I dreamed about being in a cave in the dark with a big dog who kept me warm and safe from the demons who screamed and wailed outside, and then Akaa Hunt was there, reaching for me, and I thought at first he was a demon, too, but then he wrapped me in his coat and held me close to him, and I felt safe again, with him.

But then Akaa Hunt told me in a hard voice that Ammi—*my first mother—was gone and he was taking me to someone who would keep me safe, and we traveled through the dark and the cold, and somewhere along the journey Akaa Hunt left me and went away.*

She used to cry after she dreamed those dreams, when she was little.

Then Yancy became her new mom, and she felt happy and safe and didn't have the dreams anymore.

Now, seeing Akaa Hunt again, she remembered the dreams and they seemed much more real than before. But she wasn't little now. She was eight years old and she was too old to cry. Crying was for babies.

Laila pressed her lips together and clutched the car windowsill as she stared blindly through the glass and tried not to listen as Mom and Akaa Hunt went on talking.

"Wouldn't we be safer at the hotel?"

Hunt's eyebrows lifted into the shadow of his turban. "Think so? How did they know where to find you?" He paused. "Who knew you were going to the bazaar today? Who did you tell?"

"Nobody," she stated with certainty, then felt herself go cold. With growing realization she added in a whisper, "The hotel concierge. The doorman…the cabdriver…"

Hunt was nodding. "I know, because I heard you. So could anybody else who might have been in the immediate vicinity."

"You…were *there*? But how did you—"

Once again his beard telegraphed his smile, and his eyes denied it. "Let's just say I have an interest in your comings and goings." His voice hardened and so did his eyes. "Evidently, so does someone else."

Yancy sat in stony silence while her heart raced and her mind whirled. She was both furious and frightened, so full of questions she felt she might explode, but acutely aware of all the reasons she couldn't ask them. *Not yet.*

There was Laila, of course, whose hearing was keen and her mind busy even when she appeared to have her attention focused elsewhere.

But also, there was Hunt, who never answered questions. She thought of all the times…all the questions he'd never let her ask…

"Where have you—" I would always begin.

And his mouth would come down on mine, hard and hungry, his beard stubble rough on my face and his skin smelling of gunpowder, smoke and dust, shutting off the rest.

And I would close my eyes and my mind, letting it be enough that it was to me he came to forget, that it was my clean, female body he turned to, to erase the horrors he'd seen. The ugly things he'd done.

She eased slowly back in her seat, shaken by the sure and certain knowledge that *this* time was going to be different. It had to be. Too much had changed. This time she was going to ask the questions, and this time she would not be denied the answers.

She stared through the dusty windows, and as her emotions settled and her gaze focused, once again she realized she knew approximately where they were. This was another part of Old Town Kabul, only a few kilometers but worlds apart from both the poor section they'd just left and the bustling and modern downtown.

She slid forward again.

"You live *here*?" She dipped her head, indicating the aged trees shading the quiet street ahead, the high walls of houses with intricately carved wood window screens just visible through leafy branches. She waited for acknowledgment that didn't come, then went on in a conversational tone. "I did a feature here a few years back. These houses are a couple hundred years old, at least, and most of them are owned by Kabul's oldest families, families that trace back to the days of the Silk Road. How—"

"A friend of a friend," he said, in a way that stated clearly, *And that's all I'm going to tell you.*

She must have made some sound of vexation, because he exhaled through his nose and spoke under his breath. "This isn't the time. Or the place." The slight movement of his head recalled her attention to the other pair of ears present.

His eyes met hers and she realized with a small sense of shock that there was anger in them, mirroring her own.

She pushed back into her seat again, silently seething.

He's angry? He's angry? He pops in and out of my life—my bed!—without warning, as he pleases, dumps a child on my doorstep, tells me she's his, then vanishes from the face of the earth for three years, and he's angry? Really?

In a quick-as-lightning change of mood, fear returned.

Why? What is he angry with me about? It can only be something to do with Laila. Is it the adoption? The fact that I brought her here?

What business is it of his? He has no right—

A panicky shiver rippled through her. *Did* he have the right? If he was, in fact, Laila's biological father—and she had only his word on that, after all. That, and those eyes.

Might he have a legal claim to her?

Could he take her away from me?

It was a new question, and it joined the others whirling in her mind.

Out of the maelstrom, once again one coherent thought emerged: *I have to hold it together...put on a calm face... for Laila.*

"Here we are," Akaa Hunt said.

Laila ducked her head to look out the car window. She

didn't know why she felt funny about getting out of the car and going into the house with the carved patterns over the windows, but she did. Not scared, exactly, although she did have butterflies in her stomach and her heart was beating very, very fast. It was more like the way she remembered feeling on her first day in the new school after Yancy became her new mother, because she knew something big and exciting was going to happen and she wasn't sure whether it would be good or bad.

"It's okay, honey," her mother whispered, and Laila nodded and reached for her hand. She felt like she might throw up or wet her pants, but that was so babyish she didn't want to say so.

Just inside the door, she stopped suddenly and couldn't keep from making a sound. It wasn't very loud, but her mother and Akaa Hunt both heard. They stopped and looked at her.

"What is it, sweetie?" her mother asked.

Laila frowned and wrinkled her nose. "I *smell* something."

"That would be supper," Akaa Hunt said. "I hope."

"It smells delicious," Laila's mother said and squeezed her hand in a way that meant *remember your manners!* "Doesn't it?"

"It smells like…something I remember," Laila said and added with a shrug, "but I don't know exactly what." She took a deep breath, let go of her mother's hand and walked into the room. "I remember this, too. We used to sit on pillows when I lived with *Ammi*, when I was little."

Behind her she heard her mother let out a breath and laugh a little bit. "Yes, I guess you did," she said.

But her voice sounded quivery, and Laila wondered if maybe her mother's stomach had butterflies, too.

"I think," Yancy said, taking a deep breath, "Laila and I both could use a bathroom, if you—"

"Of course." Hunt's voice and manner were crisply formal. "Just go through there, into the courtyard. Second door down on the left is the women's quarters. You should find everything you need. If not, let me know and I'll have Mehri get it for you."

"Mehri?"

"My housekeeper."

"Oh—of course. Laila? Shall we wash up before supper?"

Laila looked up at her, then reached for her hand in a way that felt oddly as though she were offering reassurance and guidance to Yancy, rather than the other way around.

In the magnificently tiled bathroom, Yancy watched her daughter slowly and methodically wash her hands, arms and face, carefully rubbing the soap into foam, squishing the foam between her fingers, rubbing it over her forearms…

How silent she is. She should be chattering away, nonstop, asking one question after another, chirping like a little bird…

She cleared her throat. "Honey, how are you doing? Are you okay?"

Laila watched her hands, washing, washing. "Yes," she said, but it lacked conviction.

"We had a pretty exciting day, didn't we?" Yancy said carefully, wanting to go to her, wanting to touch her, though something held her back. "When those men… um. When they tried to…" *When they tried to…do what?*

What did they want with us? I still don't know. She caught another breath. "I was a little scared. Were you scared?"

"Well, I was…" Laila clasped her hands together and appeared to be fascinated by the foam squishing between her interlaced fingers. "But then I saw Akaa Hunt and I wasn't scared anymore."

Yancy felt a chill shiver through her. Breathless, she said, "Really? Why not?"

Laila's shoulders lifted…fell. "Because I knew he would keep us safe. Like always."

It was evening, which in recent times had become one of Hunt's favorite times of the day. In his experience, most bad things seemed to happen at dawn. By nightfall, whatever was going to happen had happened, for better or worse. The world was shutting down, taking a breather. Even the wind stopped for dusk.

There was that, and the fact that lately it had begun to remind him of evenings when he was growing up, when the chores had all been done and the animals were quiet, well fed and bedding themselves down for the night. Dad would be out on the front porch having a smoke and surveying his kingdom while he waited to be called in to supper, and Mom banging things around in the kitchen, and good smells drifting through the windows. He remembered watching his dad and wishing he could be more like him, knowing he wasn't and never would be as good a man as Charles Grainger, and all he really wanted was to be someplace far, far away from the farm and the whole state of Nebraska.

As an adult he'd worked hard to make sure the wish came true, and he had no regrets. Except maybe *that*— having no regrets—was something he regretted.

Here in the courtyard in Old Kabul, the air smelled

of cooking—the meal they'd just eaten—and of flowers rather than hay or freshly turned earth or manure, and some kind of bird was singing a twilight song in one of the trees. Unlike his father, Hunt didn't smoke—never had—and they'd already had supper. And the tiny kingdom he surveyed wasn't his. But he *was* waiting. Waiting, not to be called *in*, but maybe—almost certainly—to be called to account.

He'd counted down the minutes before life-and-death missions with less trepidation.

He owed Yancy big-time, he knew, an explanation being the least of it. Explaining the facts wouldn't be that hard, but he had a feeling "just the facts" wasn't going to be enough for her, not this time. She was going to want to know what was going on with him, the why of it all, and how was he going to explain that when he wasn't sure he knew himself. And even if he did know, he wasn't clear on how much he was willing to tell her. Reticence was a hard habit to break. Knowledge was power, and giving that up to anyone, even the woman raising his child... He wasn't sure he was ready for that. Or if he ever would be.

That realization made him inexpressibly sad.

The carved door behind him opened and his skin shivered with awareness. He turned and watched without comment as Yancy came into the courtyard from the part of the house that had traditionally been the women's quarters. She was clutching a shawl around her shoulders. Because of the coolness of the evening, he wondered, or merely a case of nerves?

It surprised him a little that he felt the same purely physical, gut-tightening attraction to her he'd had almost from the first moment he'd laid eyes on her—not during the rescue, naturally, but later, back at the base. Sitting across from her at that table, looking into her eyes, the whole world around him fading away until it was just him and her... He'd known then he'd have her, eventually. He'd never doubted it. Just as he'd never doubted she'd be there whenever he came in off a mission, needing her.

He hadn't looked too far ahead, back then. Never given much thought to a time when she wouldn't be there. Then he'd put his daughter in her care, and everything had changed.

He'd thought he knew her pretty well, well enough at least to know she had nerves of steel. Ordinarily. But she'd been silent and withdrawn during the meal—with him, anyway—and he had an idea there was a lot churning around in that red head of hers. Because silence wasn't a normal state for Yancy Malone.

"She's asleep," she said, and he nodded.

She glanced at him as she walked past him, deeper into the shadowed courtyard, where she lifted a hand to touch a blossom hanging from a vine. "It's nice out here."

"Yes," he said, watching her. Waiting.

She turned to fully face him—as if squaring for battle. He couldn't help but think how beautiful she was with that fierceness about her.

"Dinner was wonderful. Please tell... Mehri, wasn't it?" He nodded. "Please tell her how much we—Laila and I—enjoyed it. I don't think I've ever seen or tasted so many different rice dishes. And the *qorma* was fabulous. I'm going to have to ask her for the recipe."

Seriously? It sounded as if she'd rehearsed it.

He answered with a stilted nod. "I'm sure she'll be happy to share it with you. Afghan people are justifiably proud of their cuisine, as well as their hospitality."

Her smile flickered and finally went out. Her gaze wandered away from his face and was jerked back, like a restive horse fighting the reins, to meet his, this time with defiance.

"Well?" he said. Gently rather than with impatience.

He heard the slight catch in her breathing. "Well, what?"

"I know you've been wanting to ask questions. So—ask."

Chapter 4

She stared at him a long moment more, and this time when her gaze slid away she didn't force it back. He saw the muscles in her face flinch and her mouth quirk with an attempt at a smile. As he watched the emotional struggle play across her familiar features, it came to him that this was a Yancy Malone he'd never seen before. Jolted, he realized in all the times he'd shared her bed, as intimately as he'd known the secrets of her body, he'd never once seen her angry. Or wounded. Afraid or sad.

Or if she had been, he'd been too selfishly involved with his own needs to notice.

She shrugged finally and shook her head. But still no words came.

Out of sheer self-preservation, Hunt did what he'd always done when unwanted emotions threatened to pierce his armor. He turned on the charm. He put on a smile, one that was just a bit crooked. "Don't tell me Yancy Malone doesn't have questions to ask, because I won't believe it."

She made a sound that might have passed for a laugh if the light had been poorer. If he hadn't been able to see that unfamiliar pain in her face. "I'd think you'd be happy about that."

"Come on. I always loved your questions." He paused and added with another wry smile, "It was so much fun to shut you up."

For Yancy, the unmistakable growl of intimacy in his voice brought a fresh flood of memories... A face, a voice, a body...the sound of a laugh, a remembered look, the shape of a mouth.

Almost in a panic, she thought, *But I can't remember the feel of that body...can't remember what that mouth tasted like.*

Her memories were like recalling a movie or a television show she'd seen. She couldn't seem to bring them into focus with her own reality or with the man standing before her now.

Strange to think I once shared a bed with this man— more than once. So many times...and yet I don't think I know him at all.

What was it that was so different about him?

Oh, certainly he *looked* different, with the full beard, the turban, the Afghan tunic, vest and loose-fitting trousers—though here in the privacy of his home he'd shed the turban and vest. But it was more than that. It was, she realized in a late flash of insight, not what he looked like, but the way she saw him.

When she'd first met him he'd seemed to her like an invincible man-machine, a superhero, a life-size action figure. Later he was her shadow lover who came and went in the night like a ghost. But something had happened since the last time she'd seen him, the night he'd brought Laila to her and then disappeared without a trace.

Something's changed.

Maybe I've changed.

Older now, perhaps wiser, and from the perspective of motherhood, she saw him as a mere human being, a man, one with flaws, one who'd loved a woman, fathered and then abandoned a child.

Though, oddly, he seemed no less imposing because of that.

If anything, even more so.

Yes, definitely more so.

I don't know how to talk to him now. We never talked much before. Never had to. Meaningless love-words, whispered in the darkness...laughter and sighs...forbidden thoughts and questions never voiced. It was enough then.

Not now, though. Now the reality was, they shared a child. Like it or not, difficult as it might be, she would have to learn new ways to communicate with the man who was her adopted daughter's biological father.

Shouldn't be too hard, right? Communicating is what I do.

But it was he who spoke first.

While she was still thinking how to begin, he said hoarsely, "You have to know I never intended to drop her in your lap and—"

"Disappear?" Caught unprepared, she spoke with more bitterness than she'd intended or wanted to. *Of course, it's about Laila. It's only about Laila. Remember that.*

He drew in a sharp breath. "That's not—"

"But you did," she said, giving no quarter now that she'd regained her footing, skewering him with her gaze—her interviewer's stare, the one that demanded answers, that refused to back down. "Didn't you?"

He nodded, glaring back at her like the warrior he was. "I thought I'd be able to come back for her."

"But you didn't. You didn't send word, leave me instructions, a message, *anything*." Not accusing, simply stating facts they both already knew.

"I couldn't." He didn't raise his voice, and it was like stones dropping into a well. "You know what my job is—was—like. The mission was—"

"Secret." She nodded, smiled painfully. "This is where you tell me you can't tell me anything, right?"

"I sure as hell couldn't *then*," he snapped.

"Does that mean you can…*now*?"

"Some things…" he said stiffly. "Maybe…when you're ready to listen."

She sucked in a breath and managed to keep a rein on her anger, though what she'd have loved to do more than anything just then was kick him. She managed not to, partly because it occurred to her, with her experience as an Emmy-winning reporter and hard-nosed interviewer of the famous and infamous, that his macho attitude—face set in stone, arms folded on his chest—was more defensive than imposing.

Switching gears, she said quietly, "What did you think I was going to do, Hunt? I had no experience with kids, let alone a traumatized child. I was in no way prepared for…for that. Why did you do it—bring her to *me*, of all people?"

He coughed, the universal indicator of masculine discomfort. "Well, hell, that's a no-brainer. I came to you because I knew about that outfit you belong to…that—"

"INCBRO." *And was that all, Hunt? The only reason?*

"Right. I knew you could get her to safety through them. I figured I'd come back and find her when I—" He stopped abruptly and ran a hand over his face and beard, a gesture of distraction she wouldn't have thought him capable of—the Hunt she'd known, the superhero warrior. "That's not— Look, you were the only person I could think of. That I could trust." And then, in a voice that seemed to come from the depths of his soul, he whispered, "I sure as hell never thought you were going to *adopt* her."

She didn't answer for a moment—her mind was too busy throwing up barricades and battening down hatches. *Keep your distance, Malone... Don't let your own emotions get in the way. Your job is to get him to reveal his. And his intentions. Is he going to try to take her away from me?*

But in that small silence Hunt must have seen an opening, and he took it.

"Okay, Yankee. What made *you* do it?"

It was her turn to suck in a breath—she hadn't expected him to turn it around on her. At least, not so soon.

Hoping to buy herself some time, she said sharply, "*Do it? You mean, adopt her? What kind of question is that? Why does anyone adopt a child? Because—*"

"Usually because they want one very badly," Hunt said, and though his eyes were hidden now by the deepening dusk, she could hear the steel in his voice. And the disbelief. "You said it yourself—you hadn't had any experience with kids until I dropped one in your lap. It never occurred to me you'd suddenly develop motherhood instincts. I thought you'd get her to safety through that child-bride rescue outfit you work with. I figured you'd—"

"Pass her off like a hot potato? A traumatized little girl?" Again her voice came sharper and louder than she'd planned, partly because the words he'd spoken hit so close to the mark.

Motherhood instincts? I was terrified, Hunt. Bullets

flying past my ears never scared me so much as those shimmering golden eyes gazing up into mine. And when a tear detached itself from the shimmer and slid away down her cheek... I didn't have a clue what to do. I remember kneeling down...putting my arms around her... feeling her body trembling. She was trying so hard not to cry. I think I picked her up then. I must have, because I woke up on my cot with her wrapped in my arms, sound asleep.

She paused, then went on in a half whisper. "What kind of person do you think I am?"

"I don't really know that," he said, matching his voice to hers. "Do I?"

"You know a whole lot more about me than I do about you." She threw that at him, tight and quivering with emotions, three years' worth of fear and uncertainty and unanswered questions. "I live my life in the public eye. You live yours in the shadows. You're a...a—"

"Ghost?" A single word, spoken softly in the darkness.

Her chest constricted with the pain of remembering. She gave a helpless whimper of a laugh and turned away from him.

His voice followed her. "You still haven't answered my question."

She shook her head and looked up at the night sky, where the stars were veiled by the lights of the city, as they were in New York and Los Angeles and all the other cities where she lived most of the time. Starry nights were one of the things she missed now that she was no longer reporting from remote battlefields.

"Why did I keep her with me and not hand her off to some *stranger*?" She paused, then took a careful breath and answered truthfully. "At first, I guess it was because she seemed so…lost. So scared. So wounded." *She has your eyes. Did you know that? I know it's not unusual for Afghans to have light-colored eyes…blue or green or hazel eyes. But Laila's eyes are* your *eyes.* "The way she looked at me…as if she trusted me."

"I told her she could."

How different his voice sounded. Did she only imagine it was emotion she heard? Or was she projecting her own inner turmoil onto him? Surely the Hunt Grainger she knew would never allow himself to be caught in such an unguarded moment.

But then, I really don't know him at all.

If only I could see his face, she thought, then remembered, *The same darkness protects us both.*

"And was that it?" His voice was relentless. Implacable. "Just…she looked scared? So you decided to take on the responsibility of raising a child? Come on, Yancy."

He'd had enough interrogation experience to know when someone was lying to him. Or being evasive, at least.

He knew he'd cornered her, so he wasn't surprised when she jerked around to face him, squaring off again, obviously angry, struggling to find the right words. Which was pretty amazing, considering words were ordinarily her best weapons of choice.

The qualities of the night hadn't outwardly changed—the same soft darkness, the sound of trickling water from a fountain in a neighboring garden set against the far-off percussion of city traffic—but the courtyard was no longer peaceful. Now it seemed more like a battlefield, crackling and humming with tension.

"Obviously, Laila isn't—wasn't—just any child." Yancy's voice was infused with the same tension that filled the air around them. "And even if she was, we don't simply pass them along, like…like shipping off a package on a train. Every case is different, and we always try to do what's best for the child. Sometimes that means educating the family, even paying a bride-price or school tuition so the child can stay with her parents. We only take a child away if she's an orphan or in immediate danger."

"She was—I told you that."

"In danger, yes. But not an orphan, not entirely. She had a father, someone she knew." She paused, and there was accusation in the silence. Then, in a breaking voice, she said, "I thought she had *you*."

"So, you kept her because she was mine?" It took some doing, but he managed to keep any trace of emotion out of his voice.

"Of course I did," she lashed back, then caught a breath that suggested she might not have wanted to admit that. After a moment, she said on the exhalation, "She was yours—you'd told me that—so naturally I assumed you'd be coming back for her." Again she paused, and this time when she went on it was in her reporter's voice, vibrant with controlled passion. "Which I *thought* would be a few days. Then a few weeks. But you didn't come back, and after a whole year had gone by, I thought you must be dead. *Surely* you were dead, because, I thought, how could any man abandon his own child without one word?"

Or me! The thought intruded, slipped past her defenses. *How could you abandon me?*

She rushed on before he could respond. "Anyway, by that time I'd grown so attached—" She shook her head as if throwing that word away. "Okay, I'd fallen in *love* with her. It's not hard to do, you know. I couldn't bear the thought of losing her. So I started the process of adopting her. It wasn't easy, but I'm in a unique position to get some strings pulled and cut through a lot of red tape. The adoption was final six months ago. She's my child, Hunt. My daughter."

"Did you even try to get in touch with me?"

She gave a huff of laughter. "Seriously? I'm a reporter, remember? I called in every favor, accessed every contact I had. Brick walls. Everywhere I turned, the story was the same. You'd been killed in action. The rest was classified. They wouldn't even give me your family's location so I could tell your parents they had a granddaughter. I thought— *Never mind what I thought!* Why am I answering *your* questions? You're the one who owes me an explanation. A hundred explanations."

The words seemed to ring in the quiet courtyard, like the after-humming of a struck gong. He listened, and it seemed as though he could feel the vibrations in his own chest. *A hundred explanations. Yes. And it still wouldn't be enough.*

"I'm sorry," he said stiffly.

She uttered a high sound, too sharp to be laughter. "Is that all? Seriously? Even now? Just...*I'm sorry*?"

He stared at her. His eyes felt hot and his face like stone. What could he say to her? He didn't know how to talk to her, not this way.

In the darkness, touching her...he'd felt as if the depths of her soul, the secrets of her heart, the mysteries of her mind were all accessible to him, in protected vaults to which only he held the key. And that, if he wanted to, when the time was right, he could open the doors, unlock the secrets, learn what treasures she kept hidden from the rest of the world.

That was then. In the darkness...touching.
This is now, and everything has changed.

The physical distance between them was small—an arm's length, no more. He could have reached across it and touched her—her face…her hair…her neck. He remembered the way it smelled, that soft sweet curve of neck and shoulder, hidden by the thick fall of hair, warm and musky from sleep. Memory struck like a knife in his gut so that he winced as if with physical pain. Because he knew the distance between them was a bottomless chasm, one he didn't know how to cross.

"You know I've never been able to talk about my missions," he said at last.

So, it's come back around to this. The mission. As it always would.

As Yancy gazed at him through a haze that was half tears, half anger, it appeared to her as though Hunt was moving away from her, as if she was on a fast-moving train and he was left standing on the station platform. She felt an almost overwhelming sense of grief and loss.

She made a small, helpless gesture, taking in the whole of him—clothes, beard, surroundings. "That's what this is—all this—a mission?"

"Of course." With arrogance in his voice and his arms folded on his chest, in the near-darkness he seemed to become the Afghan chieftain he pretended to be.

"And you can't tell me anything about it."

"No, I can't. Not until it's done."

"What happened today—did that have anything to do with your *mission*?"

"I don't know. I wish I did."

She turned away, choked by her own frustration, unable even to say good-night.

His words stopped her. "But I can tell you about *her.*" She looked back at him, at his silhouette against the lighter sky. "About Laila. Her mother. How it happened. If you'd care to hear."

Was there entreaty in his voice? She so wished she could see his eyes, his features—though she doubted they'd have told her much. She took a deep breath and, with great effort, said carefully, "I would. Of course."

Now there was no sound at all in the courtyard; the background noise of the city had faded away and the fountain had ceased its music. The darkness seemed to enfold the two of them in its own embrace. Wrapped in it, she could feel his heat, smell his scent. So close... too close...

She put out her hand expecting to touch his chest, meaning to hold him at bay, knowing she had no will to resist him if he chose to move closer. Her hand encountered only air. It was her perceptions that made him seem so near. To disguise the gesture she turned it into something else.

"But first—" She turned quickly, before he could guess how close she'd come to stepping into his arms. "First, just let me check on Laila. It's a strange place... I don't want her to wake and be frightened. It's been such an eventful day—"

"I'd like to come with you." She halted without turning and felt the light touch on her shoulder. "If it's okay. Please."

She nodded, shielded her feminine responses, swallowed all her maternal misgivings and protective instincts, and murmured, "Sure. Of course."

She led the way into the silent house, into the smaller of the two living rooms that were traditionally used for sleeping, as well as dining and relaxing with close family members. In this one the walls were soft buttery yellow, lit by small lamps in sconces placed high on the walls.

There were sleeping mattresses against three of the walls and pillows covered in red and orange and black patterns. On one of the mattresses, Laila slept soundly, curled on her side in her favorite position, with her cheek pillowed on her hand. Her lips were parted, and her lashes made dark shadows on skin turned golden by the lamplight.

As Yancy knelt beside the sleeping child, she felt her chest tighten and her throat ache and her fingers burn with the need to touch…to reassure herself this small beautiful creature, this miraculous being, was real…and *her daughter.* Behind her she could feel Hunt balancing himself on one knee, but she didn't look at him, afraid of what she might see in his face.

Which would be worse—to see him dispassionate, cold, aloof…the kind of man too occupied with making war to care about a child…the kind of man who could so easily walk away and leave his child in the hands of strangers and vanish without a trace? Or to see in his face the same overwhelming love that fills my heart? The kind of love that won't let go? That will fight to the last breath for his child.

She drew a shuddering breath and rose, and he did, too, almost simultaneously, one hand under her elbow to steady her. She slid away from his touch and turned on him a blind smile as she whispered, "Obviously, she's fine. Where would you like to—"

His hand on her elbow guided her back into the courtyard and to another door, this one leading into the other living room, the larger one in which Mehri had served them their dinner. Here, too, there were mattresses and brightly patterned pillows against three walls, but with a slightly raised platform of polished wood in the center. The walls here were a darker gold, the lighting, as in the sleeping room, subdued. It occurred to Yancy that

the effect of all this was warm…intimate…intensely se-
ductive, and to her extreme distress she felt an electric
current race through her body, making her palms sweat
and her pulse quicken.

"Would you like some tea?" Hunt gestured toward
the raised platform that earlier had held their dinner.

She shook her head. "It's late. I don't want to impose
on Mehri."

"She's retired for the night." He sounded oddly formal, as if, she thought, he'd slipped back into whatever
role he'd been playing. "If you want tea, I'll make it."

She couldn't help but smile. He caught it and lifted
his eyebrows.

"What, you don't think I'm capable of making tea?"

"I'm pretty sure you could do anything you set your
mind to," she said as her smile went wry, "but it's definitely a side of you I'm having a hard time imagining."

"I imagine there are a few sides of me you might not
have imagined," Hunt replied drily.

She gave a soft laugh and said, "No doubt," and it
seemed the tension between them eased…for a moment.
"But really," she added, "I don't need anything."

Hunt nodded and let a breath escape, in full acknowledgment of the words she hadn't spoken: *I don't need
anything from you except an explanation. Except the
truth.*

He gestured at a mattress and said, "Have a seat."
When she had done so, he settled himself on the same
mattress, but more than arm's length away. He didn't re-
cline or lounge, but sat upright with his knees bent, as if
he were squatting before a campfire or on lookout with
his rifle at the ready. He looked extremely uncomfortable.
After a long silent moment he frowned at his hands as if

he didn't know quite what to do with them, then draped them over the tops of his knees and cleared his throat.

"You were going to tell me how you met Laila's mother," Yancy prompted.

"Yeah. It was—" he began, then shook his head and looked around angrily, reminding Yancy of a correspondent beginning a live report only to discover a problem with the audio feed. She'd done that herself more than once.

Sympathy mixed with something else, something she couldn't bring herself to acknowledge, made her chest ache. Pushing against the pain, she uttered the question she hadn't even realized was uppermost in her mind. "Did you love her?"

He threw her a startled look, and for an instant there was something in his eyes that, in spite of the full dark beard and hollow cheeks, made him seem very young. Then he shook his head and shifted his gaze away from her, letting his knees fall into a more relaxed cross-legged position. Slightly hunched and speaking now to his clasped hands, he said, "It wasn't like that. Sometimes, in war—" He paused to clear his throat. "You have to understand, sometimes things happen you're in no way prepared for. We're supposed to be prepared for anything. I should have been. But I…wasn't. Let's just say it wasn't my finest moment." He gave her his warrior's glare. "I take full responsibility for that."

Not trusting herself to speak, Yancy only nodded, and after a moment, he went on in an expressionless drone, as if he were being debriefed for the umpteenth time.

"The mission was to take out a target—an al Qaeda leader we'd been after for a while, pretty high up on our most-wanted list. We had intel he was supposed to be at a wedding—his, actually. The location was a small village in the mountains near the Pakistani border—the bride's hometown. We knew the area would be difficult to penetrate using a ground attack, and blowing up the place with a drone strike wasn't an option if we wanted to collect any intelligence data the guy might have. So we used a chopper approach." He paused to look up at Yancy. "Like the one that later took out Bin Laden." She nodded and he smiled without humor. "Lessons were learned. Having a backup chopper, for one."

"You had one crash?"

He shook his head. "Not then. The operation went as planned, just the usual small glitches, nothing we couldn't handle." He paused long enough for Yancy to hear everything he *wasn't* saying. "We went in...took care of our objective. We were in the process of gathering intel—interviewing members of the wedding, family, guests... confiscating whatever we could carry...and this woman comes to me. I realize she's the bride—now the widow, I guess—which hits me harder than I expect it to, because she's so young. The al Qaeda guy was at least sixty, and this girl couldn't have been more than maybe eighteen... nineteen. And she's obviously scared out of her mind. She begs us to take her with us. Says her family sold her to the al Qaeda guy in exchange for protection and she doesn't know what's going to happen to her now."

"Why did she come to you?"

He gave her another look. "I speak both Farsi and Pashto. She heard me doing most of the talking during the raid." He paused, coughed and straightened a little. "Anyway, I told her we couldn't take her, obviously. We were deep in hostile territory and still had to be extracted for the mission to be a success. No way were we equipped to deal with hostages, prisoners, refugees—whatever. I mean, we *couldn't* take her." The look he gave Yancy now was steady, not asking for understanding, just stating facts.

But she did understand, both the necessity of saying no and the pain it must have caused him to do so. She nodded, and he let go a breath.

"I figured that was the end of it. But then, as we were making our way back to the choppers, here she comes running after us. Out in the open. I figure it was a miracle she didn't get killed then and there, but it was a sure bet the people left behind in that village weren't going to be happy with her.

"It was my call—you know, I figured she might have some intel that would make it worth the risk of taking her with us. But she'd delayed us just long enough. We started taking fire at the extraction point. I took one in the leg."

He says it so matter-of-factly.

Which wasn't a surprise to Yancy; she'd heard the same tone and the same stoic acceptance from countless other soldiers she'd interviewed over the years.

That's when I knew I'd been hit...

I realized my arm was gone...

Don't remember much...

My buddy next to me...

She wondered if she would ever understand the kind of courage it took to face that kind of horror every day.

"We all made it to the chopper," Hunt went on. "But we were taking some heavy fire. A couple other members of the team had been hit, and they were worse off than I was. We got off the ground, but it was obvious right away we weren't going to make enough altitude to get out of shooting range. There'd been five going in. Now there were six, thanks to me, and the chopper had evidently taken a few rounds where it hurt. It was pretty clear either a couple of us had to get off the chopper, or we were all going down.

"Zahra knew something was wrong, and when I told her what the deal was, she didn't even flinch. Just said, 'I know where to hide.' And she pointed down. We were flying over some pretty rugged terrain, but the pilot managed to find a place to put us down."

"*Us?* Why did *you* have to stay? You were wounded!"

He gave her a long look, then said quietly, "Simple logic, Yankee. We needed to lighten the load. Couldn't very well leave a girl alone in the wilderness in her bridal clothes, not after I'd already compromised her by taking her along. There were five team members in the chopper, two with life-threatening injuries. My wound wasn't life threatening. The two uninjured didn't speak Pashto and were needed to keep the injured alive until they could get back to base. Do the math."

She shook her head, though she knew he was right. "So, they put you on the ground and left you there."

"With enough supplies to last a few days—until they could send a chopper to pick us up. Zahra knew the terrain—she told me she used to tend her family's sheep in the area. She knew a cave the sheepherders used, which would be deserted at that time of year when there was no wild feed to graze."

He fell silent but didn't look at her, gazing instead at his clasped hands. She had no way of knowing how much time had passed before she saw his shoulders lift, and he drew in a breath and went on.

"It took longer than it should have for the extraction team to get to us—there were reasons, but it doesn't matter why. She took care of me. Nursed me. It was a small cave. It was cold. Hell, I can make a hundred excuses, but the bottom line is, what happened shouldn't have happened. I take full responsibility."

Of course you do, she wanted to tell him. *God forbid you should be human.*

But she kept silent, and he cleared his throat loudly. "Obviously, I had no idea she was pregnant, and neither did she. I arranged for her to be taken in by a family—friends, contacts of mine, people I knew I could trust—in a village far enough away from hers that I felt she'd be safe. I gave her a backstory—husband killed fighting the Taliban, that kind of thing—and I arranged to have money sent on a regular basis. But I was sent back to Germany for rehab, and then…well, it was almost a year before I was able to get back there to check on her." He gave a short, hard laugh. "And there she was."

"With a baby girl," Yancy said softly.

He hissed out a breath. "I knew it—she—had to be mine. Nobody in that household would have touched her, and I knew for darn sure there hadn't been anybody before me." He looked at Yancy then, and the light caught his eyes and made them glow like fire. "She was a virgin when she came to me in that cave, Yankee. And God help me, I—"

A sound cut him off—the high, thin wail of a terrified child.

Chapter 5

He wasn't in his best fighting shape but had managed to keep himself reasonably fit during the past two years spent under deep cover. Even encumbered by the extra fabric in his Afghan clothing, he was on his feet before Yancy and didn't even remember covering the distance through the darkened courtyard to the women's quarters. Pausing outside the door, he could hear her—his child, his little girl—whimpering. Hear the words she said.

"Ammi... Ammi..."

In the few seconds he waited there, Yancy was beside him. He glanced down at her and saw her looking back at him, her gaze fierce, its message unmistakable. He hardened his jaw and, without a word, stood back to allow her to go before him.

He followed her into the room, and his heart gave a queer little kick when he saw Laila kneeling on her pallet, her arms lifted to Yancy, the tears on her cheeks shining golden in the soft light of the sconce high on the wall. He wasn't used to being the fifth wheel, the odd man out, and as he watched the scene from a distance that seemed farther than the few yards it was, he realized that the unaccustomed hollowness he felt inside was loneliness.

I'm an outsider. I don't belong here.

It was much the same way he'd felt the day he'd realized that no matter how much he loved and respected his parents and valued the upbringing they'd given him, he wasn't going to follow in their footsteps. That no matter how much they wanted it, he would never be a farmer.

While he waited for his adrenaline-fueled heartbeat to return to normal rhythms, reminding himself to unclench his teeth and his fists, unfamiliar thoughts crashed through his brain, colliding with reason.

But, still, she's my child.

Yes, but it's her mother she needs now, not me.

Yancy's her mother.

But she cried, "Ammi!" Not Mommy.

I did this. My fault. My fault.

Yes, but I did what I had to do.

She needs me! I'm her father. She needs me, too.

With burning eyes he watched Yancy cuddle and comfort Laila until she finally fell asleep again. To add to his unaccustomed inner turmoil concerning his daughter, there was the continuing puzzle of Yancy.

She was the same and yet different.

Yes, she was as beautiful as ever. Yes, his attraction to her was as strong. Nothing had changed, and yet everything had changed. It wasn't only the fact that in the eyes of the law she was Laila's mother; it was more complicated even than that.

It was his own feelings he couldn't figure out. How the hell did he feel about her now—aside from wanting

her so badly he ached all over? He didn't like not knowing. Liked even less the dark and turbulent mess he encountered whenever he tried to think about it. He longed
for the way it had been between them, the simplicity of
it. Of a man and a woman, of mutual hunger, mutual
need, giving and taking in equal measures.

*There are parts of that first time I can't remember, but
I know I told her my name. I had gone to her quarters
still dirty and stinking of death and battle, filled with the
horror of it, needing to wipe it out of my head, and the
only way I could think of to do that was to bury myself
in a woman's clean, sweet body and lose myself there. I
don't remember saying much. No explanation, no asking, nothing. I looked at her and then she was there, and
I kissed her, knowing it wouldn't stop with that. And she
didn't stop me. Seemed to know what I needed without
my telling her. I wanted to cry, but instead I put all that
was inside me into making love to her.*

*She was generous with her loving. She gave it all,
nothing held back, even though I hadn't showered or
shaved, and I know my beard marked her redhead-fair
skin. I probably marked her other places, too, though
not intentionally. Afterward—too quickly it was over—
she didn't give me a chance to feel ashamed. She smiled
up at me and touched my lips with her fingers, and said,
"Hello again, soldier."*

"She's asleep," Yancy whispered, and he nodded. "I
think I should sleep here with her…in case she wakes
up again."

"It was a nightmare?" His voice was hoarse, raw with
remembering.

She nodded, looking not at him but back over her shoulder at the sleeping child.

"Does she have them often?"

She pulled her gaze back to him, but it slid quickly away. "She did at first. But she hasn't had one for a long time. Probably what happened today…"

Again Hunt nodded. "It was probably seeing me that set her off—made her remember."

She opened her mouth to deny it, then shook her head and shrugged. "Maybe. Probably. I don't know."

He said, "Yankee—" just as she hitched in a breath to say more, so he yielded to her. The look she angled up at him was dark and troubled.

"Hunt, what happened today? Was it—"

Breath exploded from his lungs, and for the second time he said, "I wish to God I knew."

"I thought Kabul was secure—relatively. There haven't been any bombings or kidnappings since the drawdown. And now—and here *you* are, and… Hunt, tell me the truth. Is it *Laila* they were after? What's going on that I should know about?"

He touched her face, unable to tell her what was in his heart just as he'd been unable to tell her then, that first time. Only now, though he needed her as much, wanted her as badly, this time there was no welcome, no giving, no compassion in the eyes that bored into his. Only questions and anger and fear.

"Yankee," he whispered, "all I can tell you is that I didn't mean for this to happen. I didn't mean for you to know…about me. I wish I could tell you more, but I can't. I hope you can understand."

She stepped back, away from his touch. "I wish I didn't, but I do." Her voice was soft as a sigh. "That's what makes it so hard."

She closed the door. Gently.

He stood for a long moment, her image burned onto his retinas. Then he turned and went upstairs to his room, where he accessed the secret cubbyhole that housed his computer and COM link. As he waited for the system to power up, his mind was busy composing the report of the day's events he'd be sending off to central command. That, and the questions he wanted answers to.

Was it Laila those men were after?

Or Yancy?

Was it a random kidnapping, revenge or part of a much larger plot?

And, most important, who is behind it—the Taliban or al Qaeda?

Laila was awake, but she didn't open her eyes. Not yet. She was thinking. And she felt scared. And she didn't know why. There was *something* scary lurking in her memory, just out of reach, and she knew that if she tried too hard to see it, it would only shrink back into the shadows. Whatever it was, it made her feel cold and quivery in her stomach.

She thought maybe it was a dream, and if she opened her eyes it would be gone. So, even though she was afraid to do it, she summoned all her courage and opened her eyes.

The scary dream-thing went away, all right, but now she didn't know where she was. This wasn't her room back in Virginia or her mom's room or even the hotel room they'd slept in the other night. Her bed was a soft pillowy thing, and when she reached out her arm she could touch the floor.

Laila pushed herself up on her elbows and swiped her hair out of her eyes, and there was her mom, standing a little ways away, smiling at her and brushing her pretty red hair.

"Good morning, sweet pea."

Her mom always called her silly things like *sweet pea* and *pumpkin* and *honey*. She said it was because she had grown up in Virginia, and that it meant you loved someone very much. Laila just knew it made her feel warm and good inside, and hearing it now made her smile.

And also she remembered.

Her mom was wearing the same brown dress from yesterday, and the pretty scarf she'd bought at the market was draped around her shoulders, instead of over her head, covering up her hair. Laila remembered she'd had to wear a scarf over her head, too. She remembered the men who had crowded around them, and how her mom had stumbled on purpose and tripped one and made them fall, and how she had grabbed hold of Laila's hand and they had run very fast.

She remembered Akaa Hunt.

This was his house.

"Come on, sweetie pie. Aren't you going to get up and dressed?" Her mom dropped her brush into her purse, which was sitting open on the pillowy mattress beside her. "I'm sure breakfast must be ready."

Laila scooted herself up onto her knees. "Is Akaa Hunt going to eat breakfast with us?"

"I imagine so." Her mom looked in her purse, found a lipstick, opened it, stared at it, then put it back. "If he hasn't already eaten." She was frowning the way she did sometimes that meant she was thinking hard, not that she was angry. Then she looked up and smiled. "Okay—how about a bath?"

Laila found the bath very interesting. It was in the floor and made of tile and had little steps to go down into it, like a very small swimming pool. Her mom ran some water into it, which wasn't very hot, only just warm. Laila stretched out in it on her stomach and let it lap against her chin while she thought about her mom and Akaa Hunt. She wasn't sure why, but she liked having them with her. Both of them. Together. They made her feel safe. And happy.

Almost like...

But she pushed that thought out of her head, because she didn't want to wish for something that probably wasn't ever going to come true.

Still, she watched them closely while she ate her breakfast of eggs cooked with vegetables, sweet flat bread and soft cheese with raisins, sitting on the cushions on the floor the way they had last night at dinner. She pretended not to watch them, of course, making a point to study each bite carefully before putting it into her mouth and closing her eyes while she sipped her cup of sweet milk and tea. But she listened.

Akaa Hunt said he would take them to the hotel, but only to get their things. Laila's mom said that was nice of him but not necessary, if he would call a taxicab for them. Akaa Hunt said it *was* necessary, because they would be staying with him. Laila's heart jumped when she heard that! Then Akaa Hunt made his voice very soft and she had to strain so hard to hear she could almost feel her ears growing bigger, and he said, "Until I get to the bottom of what happened yesterday."

Laila's mom didn't answer.

Laila said loudly, "Are we going to see a farm today? You said we could, Mom. You *promised.*"

Mom opened her mouth but didn't say anything. Akaa Hunt said, "Out of the question."

Laila felt a lump growing in her throat and was afraid

she might cry. She didn't want to cry in front of Akaa Hunt. She whispered, "You promised," then stared hard at Akaa Hunt, willing the tears to go back inside her head and out of her eyes.

Akaa Hunt looked back at her, frowning in a way that made him look very fierce but for some reason didn't scare Laila one bit. She kept on looking at him, and after a moment, he turned the fierce look on Laila's mom and asked in a growly voice, "Where is this farm? Whose is it? How did you arrange it?"

Laila's mom cleared her throat and explained. "The family of one of our translators has a farm. It's not far away—just south of the city, off the Kabul-Gardez Highway. It's a secure sector." She lowered her voice so Laila had to strain to hear again. "It's completely safe, Hunt. You must know I wouldn't even consider it otherwise."

Akaa Hunt said something Laila couldn't hear. Then he looked back at Laila with that frowning face and said, "Okay, you can go—under one condition. I'm coming with you."

Laila's mom lifted her eyebrows and her lips got tight, as if she might be about to say no. Instead, she looked at Laila and said in a company voice, "How about it, Laila? Is it all right with you if Hunt comes with us to visit the farm?"

Laila shrugged and said, "Sure," hiding her face behind her cup of sweet milk and tea.

Inside, her heart was dancing.

Riding along the dusty highway in Hunt's dusty Mercedes, watching the dusty land go by beyond his austere profile, Yancy felt as if she'd entered the Land of Oz— only in reverse, going from a Technicolor world to one of sepia tones, where even the familiar seemed unreal.

The car was ordinary, the highway one she'd traveled before. She was familiar with the rumbling trucks and crowded buses, the occasional donkey cart clanking along the shoulder. The landscape of cultivated fields against a backdrop of dun-colored hills, broken here and there by a cluster of mud-brick houses, was one she'd passed through before. The man's profile was familiar to her, too, most often gently silhouetted against the glow of lantern light and molded with shadows.

Separately, these things were commonplace, unremarkable. Taken together, they seemed otherworldly. Dreamlike.

Yesterday at this time she'd been shopping in a Kabul marketplace with her daughter, picking out presents for her sister, Miranda, enjoying Laila's delight in rediscovering her roots. If Hunt had entered her thoughts, it had been with poignant regret that Laila's father could not have lived to see her grow up. Her life had seemed secure, her paths clear, her choices her own to make, for both herself and for her daughter.

Then, in a matter of minutes, everything had changed.

Today, not only was Laila's father alive, but he was driving them in his car. He had taken control of their lives—hers and her daughter's. And on this outwardly peaceful, sunny day, Yancy felt engulfed by clouds of mystery, uncertainty and fear.

Fear? Why now, when I've never been afraid before, not in a decade of reporting from battlefields and smoking ruins?

Yes...but then I didn't have a child.

Yancy turned to glance back at Laila, who was gazing out at the passing scene, her forehead pressed against the window glass. And she felt a cold, squeezing sensation around her heart.

"Why did you do it?" Hunt's voice was low, meant for her ears only. He moved his head slightly, indicating the little girl sitting so quietly in the backseat. "Why did you bring her here?"

Yancy shifted to face forward again and spoke in tones as soft as his. "Here—to Afghanistan? It's where she was born. It's her heritage. I thought she should know—"

He nodded. "But why now?"

"Because," she began, then lowered her voice even further. "Because I thought it might be now or never. In a few weeks the last of the coalition forces will be gone. Who knows what will happen then? With Taliban forces strong in the border regions, how long will the current stability last? If the Taliban regains control—"

"There are people working hard to make sure that doesn't happen," Hunt interrupted, his voice hard.

On the verge of a reply, Yancy turned instead to gaze at him in silent understanding. The knowledge came to her in the quiet way that made her mind whisper, *Of course.*

Of course. He is one of those people.

Without his having to say another word, she understood that this was his mission, the goal he'd been working toward for three years, if not longer. He'd been working undercover, living as a native, a tribal elder, working to forge coalitions to resist the Taliban. It came down on her all at once, the understanding of why his identity must be kept absolutely secret at all costs, the realization of how she and Laila must have jeopardized his mission and his cover, and how much he'd risked by intervening in their attempted kidnapping. How much he was risking by being here with her now, and with Laila.

Her heart hammered wildly as the revelations rocketed through her mind. The words she couldn't say all but deafened her.

Oh, my God.

But she couldn't say even that much.

The lamb wriggled free of her grasp, but Laila didn't seem to mind. She stood clapping her hands as the lamb scampered back to its mother, and her laughter carried across the field on the breeze, the sound reminding Hunt of the wind chime that hung on his mother's front porch back in Nebraska.

It was the second time in less than twenty-four hours he'd thought of the old home place, which had to be a record of some kind.

Beside him Yancy stirred, and he knew she'd turned her head to look at him.

"Thank you," she said softly.

"What for?"

"For this. You know..." She tilted her head toward the little girl doing her best to imitate the lambs hopping in the field.

He waited, and when she didn't continue he shrugged and said, "You arranged it. Seemed important to you. To her."

He heard a soft exhalation. "It was the only thing she asked for, when we were planning this trip. To see some lambs and goats. And donkeys," she added with a small laugh. "I guess she remembers playing with them when she was little. And it's not like she's had much chance to see farm animals, living in New York and DC as we do."

"No farmers in your family, I gather."

He was pretty sure he'd said it without inflection, but it blipped on her reporter's radar anyway. The look she gave him was keen, inquisitive as a cat's.

"Nope," she said, "I'm a city girl through and through. What about you?"

So he told her, because he could think of no reason he shouldn't. "I grew up on a farm. Not sheep, though. Cattle and hogs, corn and hay, mostly." He added, as an afterthought, "My mom had chickens."

Again he felt her gaze and waited for the inevitable questions. Instead, she nodded and muttered—a trifle smugly, "I thought so."

He gave a short laugh, amused rather than annoyed. He'd forgotten what a top-notch reporter she was. "Oh, yeah? Why?"

"I noticed the way you were with our host, when he was showing us around." She nodded toward the man now joining Laila in the field, the flock that had come pushing and shoving to surround him and the child. "You seemed comfortable. And knowledgeable." He nodded but didn't say anything, and after a moment, she asked, "Where was it? Your family's farm."

"Not was—is. They're still there, on the farm where I grew up." He paused and again couldn't think of any real reason not to tell her. "It's in Nebraska."

She smiled. "Of course." They were both silent, watching Laila, who was obviously delighted by the jostling sheep, not at all afraid. Then Yancy drew a breath and said in a carefully neutral voice, "Do they know you're alive?"

"Yes," he said, and the breath came out ragged and uneven. "I probably broke some rules, but I did manage to get word to them."

The silence stretched between them. He could feel the anger and hurt radiating from her like body heat, hear the silent question that had to be screaming inside her head: *You got word to them, yet you couldn't have done the same for me?*

"Yankee," he began. "You—" she said at the same time. And they were both silenced by the deep hum coming from beneath his tunic.

His satellite phone. The phone he carried with him at all times and which was supposedly used only for emergencies.

Yancy watched him reach inside his tunic, pull out a sat phone and put it to his ear. In the split second before he jerked around, turning his back to her, she saw a frown darken his face. She clenched her fists and bit back her questions while frustration, a hint of relief and a growing unease made chaos of her emotions.

Part of her wanted to scream at him, *If you were able to let your parents know you were alive, couldn't you have let me know, too?*

For Laila's sake, she told herself. *Of course, for Laila's sake.*

At the same time she was glad for the distraction, giving her the chance to bury the hurt deeply enough that he'd never know how devastated she'd been, all those years believing him dead. Believing him gone forever, without a word of goodbye. She'd fortified herself against that kind of loss…she'd thought.

I did! I did protect myself. It's not about me. But Laila? How can I forgive him for abandoning her?

But all that came and went in seconds as she watched the tension gather in Hunt's shoulders, and the awareness that something was obviously wrong became a beeping on her reporter's radar that drowned all other thought.

"What is it?" she asked in hushed tones when he finally turned back to her, the phone clutched in one fist.

His face seemed carved from stone; his eyes glittered,

bright as jewels. "Car bomb," he said, his voice clipped, carefully devoid of emotion. "Downtown Kabul."

She caught a breath in an involuntary gasp. "Oh, God. I thought—"

"Yeah, I did, too. It seems I was wrong."

"Casualties?" Calm settled over her as years of experience and training took over. *Get the facts: who, what, where, when, why, how.* "Who was it? The Taliban? Where—"

"Six dead—so far. Dozens injured. The Taliban is claiming responsibility."

His eyes bored into hers, and just like that, her unease returned, clutched at her chest, twisted in her belly. "What is it? What aren't you telling me?"

"Yankee—" He put his hand on her arm, and she shook it off.

"Hunt—" She gasped out his name while a dozen scenarios, a dozen reasons for the way he was acting, rocketed through her head. Whatever it was, it had to be bad. Awful. What could a car bombing in Kabul possibly have to do with—

He took a deep breath and answered. "The target appears to have been WNN headquarters."

Chapter 6

He might as well have spoken to her in a foreign language. She stared at him while the syllables fell flat on her ears and echoed incomprehensibly in her mind. She repeated them, like someone of limited intelligence.

"W…N…N?"

He nodded and again reached to take her arm. "Yankee—"

And again she pulled away. "World News—my network—our Kabul bureau, the offices where I—" Her head filled with images, a montage of all the tragic and gruesome violence she'd seen and reported on in her calm, veteran correspondent's voice from her professional distance, caring with her mind but never with her gut, her heart, her soul. But these were her friends, colleagues, people she'd worked with under the most trying, even dangerous circumstances, and inevitably bonded by that. She knew their families, their children.

Familiar faces swirled into the violence and gore in her mind, and she felt as if her head would explode.

"My God," she whispered, hands clamped to her head as if to hold it together. "Why? I don't understand. They've never attacked the news media specifically before. Yes, they've kidnapped and detained journalists, cameramen, but never anything like this. And why *now*? With the end of the war so close?"

"I don't know why. I have an idea, but I don't want to talk about it here." His face was grim, his lips a thin, angry line. He glanced toward the field where Laila was still enthralled with the antics of the lambs, her laughter an ironically sweet descant to the ominous pounding of Yancy's heart.

"Hunt, we have to get back there. I have to be there. We need to leave—*now*."

He faced her and spoke with icy calm. "Yankee, get hold of yourself. Remember who you are. And *where* you are. And more importantly, who you're with."

His words were like a splash of cold water. She caught a breath, threw a quick look toward the field, where the farmer had already started toward them, having evidently realized something was amiss.

"I won't have you upsetting her," Hunt said softly.

"*You* won't—" The spark of anger flared only briefly because, of course, he was right. She nodded.

"I'll try to explain our breach of etiquette to our host, since we'll be leaving before sharing in the meal his wife has no doubt spent days preparing," Hunt said in an undertone as he went to intercept the farmer.

Cheeks flushed and eyes glowing, Laila bounced up to Yancy's side. "Did you see me, Mom? Did you see that one lamb? It jumped straight up in the air, like *this*."

She proceeded to demonstrate, which gave Yancy

time to put on her mom-face before bending, laughing, to hug her daughter. Over Laila's head she watched Hunt soothing their host with what appeared to be extravagant apologies to both him and his wife, and promises to come again and stay for a meal next time. The leaden feeling in her stomach told Yancy it was a promise they most likely wouldn't be able to keep.

For the first half hour of the drive back to Kabul, Yancy and Hunt sat in silence while Laila chattered excitedly about the lambs and goats she'd gotten to play with, oblivious to any ominous undercurrents. Yancy listened and made appropriate responses, but her mind was casting about furiously for answers that weren't available to her, while her chest ached with grief and worry and her face felt stiff with the pressure of holding back tears and forcing smiles instead.

Who is it? Who's hurt...dead? Is it Max, the cameraman, who just got married last fall? Or Kevin, with his annoying addiction to country music and insistence on always playing Texas Hold'em when they had to overnight in some godforsaken outpost. Oh, God, please don't let it be Doug, with two little kids at home...

"I have to go there," she said in a low voice, having confirmed with a glance toward the backseat that the silence did indeed mean Laila had finally fallen asleep. "Those are my friends, Hunt. I know them. I've worked with them for years. How can I not?"

Hunt's glance flicked toward the rearview mirror. "You have a child with you. You can't very well go dashing off to a war zone." His voice was hard, almost derisive.

Yancy swallowed a retort, again because he was right. She couldn't take Laila to what would almost certainly be a scene of chaos and carnage. She chewed her lip for a moment, thinking about it, then said, "Okay, how 'bout this? You can drop me off somewhere downtown. You keep Laila with you, and I can make my own way to the scene—"

He was already shaking his head. "No way," he said flatly. "I'm not letting either one of you out of my sight."

Yancy subsided into one of the loudest silences Hunt had ever heard, but he wasn't naive enough to take the silence for acquiescence. He wouldn't put it past her to try to find some way of getting to the scene of that bombing, and how could he blame her? He'd do the same thing, in her shoes. The fact was, if it was his people maybe killed or injured, there wasn't any force on earth that would keep him away.

He mulled it over while he navigated through Kabul traffic and the car's interior filled up with tension and frustration until he almost thought he could see it— like smoke. He pulled the car up in front of his house and turned off the engine, then glanced over at Yancy. She hadn't moved a muscle, and her features were set in an expression that looked to him more obstinate than obedient.

Swearing under his breath, he got out of the car and opened the door to the backseat. Laila stirred when he picked her up, and he had only a second or two to remember the way she'd felt in his arms three years ago, the way her thin little arms had clung so tightly to his neck, the way her warm tears had wet his neck and the collar of his shirt. To marvel at how much she'd grown… and to feel a pang at how she'd grown *up*.

Too soon, she was awake and squirming to be put down because she was too big now to be carried like a baby.

Clinging to his hand, she turned to look at Yancy, still sitting like a statue in the front seat of the car. "Isn't Mom coming? Come on, Mom. We're here."

Hunt paused and his eyes met Yancy's, hers swimming with grief and worry and fear. Anger, too.

"Well, kid, here's the deal," he said to Laila. "Your mom and I have to go to the hotel and get your stuff, because you're going to be staying here with me. And *you*—" he put a hand on top of her head to quell her delighted hopping "—are going to stay here and help Mehri fix dinner, so when we get back we can all eat together. How's that?"

Laila considered the proposal, gnawing on her lip, then aimed a winsome gaze at him from under her eyelashes. "Can I have some ice cream? It's prob'ly going to be a lo-ong time before you come back, and I'm already hungry."

Oh, Lord, she's a charmer already, he thought, and he wondered what she was going to be like at fifteen. And whether he would be there to witness it.

"If it's okay with your mom," he said gruffly, looking again at Yancy. This time the glow in her eyes gave him an uncomfortable feeling in his chest.

Yancy watched her daughter go into the house with Hunt's housekeeper, hopping excitedly at the prospect of helping in the kitchen. When the front door had closed solidly after them, she hurried back to the car and climbed into the passenger seat, turning to Hunt as she slammed the door. She opened her mouth to speak, but he was already shaking his head.

"Don't even think about it."

"But—"

"You know what it will be like down there. You won't be able to get within blocks of the scene."

"The hospitals, then. I have to know——"

"Again—you know it's going to be a while before they get any of the victims ID'd, and then they're not going to release names until families have been notified. There's nothing you can do, Yankee."

"Then why did you— Why are we—"

He drew in a breath and put the ancient Mercedes in gear. "Just what I said to Laila. I'm taking you to your hotel to get your things. You'll stay with me until I can get you out of the country."

She was silent for a long moment. The old car moved noisily along the quiet, shaded street while a cold prickling began in her scalp and crawled down her spine. At last she said, "Hunt, what do you know?"

He made an impatient sound. "I don't *know* anything. Put away your mama-bear protective instincts for a minute and *think*. Yesterday you and Laila were almost kidnapped in a busy marketplace. Today a bomb targets a network news bureau's downtown offices. *Your* network. Coincidence? Not likely." He threw her a glance. "I don't think what happened yesterday had anything to do with Laila. I think the target was—and is—you."

"Me!" It burst from her in reflexive protest, but she couldn't argue with him. The cold that was spreading now to the pit of her stomach told her he might be right. "The Taliban." She whispered it. "Because of—"

He nodded. "INCBRO. Think about it. You're not only rescuing child brides, but you've been convincing their families to have their daughters educated instead of selling them off like cattle. The Taliban wants to regain control in Afghanistan after the Americans leave, and education, especially for women, is something they can't tolerate. Hell, they've killed people for a lot less."

Again Yancy sat silent. Her brain felt paralyzed with the implications. *If that's true, then I'm responsible for the bombing. For my friends...*

And with fear. *I've put Laila—my child—in terrible danger.*

"Oh, God," she whispered at last.

"Is there anyplace you could go? Someplace the Taliban wouldn't be able to find you?"

She stared at his hands where they gripped the steering wheel, mesmerized by their size and strength while a memory came unbidden. *Those same hands touching me...with such gentleness and terrible intimacy...* She shivered and shifted restlessly as she shook her head. "What good would it do? If the Taliban wants me dead, they'll track me down—"

"If the Taliban wanted you dead, you'd be dead." His voice had turned hard. "They're sending you a message."

"A message!" she cried out in anguish. "By killing my friends?"

"Exactly. What they want," he said more gently, "is to get you and your organization out of Afghanistan. You're the organizer, the face of INCBRO, and you're high profile. But if they kill you, someone else will just pick up the flag...right? But if they make it clear they'll keep killing people you care about until you back off, they know you'll back off."

Her every instinct wanted to deny it. She sat silently, wanting to scream at him, to argue, to tell him—

"You know I'm right," he said softly, and as traffic slowed to a crawl, he turned to look at her.

The pain and compassion in his eyes stunned her.

He really cares about them. These people. This country. His mission.

He would have to care, she realized, to have given so much of his life for them. His sacrifice wasn't only about protecting his own country—it was about saving theirs.

She nodded and, as her own eyes burned and blurred with tears, turned her face away from that pain-filled gaze.

"So… Laila and I need to disappear, right?" There was no need for him to confirm it, and he didn't. She drew a steadying breath. "Okay. I, um…I think I might know of a place."

She stretched around to grope in the backseat for her purse, then settled again with it on her lap. She sat for a moment without opening it. Her hands felt unsteady as they rested on top of the buckled flap, but her eyes could detect no sign of shaking. After a moment, she opened it and took out a folded envelope, its thick, expensive paper making it easy to find in the crowded depths of the purse. She opened the envelope and extracted two folded pieces of paper, one of which was in sharp contrast to the quality of the envelope. It was cheap lined paper, like the kind schoolchildren used, and the writing on it was by hand. The second sheet of paper was of the same quality as the envelope and contained a typed translation of the first letter. Hunt glanced at the papers as she held them in her hands but made no comment and asked no questions.

She held the letters until he had parked in the hotel's outdoor parking lot and turned off the engine. He took the letters from her, glanced at the handwritten one, then began to read the typewritten translation. Yancy closed her eyes and followed the words in her mind, as they were imprinted indelibly in her memory:

My Dear Yancy,

First off, my name is Sam Malone, though for some reason many have preferred to call me by the nickname Sierra, and I happen to be your grandfather.

I am a very old man now, and I've lived a full and interesting life, during which I managed to amass a considerable fortune and squander the love of three beautiful women. As a result, I was not privileged to know most of my own children, although I did at least get to see my son, your father, grow up. It is my deepest regret that I did not find more time to spend with him when I had the chance. But this is not the time for regrets, and I can't change the past anyhow.

Since I have outlived all of my wives and my children, it is my desire to share my earthly treasure with my grandchildren, any that may chance to survive me, and it is this last wish that has led me to write this letter to you. I have sent one to your sister, Miranda, too, of course. If you are not too dead set against me and would care to come to my ranch to collect your inheritance, I do not believe you would be sorry.

My lawyer will no doubt include with this letter the information you need to contact him to make the necessary arrangements.

Yours very truly,

Sam Malone

Hunt looked up from the letter to find Yancy watching him, waiting quietly for his reaction. "Sam Malone." He tapped the lined paper with its handwritten, barely legible scrawl. "Not...*the* Sam Malone? The legendary billionaire recluse—"

"Yep," she said, one corner of her mouth quirking upward, probably in appreciation of his reaction, he thought. "The very same."

"How—"

"He was my father's father—hence my surname, Malone. My grandmother was his third wife, Katherine. She was old New York money. My dad was their only child."

He stared down at the letters in his hands, still barely able to take it in. "My God, is he still alive? He's got to be—"

"As the letter says, a very old man. To tell you the truth, I don't know how old he is—I'm not sure anyone does. Including him."

"I take it you've never met the man?"

"I may have, when my sister and I were very small, but I don't remember it. Miranda and I were only five when our parents were killed, and I don't remember ever seeing my dad's parents after that. We were staying with my mother's family in Virginia while they made that last trip to Africa. We wanted to go with them—I remember Miranda throwing a screaming fit about it—but they insisted we were too young." She drew a shaky breath. "They promised us we could go on the next trip. I guess we were lucky we weren't on that plane, or I wouldn't be here now, would I?"

Hunt was studying the typed version of the letter, probably written by the old man's lawyer. It concluded with his contact information, an address somewhere in Los Angeles, phone number, email address. "Have you contacted him?"

She shook her head. "I got the letter as I was knee-deep in preparations for this trip. I didn't know what to think. Frankly, it came as a complete shock. I hadn't even thought about that side of my family in…well, years."

"From the way this letter's worded, sounds like he expects you to have some sort of beef with him. Do you?"

"No—why would I? As I said, I barely know him. It does sound as if there are others—cousins of mine, I suppose they'd be, and isn't that weird? Maybe they have reason—"

"So you wouldn't have a problem taking him up on the invitation?"

"I— No. I mean, again, why would I? Of course—"

He was barely listening to her response. "I imagine he'd have plenty of security, with his money and fanaticism about privacy."

"Do you really believe this is necessary?"

He looked back at her, seeing the strain in her face, the anguish in her eyes, refusing to think about the vulnerability in her mouth, the way strands of her hair licked across her cheeks like flames. He couldn't think now about what she'd been to him, his refuge and comfort and bastion against the evil and horror that had been his daily mission. Her face the one he called up to banish the nightmares, her voice, her laughter the music that renewed his soul. All he could think about was the job he had to do now.

And that meant first getting her and Laila out of the country and to a safe place.

He didn't mince words. "Yes. You're getting your things and getting out of here. And I'd rather you didn't use your cell phone."

He pulled the keys from the ignition and opened the door.

Yancy stayed where she was. Conflict churned inside

her. Emotions she was used to suppressing boiled to the surface, defying her every effort to push them back down.

"Yancy?"

She could only shake her head, afraid to speak. She could barely see through the fog of grief and rage and fear that had engulfed her—so suddenly she'd had no warning, no defense.

She was aware of the car door closing, of something touching her bowed head and then her shoulder. Strong hands turned her; strong arms gathered her in. Shaking with silent sobs, she buried her face in the soft fabric of his tunic and let herself accept, for just a moment, the solace and safety he offered. It felt so good being there in his arms, his heartbeat in her ear, his warmth seeping into her shock-chilled body. He smelled of laundry soap and dust and sunshine, something at once familiar and alien—the smell of Afghanistan, perhaps. She felt his hand stroking her hair and realized that, in all the times they'd been together in intimate circumstances, he'd never before held her just like this.

It took all her strength to pull away. For a long moment she looked into his eyes, blazing golden in the darkness of his skin and beard.

"You have to do this," he whispered. "For Laila."

She nodded, then turned to face front. "Yes," she said. "For Laila."

From the Memoirs of Sierra Sam Malone:

> *Living in Hollywood as long as I did, I had attended my share of black-tie affairs—white-tie, too, although I never was clear on the difference between the two. But that night in New York City I could tell right away was different. People in*

Hollywood wear tuxedos like they're on cam-
era, which I guess is not a big surprise since they
usually are. That crowd at the Waldorf, though,
they wore their tuxes like I'd wear my Levi's and
boots—you know, like they were comfortable in
'em. The women, too, and don't get me wrong,
they were as beautiful and rich as any I'd met in
Hollywood, just not as flashy about it. A whole lot
less skin showing, for one thing, though it wasn't
only that. Like the men, these women dressed like
they were born to it, and didn't have a thing to
prove to anybody.

At that time in my life, I didn't have anything to
prove, either, so I felt right at home.

I was there for two reasons. First, because I
had more money than I knew what to do with, and
I was aiming to give a bunch of it away. I don't
recall the name of the charity; I'd been trying my
best to give my money away ever since my second
wife took a one-way walk into the Pacific Ocean,
and I guess it doesn't take a head-doc to figure
out I was carrying around a load of guilt. And it
didn't bother me a bit that my money was newer
than some of those tuxedos they were wearing,
because it seemed to me it ought to buy the same
amount of redemption.

Anyway, it wasn't long before the smell of money
and expensive perfume in that ballroom got to be a
little heavy for a man accustomed to the wide-open
deserts and mountains of Southern California, so
I stepped out onto a balcony to have a smoke and
get away from the crowd for a bit. I lit up and
was looking down at the bright shiny people down
below, biding my time until I figured I could write

my check and get on out of there, when she slipped through the curtains and came to join me.

She acknowledged my presence with a nod but didn't say a word, giving me the idea she knew who I was, so I didn't introduce myself, either, just nodded back. She took out a cigarette, so I offered her a light, like any man would have done. Smoking wasn't the taboo then that it is now, so I didn't think any less of her for doing so, and we shared the silence in a comfortable way, like we'd known each other for a long time.

After a while, she turned her back on the ballroom and gave me a long, measuring look.

I gave her one right back. It was hard to know what she was thinking, which naturally made her interesting to me. I can tell when a woman is flirting with me, and she wasn't.

She wasn't what you'd call pretty, but she wasn't hard on the eyes, either, just a little too bony for my own personal taste. She had red-brown hair and blue eyes and freckles and a wide mouth, and her gown was a shade of dark blue that didn't do much for her except where it showed a bit of skin down the middle of her back. She held her cigarette discreetly down at her side, not up waving in the air with her elbow bent, like most women did. I noticed she wasn't wearing a ring.

"I guess you don't care for crowds," she said. Her voice was low and throaty, and her accent was an upper-crust drawl. "Neither do I. I'm Katherine Beaumont, by the way." She held out her hand.

I took it and found it strong and firm. "Sam Malone."

She nodded and said, "Yes." She went on studying me with intelligence in her eyes.

I took a pull of my cigar and squinted one-eyed through its smoke. "Miss Beaumont—"

"Katherine."

"Katherine... Is there something I can do for you?"

Instead of answering, she turned again to look over the balcony wall at the crowd down below. "I have heard that you are considering a run for Congress."

"Some have made that suggestion," I said, being careful since I didn't know what she was leading up to.

She looked at me now along one shoulder, and I could see a smile in her eyes. "Don't you think your reputation might be a bit too scandalous for politics?"

I nodded and felt easy enough to smile back at her. "Some have made that suggestion, too."

She put out her cigarette in the tall ashtray there by the balcony wall and faced me, and now I could see by the way her hands moved that the cigarette had been more of a crutch to her than a pleasure. She was nervous, and doing a fair job of hiding it. "If respectability is what you want," she said in a manner more forthright than was usual for a woman, "I have a proposition for you."

"Is that a fact?" I said, smiling inside.

"Marry me," she said.

I don't shock easy, but I'll admit that set me back. I think I said something, making light of it. "Katherine, I believe that's called a proposal, not a proposition."

But I could see she was dead serious. She tipped her head back and her gaze didn't flinch. She didn't smile, exactly, but that wide mouth of hers kind of quirked off center.

"My family has all the respectability you'd ever need, if you should decide on a career in politics."

I rubbed on the back of my neck and I might have laughed a little. "I expect that's true. But you know I'm gonna ask, what's to your benefit in this proposition?"

"Your money, of course." But now her eyes wouldn't meet mine, and she went looking in her little shiny silver handbag and pulled out a jeweled cigarette case. She took one out and I lit it for her, and she blew smoke, and now that she had her crutch back in her hand, she plowed on. "My family's dead broke, you know."

I did know but didn't say so. I knew the Beaumont family's fortune had been built on some industries that didn't have much of a future in the modern world, and evidently whoever held the purse strings hadn't had enough sense to diversify while they had the chance. "Sorry to hear that," I said.

"Thank you," she said in that dry, upper-class drawl, then pushed on in her no-nonsense way. "The fact is, we are on the verge of losing our family home. In exchange for respectability, I would expect you to save it for us."

"That's it? Purely a business deal, my money buys your family's position?" It didn't seem to me like much of a deal for a beautiful woman to make—and I was beginning to see that she was beautiful, in her own way.

"Not quite." Now for the first time the hand that was holding the cigarette came up, like she was brandishing a sword. *"There's something I want from you, Mr. Malone."*

I felt my chest get tight, and I said, *"And what would that be, Miss Beaumont?"*

"A child," she said and let out a long stream of smoke, slowly. Then she stubbed out the cigarette, though she'd barely started on it. *"I find myself approaching what I believe is usually referred to as 'a certain age.' And, to my surprise, I find that I want very much to be a mother."*

I coughed, or some such thing, for the moment not having a word to say. *"Miss Beaumont—Katherine,"* I finally said, *"I would find it hard to believe you can't find someone who would be happy, to, uh—"*

"Oh, yes," she interrupted in that dusty drawl, *"I am sure my family name still has some capital attached to it. Mr. Malone, I have spent—let's call it the blossom of my youth, waiting for the right person to come along, but that has not happened. Which is rather a blessing, I find. Without the distraction of emotions, I can better search for the person with the attributes I would like to see in the father of my child. I believe you would do very well in that capacity. You are passably good-looking, if not overly handsome. You are possessed of a strong physique and appear to be in good health. You are certainly of high intelligence—"*

"If not of good character."

She brushed that aside like a horsefly. *"Character can be taught. In any case, I believe I have enough character for the both of us."* She paused, but for the life of me I still couldn't think what to say.

She took a breath and plunged. "So, Mr. Malone, what do you think of my proposition—or proposal, if you wish. Is a partnership with me on those terms something you might consider?"

In my day I'd had offers with a lot less promise, so I didn't keep her in suspense. "Kate," I said, and I held out my hand. "If I am to be the father of your child, then I believe you ought to call me Sam."

PART II

June Canyon, California

Chapter 7

Listening to the tread of footsteps climbing the stairs, Sam shuffled the pages he'd been reading into some semblance of order and returned them to the desk drawer from which they'd come. He didn't hurry—he knew by the sound of the footsteps who was about to pay a visit to his tower refuge.

This evening's visitor wasn't Josie—her step was lighter, quicker, partly because she had those short little legs, partly because the woman had more energy than she knew what to do with. And it wasn't Sage, who also had a light step in spite of the boots he normally wore. Probably the Indian side of him, Sam thought, knowing that was a cliché right out of old Hollywood, a fact that didn't bother him in the least. The boy was his own flesh and blood, after all, though he'd earned his father's respect in his own right.

No, these steps were steady and strong—businesslike

and no-nonsense—like the person making them, the one other person who could knock on Sam Malone's door any time of the day or night and know he'd be admitted.

"Come on in, Branson, gol'dammit," he snapped, when the steps paused outside the door, just before the knock came. "Are you gonna keep me waitin' here in suspense all night?"

The heavy door creaked open and his lawyer slipped into the room. "Psychic too, now, are you?"

Sam responded to that with the snort it deserved. "Got good hearing, is all. I may not recall how old I am, but I've got my hearing and my eyesight and I can still pee standin' up, which is about all a man can ask for. So what's the news? She comin' or ain't she?"

"She's coming."

Strong emotions never had come easy to Sam Malone, so all he did was scowl and snort and ask, "When?"

The lawyer glanced at a paper in his hand, which Sam knew damn well he didn't need to do. He cleared his throat, though most likely he didn't need to do that, either. "She will be arriving at Meadows Field tomorrow afternoon. I offered to pick her up, but she said she prefers to rent a car."

Laughter tickled through Sam's chest and gusted forth like a sneeze. "Just like her grandmother—independent as a mule." He was silent for a moment, remembering.

"She's bringing the child, of course."

"Well, she'd have to, I guess. Just what we need, another rug rat around the place. What the hell—it'll make Josie happy."

Branson put the paper carefully on Sam's desk and frowned at it for a second or two. "Let's hope the child isn't all she brings with her. That trouble in Afghanistan..."

Sam snorted. "You figure the Taliban'll track her here? Bring 'em on, I say."

Branson gave a small put-upon sigh. "Well, security has been notified. Though I'd really rather not get into a full-scale war."

"What about the other one? The sister—Miranda?"

"Nothing definite yet. According to my sources, she's gotten herself into a bit of trouble down there in LA. She may have to sort that out first."

Sam's spine straightened right up, and he was an old warhorse hearing bugles. "What kind of trouble? Anything we can do to get her out of it?"

Branson gave him a crooked smile, one old Duke Wayne woulda' been proud of. "I know you'd like to go riding off to her rescue, guns blazing—"

"Damn right!"

"—but I don't think that's necessary this time, Sam. At least, not yet."

Sam scowled at him. "Well, you'll be keeping an eye on things. I trust you to tell me if it's time to step in." He pulled a bandanna handkerchief out of his pocket, blew his nose and growled into it. "Lost one grandchild. Ain't about to lose another." He pointed at his lawyer with the bandanna flapping from his clenched fist. "You make damn sure that don't happen, you hear me, boy? You look after those girls, whatever it takes."

"I will, Sam," the lawyer said in his quiet way, and Sam knew he would.

He knew Alex Branson would protect those girls with his life, if it came to that.

And so would he, Sam Malone.

Jethro Jefferson Fox III, mostly known as J.J., former San Bernardino County sheriff's deputy currently on disability leave, laid aside his guitar and eyed his crutches. The umbrella's shade had moved and it had gotten too hot where he was sitting, there on the patio overlooking the valley, and he was thinking it was time to go find some air-conditioning.

He changed his mind when the kitchen door slid open and Rachel came out onto the patio to join him. She was wearing a sleeveless smock-type thing that came to her knees, which J.J. knew was because she was still self-conscious about her body. It had been more than two months since he'd helped her bring her son, Sean, into the world, and he still hadn't been able to convince her a few bulges and pooches were normal and nothing to be ashamed of, and that she was still the most beautiful woman he'd ever seen in his life. He meant to keep working on that, though, if it took him the rest of his life.

What he really wanted was to make that official, but he couldn't see how he could ask an heiress to marry him when he was looking at one more surgery on his leg at least and months of rehab after that. And even then he didn't know if he'd have a job to go back to. He'd been a sheriff's department homicide detective once and wanted nothing more than to be one again, but the question was whether the department would have any use for a cop with a leg that had been patched together with bits and pieces and cold hard steel. He was pretty sure Rachel wouldn't care about any of that, and he knew for darn sure Sean didn't, but the thing was, J.J. did. He cared a lot. He wanted to be a whole man, a worthy husband to Rachel and a better dad to Sean than the one he himself had had.

Right now, Rachel had Sean in one of those carry-packs, strapped to her chest. The little guy had his head up like a little periscope and was looking around, taking in the world with his big dark eyes. He'd changed a lot in two months, but his black hair still stuck straight up like a silky-soft paintbrush.

Rachel came to Sean and kissed him slowly and sweetly, warm and breathless and smelling like the baby. He held out his arms and she unstrapped the kid and lowered him into J.J.'s lap. Sean immediately waved his hand in the general direction of J.J.'s chin; for some reason J.J. hadn't yet figured out, the kid seemed to like the feel of beard stubble, though he hadn't quite figured out how to grab on to it yet.

"Did you hear?" Rachel asked as she adjusted the umbrella so it shaded the three of them. J.J.'s reply was unintelligible as Sean's clumsily exploring fingers were now in his mouth. She dropped into a chair, smiling and radiant. "They've heard from another one."

"Another—"

"Granddaughter. Sam's. Her name is Yancy, and she's got a twin sister named Miranda—they haven't heard from her yet. Their father was Sam's son with his third wife, Katherine, so their name is Malone."

J.J. shifted the baby in his lap. "Yancy Malone. Where have I heard that name?"

"You've probably seen her on the news. Until a couple of years ago she was WNN's chief Middle Eastern correspondent, but Josie told me she adopted a little girl from Afghanistan and stopped going to war zones after that. According to Josie, the little girl's name is Laila, and she's eight."

"So she's bringing the kid with her, I guess."

"Well, of course."

"Ah, hell. More rug rats."

Rachel smiled and nudged him with her foot. "They're coming tomorrow. I can't wait to meet them. It's going to be so nice to have another child staying here. And I get to meet my cousin!"

J.J. grunted. "Let's hope it's a real one this time."

Rachel's smile vanished. "Oh, Jethro, we're all heartbroken about Sunny. But Abby's a darling, she really is, and I know you'd like her, too, if you'd give her a chance—"

"And overlook the small matter that she committed fraud? Impersonated an heiress?"

"Yes," Rachel said firmly. "Sam has forgiven her, and so has Sage, so I think you could stop thinking like a cop and get over it, as well."

"Huh." He leaned over to make a face at the baby, who produced a drooly smile in return that made his heart do weird things. The truth was, he hadn't been thinking like a cop for quite a while now—since about the time he'd come way too close to losing both Rachel and his leg. "Well, let's hope this one comes with a little less drama."

"Yes," Rachel said softly, gazing at him and her son with love in her eyes. "Let's hope."

Sage Rivera-Begay got home from a long hot afternoon spent doctoring and ear-tagging calves to find his house enveloped in silence. Having lived alone for most of his adult life, the disappointment he felt surprised him.

"Hey, Sunshine?" he called, not expecting an answer. But he heard the soft thud of footsteps and Pia, aka the Cat From Hell, came stalking into the kitchen like a mountain lion on the prowl. Pia was the only cat he'd ever known whose footsteps were actually audible. So much, he thought, for "little cat feet."

He took off his hat—not a cowboy hat, but the Australian outback-style canvas hat he preferred in the dry Southern California desert heat—and hung it on the rack beside the door. Then he unbound his braid to let it hang free down his back.

"Hello, *tuugakut*," he said, speaking to the cat as he always did in Pakanapul, his mother's native language. He stooped to let her sniff his hand, then gave her a brief head scratch, something she seemed to tolerate only from him. The cat replied with a chirp of appreciation, then went off to check out her food dish while Sage went in search of his roommate.

Roommate?

He grimaced in dissatisfaction at the term but couldn't think what to replace it with. Abigail Lindgren had been sharing his house and his bed for only a couple of weeks now, and after the first night, neither of them had spoken again of *forever*. In his own mind and heart, he knew it was—for him, anyway. He hoped Abby knew it, too, but he couldn't be certain she truly believed it. He had an idea how he might help her with that, but he also knew she still had a lot of healing to do. The last thing he wanted to do was dump something huge and life changing on her when she was trying to wrap her head around the things that had happened to her in the last few weeks. Patience, he told himself. *The right time will come, and when it does, you will know it.*

He found Abby where he'd thought he might, in the old barn sitting cross-legged halfway up a stair-stepped stack of hay. Early as it was, the sun had already set behind the high hill to the west, and in the deep shadows he might have missed her if he hadn't known where to look. And if the sunlight gleam of her fair hair hadn't shone like a beacon in the twilight.

Sunshine. She may not be Sam's granddaughter Sunshine Blue Wells, but she was and would always be *his* Sunshine.

Though he tried to slip into the barn as stealthily as his heritage might have decreed, in an instant the lapful of kittens she'd been petting shot off in five different directions and vanished. Abby gave a little gasp of disappointment, but, in a way that made his chest swell, her face lit up when she saw it was him.

"Well," she said in the husky voice he loved, "I *thought* I had them tamed."

He scaled the haystack and leaned in to kiss her before seating himself on the bale beside her. "Granny Calico's babies?"

"Yeah… I'm hoping if I can get them tame enough, I can take them all to the vet…get them spayed and neutered." She sighed, and gathering her hair in one hand, she drew it over her shoulder, leaving her neck exposed.

It was an invitation he couldn't ignore.

She sucked in a breath, laughed and protested weakly. "I'm all dusty. And sweaty."

"Um…that's okay. So am I. And I smell like horse."

"Um…that's okay. I like horses."

The highly enjoyable interlude that followed ended abruptly when she gave a little gasp and pulled away. "Oh—I almost forgot. Your mom called."

"Uh-huh… What did she want?"

"They heard from another one of Sam's granddaughters. She's coming tomorrow." Her tone was light to match her smile, but he didn't miss the shadows in her eyes.

Carefully, he said, "Oh, yeah? Which one?"

"The television journalist—Yancy." He nodded, and she went on. "Turns out she's got a little girl—adopted, from Afghanistan. She's eight." He nodded again. "She's coming, too. Everyone's really excited." And now her smile, which had become more and more forced, faded completely. She looked away, and he knew she was remembering how, not so long ago, all the excitement had been for *her*.

For the person she was pretending to be.

He cupped her chin and gently urged her to face him, but she stubbornly kept her eyes lowered. "Hey," he said softly, "you know what happened to Sunny wasn't your fault." She nodded but still didn't meet his gaze. "You're here, and you're part of us now."

"But I'm not family," she whispered. "You know it, I know it, and they know it."

You could be, he wanted to say as he gathered her into his arms. *You will be, when you marry me.*

But he knew it still wasn't the right time to say it. So he kept silent and simply held her, and hoped he would know the right time when it came.

Laila's voice came plaintively from the backseat. "Mom... I think I have to throw up. Really this time."

With a glance in her rearview mirror, Yancy flipped on her signal and, a few curves farther along, pulled into a turnout. She unbuckled her seat belt and swiveled to look at her daughter, whose head was lolling pitifully over the side of her booster seat.

"Are you sure, sweetheart? The GPS says we only have a little bit more of the curvy road to go. If you keep your eyes on the road ahead—"

"I can't *see* the road ahead from back here. I don't see why I have to ride in a baby chair anyway. I don't see why I can't ride up front with you. I'm eight years old, Mom." Grumpily, Laila unsnapped her belt and hitched herself out of the booster seat.

Yancy sighed and got out of the car. "You know what the man at the car rental place said," she reminded Laila as she opened the rear passenger door for her. "You are too small for the front seat belt *and* the air bag. And if you're going to sit on a booster seat, you have to be in the back. End of story. So stop complaining and hop out and walk around a little bit. That will make you feel better. And let's try not to stop anymore, okay? We still have a way to go to get to Grandpa's house."

Grandpa's house. How homey that sounds, as if it's over the river and through the woods, and we've done it a hundred times before. Not the hideaway of some eccentric reclusive billionaire I don't even remember.

Oh, I do hope this isn't a huge mistake.

"Well, I hope he's nice," Laila said in a tone that suggested she wasn't holding out much hope.

She'd been in a mood ever since they'd left Kabul, disappointed, Yancy knew, at having their trip cut short and clearly less than satisfied with the explanation she'd been given as to why they had to leave *right now*, when they'd barely had any time at all with Akaa Hunt.

Better get used to that, baby girl, because that's all anyone ever gets with Hunt Grainger. A few crazy, unexpected stolen minutes and then years of silence. And how much harder it would be if you knew he wasn't your uncle, but your daddy.

Yancy's chest shivered, and she took a few calming breaths before saying brightly, "Oh, I'm sure he is. And Mr. Branson told us there's a pool, remember? And horses."

Laila muttered, "Well, that's just great," kicking at a bit of rock Yancy was pretty sure had recently fallen from the mountainside looming above them. "Only I don't know how to ride a horse."

"Then you will have to learn, won't you? Come on—hop back in here. The sooner we get on the road, the sooner we'll be there."

It was a good thing, Yancy thought, that this time of year, mid-June, there was still lots of daylight left.

As she had promised Laila, after only a few more of those hair-raising twists and turns, the road widened out into a four-lane highway that swooped across bridges and sliced through mountains, making it possible for her to drive at freeway speeds. Now she could even find moments to notice the scenery. And she had to admit the river canyon was rather awesome, even if the mountainsides were dry and brown and some slopes showed signs of fairly recent wildfire.

The truth was, none of it seemed real. The scenery, beautiful as it was, seemed to flash by like the vista in a driver-training simulator while her eyes focused narrowly on the road ahead, and her mind was left free to wander into places she really didn't want to go.

Blood and smoke and crowds and chaos in the streets of Kabul, and the voices on the news:

At least seven confirmed dead...

Forty injured...names of victims have not been released...

Taliban appears to have been responsible...

Hunt's eyes boring into mine as he says goodbye at the airport.

The feel of his hand...just his hand, touching mine so briefly. Naturally, he wouldn't—couldn't—hug me the way he hugged Laila.

The image of Hunt kneeling down so a little girl could wrap her arms around his neck and bury her face in his tunic, and her shoulders shaking because she was trying so hard not to sob.

And as I watch them I'm drawing shuddering breaths to keep from bursting into tears.

Now, remembering, she was drawing the same kind of breaths as she glanced in the rearview mirror to confirm what the silence from the backseat had suggested, that Laila had indeed fallen asleep. Then, and only then, did she allow herself to grip the steering wheel with convulsive anguish while her face tightened in a grimace of rage and grief.

Damn you, Hunt. Why couldn't you have just stayed dead?

But the spasm was brief. By the time the freeway section of highway had narrowed once more to a winding two-lane road, Yancy had herself well in hand. This was partly due to her years of experience working in front of cameras in the most stressful and emotionally fraught situations imaginable. But there was also the fact that her own inquiring mind had begun increasingly to wonder why her grandfather had chosen such an odd location for his hideaway. To call the area "bucolic" was probably an understatement. Definitely not the sort of place she'd have thought an eccentric and reclusive billionaire would find to his liking.

But then, she supposed, that was what made him eccentric.

After passing through a town, of sorts, one that seemed to boast stores, fast-food restaurants, motels, gas stations and even some county services like fire and sheriff's departments and a public library, the highway wound along the shores of a man-made lake. Judging by the distance between its choppy waters and the high-water mark carved into the rocky hillsides, the lake was at a low ebb.

The highway then straightened out and arrowed through a valley where black and brown cattle grazed in lush green pastures. Beyond the pastures, against more of the dry brown mountains, a thick bank of trees suggested a river's course. Although, after her GPS instructed her to turn left at an elementary school onto June Canyon Road, and she had driven between more of those verdant fields and across a narrow bridge, she found the bridge traversed only a sandy streambed, with not so much as a trickle of water flowing beneath it.

A drought-stricken land, she thought and felt a pang of homesickness for the summer rains and green Virginia forests of her childhood.

Leaving the riparian woods behind, the paved road narrowed and began to climb, zigzagging its way up a hillside covered with boulders and brush. Higher up, the brush gave way to juniper, manzanita and some sort of long-needled bluish-gray pine trees Yancy didn't know the name of. And the pavement gave way to rutted and rock-studded dirt. After one particularly hard jolt, Yancy swore aloud, glancing in the mirror to make sure Laila was still sleeping through all of this.

This can't be right, she thought, although the rental car's GPS still maintained her destination lay some distance ahead on this very road. Her misgivings grew stronger as the road continued to wind and dip and climb its way up and up, deeper into a wide canyon while the river course and pastures, the occasional house and finally all signs of human habitation fell away below. Nowhere could she see anything that might suggest the location of the guarded compound of a reclusive billionaire. Where, she wondered, were the walls, the gates, the high-tech security?

At last, when nothing lay ahead of her but granite crags and timber-covered mountains, she caught a glimpse, off to the left, beyond a grove of stately pines and poplar trees, of a red-tile roof and a green meadow where horses grazed. A short distance farther on, the dirt road—a track, really—cut sharply to the left then dipped down into a deep ravine where willows grew and a shallow stream ran chuckling across concrete paving, before making a stomach-dropping climb up the other side.

"Should have rented a four-wheel drive," Yancy muttered as she downshifted into the lowest gear and gunned the engine, nursing the compact sedan up the steep track and out of the ravine.

The truth was, she'd been on worse roads.

And now suddenly the road was graded and smooth and relatively straight, though still dirt, leading to a T intersection. There Yancy stopped the car and sat for a moment, gazing at the view. Which she had to admit was quite beautiful.

Straight ahead, behind a barbed-wire fence, lay a long meadow—or pasture?—with lush green grass and some sort of little yellow flowers, and some taller blue ones she thought might be cornflowers. A half-dozen or so horses had stopped their placid grazing and now stood with heads turned and ears cocked to watch the new arrival with lazy curiosity. On the far side of the meadow, a line of trees marked yet another streambed, this one following the base of the granite mountainside that formed the western side of the canyon. The sun had already set behind the mountain, veiling the canyon's floor and the car in which she sat in soft lavender shadow.

From the backseat came a gusty waking-up exhalation and a sleepy voice. "Why are we stopping? Are we there?"

"Almost," Yancy said, turning to smile at her sleep-grumpy child.

"Where is it? I don't see any houses."

"I'm not sure." Looking to her right, Yancy could see

barns and corrals and a small house nestled behind huge cottonwood trees. Could the house possibly be built of *adobe*?

Oh, surely not, she thought. *Eccentric* was one thing, but she doubted her billionaire grandfather would be living in a tiny old adobe ranch house.

Left, the road was paved. "This way, I think," she announced in a voice more sure than she felt.

The paved road meandered among the pines and poplars she'd glimpsed from across the ravine, the shadows deepening as they passed rose beds and flower gardens and a long, low whitewashed adobe building with red-tile roof that might have been a stable. Or a garage?

Ahead and to the left, perched on the side of the mountain, a villa stood like a sentinel overlooking the valley. It resembled a Spanish monastery, even to the bell tower at one end, though the bell had evidently been removed and windows put in the openings. The top of the tower caught the last of the sun's rays, turning the windows to golden mirrors.

With her eyes glued to the view of the villa and its tower, Yancy didn't see the two people strolling down the road, hand in hand, accompanied by a shaggy black-and-white dog, until Laila said, "Mommy, look!"

Yancy jerked her eyes back to the road and stomped on the brake, but the couple—and the dog—had already moved to the side and stood waiting with welcoming smiles. Her first thought was that they were two of the most beautiful people she had ever seen. And a study in opposites, the man dusky dark, the woman Nordic fair. Both wore their hair in single long braids hanging down their backs, one pale blond, the other glossy black. The man wore work clothes—jeans and a long-sleeved cotton shirt—and boots. The woman wore a tank top, shorts and athletic shoes, and her legs were long and slim and smooth.

Yancy opened her window and leaned out. "Hi—am I in the right place? I'm looking for Sam Malone's, uh…"

The man smiled, showing beautiful teeth. "This is it, just keep going. I'm guessing you're Yancy, right?"

"Yes, and this is Laila." She half turned to make room for her daughter, who was now wide-awake, crowded against her shoulder and gazing out the open window at the dog, who sat on his haunches grinning back at her and panting.

The man stepped forward, holding out his hand. "I'm Sage—I manage the ranch. That's my place down there— the adobe." With the hand still holding the woman's, he drew her forward. "And this is Abby."

They exchanged hellos and handshakes, and Yancy, looking from one to the other, asked, "Forgive me, but… are you relatives of mine?"

Sage made a rueful face and rubbed one sun-browned hand over his glossy hair. "I'm, uh, your uncle, actually."

"Uncle! But you don't— I didn't know my father had any living siblings."

"Just found out myself, not too long ago," Sage said with a dry laugh. "Don't worry. I'm sure you'll learn all the family scandals soon enough."

"And… Abby? Are you one of Sam's—"

The woman gave her head a rapid shake and glanced at her shoes. "Oh, no—no relation."

"Not blood," Sage said, looking at his companion and giving her hand a squeeze and a tug, insisting she return his gaze. "But she's family."

There was an awkward pause during which the dog got up, ambled over to the car and put his paws on the windowsill. He panted juicily on Yancy's shoulder, ignored Sage's command to "get down, Freckles" and gave Laila's face a swipe with his tongue. There followed a few moments of chaos while Laila gasped and giggled and shrieked and Sage gave futile orders to the dog, who was trying his best to climb into the car through the open window.

"Sorry about that," Sage said, when order had been restored and the dog was once more sitting, panting, beside him, now held there by a firm grip on his collar. "This is Freckles. He loves everybody, especially company. Hope he didn't scare you."

"It's all right," Laila said with dignity. "I like *dogs*. But I do not like horses."

"Ah," said Sage. "What about cats?"

Laila considered, head to one side. "I'm not sure. I've never had a cat."

"Well, you probably won't like Abby's cat. She's kind of hard to get along with."

"But," said Abby, "there are lots of other cats—baby kittens, too."

"I might like baby kittens," Laila said thoughtfully. "What else do you have?"

"Chickens," said Abby. "And cows and calves."

"Do you got any—"

"*Have*, Laila!"

"Do you *have* any goats?"

"Sorry, no goats."

"What about donkeys?"

"Nope—no donkeys, either."

Laila subsided with a heart-wrenching sigh. "I *knew* it."

"We were just heading up to the big house for supper," Sage said, then smiled at Laila. "Would you like to walk with us? It'd make Freckles happy, and you'd probably like a chance to stretch your legs, after that drive up the canyon." He shifted his dark-eyed gaze to Yancy. "If it's okay with your mom."

Yancy said, "Oh—sure. Laila?"

Laila had the door open already and was immediately engulfed in ecstatic, wriggling dog. For a moment all three adults watched the giggling child try—not very hard—to avoid the canine kisses. Then Yancy gave a breathy laugh and said, "Okay, I guess that's settled. Where should I—"

"Just park in the driveway by the front steps for now. There will be a welcoming committee, so don't worry about unpacking anything. My mother will take you in hand the minute you set one foot on the ground anyway. We'll see to everything after you've had something to eat and met the rest of the family."

"Will that include my, uh…grandfather?"

Sage's smile was wry. "No telling. We never know where or when he'll decide to make an appearance. Sam spends most of his time in the high country, these summer days. Or the tower." He tilted his head toward the gilded windows showing through the trees. "He pretty much does his own thing."

"So I've heard," Yancy said with an answering smile.

With a nod of thanks, she put the car in gear and rolled on up the curving drive. In the rearview mirror she saw the young couple smiling indulgently at the antics of the child and the dog as they resumed their unhurried stroll, hand in hand. For some reason the term "significant other" popped into her mind, and she felt an odd little pang in the vicinity of her heart. Because it was unfamiliar to her, it was a moment or two before she recognized it as envy.

I want that. Why can't I have what they have? Is there a significant other for me?

A face popped into her mind—a face with angular features and dark skin, golden eyes and a mouth that smiled with heart-melting charm, and dark stubble lately grown into a full beard. The pang of envy became an ache of yearning, and with an audible gasp and a shake of her head, she forced it away.

She would not yearn. She had no business yearning, not for a man who came and went like a shadow and could never give her more comfort or companionship than shadows would, even if just the memory of him made her heart quicken and pulses pound. If she was going to yearn, it would be for a man she could count on to be her friend and partner and to help her make a life of security and stability for Laila, first of all, and for their future children.

Her stomach quivered at the thought of future children. *But not Hunt's. They could never be Hunt's.*

She focused with stern resolve on the shadowed lane and the new family and the unknown that lay ahead.

Chapter 8

Dinner was over. At least, nobody was eating anymore, and the grown-ups were sitting around the table talking, and the baby was asleep in his mother's arms, and Laila was bored. She squirmed around in her chair for a while, hoping someone would notice and tell her she could be excused and maybe tell her what to do or where to go, since she had no idea herself what there was to do in this strange place.

But nobody did notice her, and finally she leaned against her mother's arm and whispered, "Mom…can I be excused now?"

Her mom said, "Well, I don't…" and looked at Josie, the lady who had cooked their dinner and was Sage's mom, and then at Sage.

Josie smiled at Laila and said, "Sure, sweetie, you just make yourself right at home."

"Can I go outside?" Laila asked, aiming the question at Josie since she seemed to be the boss of the house.

"Yes, you sure can." Josie got up and came around to help Laila scoot back her chair.

"Don't get lost," said the big man with the blond hair and the broken leg so he had to walk on crutches. "And watch out for rattlesnakes."

Laila caught her breath and looked quickly at him. She thought she saw a twinkle in his eyes, so maybe he was just teasing.

Josie made a shooing-away motion toward the others. "Oh, don't pay any attention to him. You go on out and explore all you want to. Just you be careful around the pool, okay? Here—you can go right through here." And she opened up the sliding door to the patio that looked out over the pool, and what seemed to be the whole world spread out below. "Just go down those steps, and there's a gate you can go through to get to the front."

Laila mumbled her thanks as she slipped through the door and tried not to run across the patio.

All she wanted to do was get away from *everyone*. She wanted to be by herself for a while. She needed to do that, sometimes, just find a quiet place and think about things. She'd been that way ever since she was little, because she could remember being in a snug hiding place with only a dog for company. She remembered she'd felt safe there.

She pushed the memory away before it could become scary, the way it did sometimes.

At the bottom of the steps she came to a gate with a latch that wasn't too high up for her to reach. She opened it, and there was Freckles waiting for her on the other side, wagging his tail so hard it made him wag all over. "Hi, Freckles," she said and gave him a hug. Then she noticed another dog waiting patiently a little ways away. This one had a lot of wrinkles and long floppy ears and sad eyes, so she gave that dog a hug, too.

Freckles went trotting off along the stone pathway that led around to the front of the big house, so Laila followed. The sad-faced dog ambled along beside her, keeping pace without seeming to hurry. Crossing the wide paved space in front of the house, Laila broke into a hop and then almost a run, before she remembered she wasn't going to be happy in this strange new place her mom had brought her to.

It wasn't that it was a bad place. The air was warm and smelled good, and even if there weren't any goats, there were lots of other animals, although it was too bad there had to be *horses*. There was lots of space, and trees and mountains, and the people seemed nice, too.

It wouldn't be that bad, Laila thought with a sigh, kicking at the pavement, if only…

If only Akaa Hunt was here.

She did *not* understand why they'd had to leave Afghanistan just when they were all having such a good time together—she and Mom and Akaa Hunt. It was funny, but she hadn't thought about Akaa Hunt for a long time before that, hadn't even remembered him clearly. But then she'd seen him again, and it was as if he'd always been there inside her. She remembered him very well now, and she missed him a *lot*. She missed him so much, if she was much, much younger she might even cry.

Being with Akaa Hunt had made her happy. For a little while it had been almost like having a dad.

More than anything in the world, Laila wanted a dad. Almost everyone she knew had one. Even if their parents were divorced and the dad didn't live in the same house, at least he got to take them to the zoo and come to their soccer games and take them for ice cream after. *Pistachio*, Laila thought and had to swallow hard to make the lump in her throat go away.

She didn't want to be happy in the new place, but she didn't like being sad, either. She decided it would be okay to run for a little bit, especially since it would make Freckles happy. So she skipped and hopped and stooped to pick up a stick and threw it for Freckles to chase, then ran after him and pretended like she wanted to take the stick away from him. She was having a pretty good time until she noticed they were getting close to the fence and the field where the horses lived.

Laila really didn't want to see those horses, and besides, it was starting to get kind of dark. She called to Freckles to come back. But Freckles kept going. The sad-faced dog went trotting on ahead, too, and before she knew it, both dogs had disappeared around a bend in the road, leaving her all alone.

Laila didn't want to be left alone in the almost-dark even more than she didn't want to see horses, so after a moment, she gave a big sigh and followed the dogs.

When she came around the bend, she was very close to the fence and the field beyond, and there were a whole bunch of horses right up next to the fence. A man was standing there, too, leaning against a fence post, and the horses were gathered around him the same way the kids on Laila's soccer team gathered around the coach when she was telling them something important. The dogs were there, and the man had turned away from the horses to pet them and rumple their ears. Then he looked up and saw Laila.

The man straightened up and nodded his head toward her and said, "Howdy."

Laila almost giggled. It wasn't every day someone said "howdy" to her, although she did know it was a greeting, like the way people in Virginia, where Mom's family lived, said "hey" instead of "hi." She didn't answer, though, because she'd never seen this man before, and she knew she wasn't supposed to talk to strangers.

But...the dogs seemed to know him, didn't they? That must mean he was somebody who lived here. And if he lived here, he wasn't really a stranger.

As she hesitated, the man jerked his head in a way that meant *come* and said in a growly voice, "Well, get on over here, where I can see you. I'm old and I don't see so good when the light's bad."

Even though it was getting dark, Laila could see the man was pretty old. His hair was white, and he had a beard that was white, too. Both Freckles and the sad dog were sitting on their haunches beside his feet, grinning with their tongues hanging out, so she was pretty sure he wasn't a danger. Still, she stayed where she was.

"What's the matter? Cat got yer tongue?"

"No," said Laila, deeply affronted, "it's right here in my mouth, where it belongs."

"Ha! So you ain't dumb. Well, then, tell me your name, little girl."

She hesitated another moment, then gave in. "I'm Laila."

"Ah. Pretty name."

"What's *your* name?"

"It's Sam. Sam Malone. I'm your mother's grandpa—what do you think of that?"

"Oh," said Laila.

Sam scratched his beard. "So, I reckon that makes me your great-grandpa, don't it?"

Laila shook her head. "I'm adopted."

"So what? Your mama's your mama, and I'm her grandpa, so I'm your great-grandpa. So you've got no call to be afraid of me."

"I'm not afraid of *you*," said Laila. "Just *them*."

"Them?" Sam looked around in surprise, then over his shoulder at the horses, then back at Laila. "You mean these fellas here?"

Laila nodded. "I don't like horses."

Sam jerked his head back. "What? Nobody doesn't like horses."

"Well, I don't. They're very big. And snorty and stampy."

Sam looked at her for a long time, scratching his beard. Then he said, "Well, now, I can't argue with that. They are big. And they do snort and stamp, and they can kick and bite like a sonofagun. But that just makes it all the sweeter when you can get one to eat out of your hand and let you take a ride on his back, don't it?"

Laila looked at him out of the corner of her eye and didn't say anything. He made that *come here* motion with his hand again. And although she really didn't want to go, somehow her feet seemed to, and in a moment there she was, standing right beside Sam and the fence and those horses. They seemed even bigger up close. Their heads hung over the fence, right above hers.

"Show you what I mean," said Sam. "Here, now, give me your hand."

Laila looked up at him. His eyes were very bright and there were deep wrinkles around them, and even though her knees felt funny, she slowly held out her hand. His fingers were cool and dry and strong. Then she felt something cool and moist, and she looked down in surprise at the piece of apple lying in her palm.

"Now, you just hold up your hand like that, and this fella here—his name's Old Paint, and he's a good old fella—he'll take that apple right offa your hand."

"What if he bites me? You said they bite."

Sam scratched his chin whiskers some more. "Well, now, if this horse were to bite your fingers it'd be because he mistook 'em for somethin' good to eat. That's why you have to keep your hand flat, like a plate, see? Now go ahead—try it."

"O…kay." Laila wasn't at all convinced, but she didn't want Sam to think she was a scaredy-cat. "But if I get bit, my mom isn't going to like it *at all*."

Sam made a snorting noise and took her hand and lifted it way up high. The horse made a sound that was almost the same as Sam's, and Laila caught her breath and closed her eyes and held very still, and she felt a gust of warm breath, and then something soft—like velvet—nuzzled her hand. A giggle rose into her throat and she bit her lip to hold it back.

"There, now," said Sam. "Better count those fingers."

The horse bobbed his head up and down and crunched on the piece of apple. Laila couldn't hold back the giggle any longer. It burst from her, and she wiped her empty hand on her pants and said, "That tickled!"

"See, now, horses aren't so bad, once you get to know 'em."

"Maybe," said Laila. "But I still like goats better."

"Goats!" Sam jerked back as if she'd said a bad word. "Don't tell me that. Goats are smelly things, and stubborner than a goldarn mule."

"Aren't either! Only the daddy goats smell bad. They're funny and friendly, and their babies are soft and tiny and *cute*."

Laila was furious. And then suddenly she wasn't. Instead, she had that lonely feeling again, like she missed something—or someone—so badly she hurt inside. She was afraid she might cry, and she really, *really* didn't want to, not in front of Sam.

"You sure do like to argue," Sam said.

She took a deep breath, but it didn't help much, and

her voice came out sounding very small and trembly. "I don't either. I just like *goats*, that's all. We had goats— I remember them. From when I was little. When I lived with my first mom."

She stood stiff and tall, with her hands curled into fists, glaring up at Sam, and Sam glared back at her from what seemed a great height, glared from underneath his bristly white eyebrows.

"Huh," said Sam. "Looks like somebody's come to fetch you. 'Bout time, too."

Laila heard footsteps crunching and turned around to watch a dark man-shape coming down the paved road. When he got closer, she saw that it was Sage, the man with the beautiful long black hair who had met her and Mom in the lane when they'd first arrived. She remembered his girlfriend's name was Abby, and she had a braid like Sage's, only blond.

Freckles had gone to dance around him as he came toward them on the darkening road. He paused to ruffle the dog's fur with his hands and said, "Hey, kiddo, it's getting pretty dark. Your mom sent me out to look for you." He waited a moment, then said, "I see you've met Sam."

"Ha!" Sam stomped past Laila and Sage and headed up the road, muttering to himself. "Kid doesn't like horses. Never heard of a kid didn't like horses. Argues a lot, too."

After a few steps, he turned around and pointed his walking stick at Sage and said in a scratchy, growly voice, "Get the kid some goldarn goats." Then he turned back and stomped off into the night.

Sage looked down at Laila. "Goats?"

She nodded. And she didn't feel lonely or sad or mad anymore. She felt light, as if she had bubbles inside, as she ran up the road ahead of Sage, with Freckles bounding on one side of her and the sad dog trotting along on the other.

The courtyard was empty but not still. The moon was high and almost full, and the warm summer night was filled with sounds. Yancy could identify most of them: the frogs and crickets and trickling of water from the Spanish-style fountain nearby, the mooing of cattle far off in the valley. The murmur of voices from one of the bedrooms farther down the veranda. Even the unfamiliar yip-yipping chorus from the not-so-distant hills that she was pretty sure must be coyotes. The smells were familiar, too: the sweetness of roses, lilies and honeysuckle, mingled with the spice of sage and pine, and the earthiness of pasture and stream and farm animals.

So familiar, and yet somehow being here filled her with vague feelings of longing and discontent.

There was sadness, deep and aching grief over the loss of friends and colleagues—*that* she understood. And she knew she'd done the best thing she could, bringing Laila here, so it wasn't that, either. If Hunt was right, her continuing presence in Afghanistan would only put more people she cared about in danger, and most of all, Laila. Coming here to her grandfather's ranch was the perfect solution. Laila would be safe here, even happy. She'd barely been able to stop talking about the goats Sage was going to get for her—*Because Sam said so!*—and she'd fed a horse an apple—*And it didn't bite me!*—and she was in love with the dogs, Freckles and the one with the "sad face."

She actually met Sam Malone.

The thought brought a smile to her lips and a soft chuckle to join the night's symphony.

But the smile and the laughter died quickly to be replaced by that aching emptiness.

It's Hunt, dammit. Damn him. I miss him.

She hadn't expected it. She hadn't known how much seeing him again would bring it all back. So vividly. So vividly she could taste him…feel his touch. Smell him on her skin. Those moments in the car when he'd held her and she'd hidden her face against his chest… He'd never held her just that way before. Ever.

In exasperation, she blew out a breath, waggled her shoulders and gazed up at the milky sky. *Damn the man!* For so many years she'd called him Ghost, as he'd flitted in and out of her life—*and bed*—without warning. He'd haunted her then, too, but never like this.

Because she'd had no expectations of him then—until he'd dropped his daughter into her lap and disappeared.

Finally, after hearing no word from him for years, she'd given him up for dead, come to accept that and shifted his memory to the attic of her mind. Having him turn up again had not only brought all the old memories back in vivid living color, but something had changed profoundly about the *way* he occupied her thoughts.

Before, she'd kept him in his own little compartment, one she could close the door on when she needed to concentrate on her job, her life—or bring out to hug close to her heart in secret. But now he filled her head, owned her thoughts, gave her no respite at all. He was always *there*. She couldn't get him out of her mind.

Before, she'd thought of him with inner shivers of desire, excitement, anticipation, yes, and sometimes longing. Now he aroused in her every kind of emotion she could imagine herself capable of: anger, panic, elation, desire, joy, helplessness, dread, confusion. Fear. And all the nuances in between and in combination thereof.

And love? What about love? Do I feel that, too?

No. Of course I don't love him. How could I? I don't even know him!

He was a complication in her life; *that* she was sure of. Hers and Laila's.

Maybe more than a complication. Maybe even...a threat?

What if he wants to be a part of Laila's life? She would love that, and I want that for her. But how could it possibly work?

Worse—what if he— Oh, God, what if he wants to take her back?

Could he do that?

He's her father!

The night was balmy, but she shivered and goose bumps roughened the skin on her bare arms. She rubbed at her arms, reminding herself that she had no reason to be afraid; she and Laila were safe here.

Safe from the Taliban, yes. But...from Hunt?

Flat on his belly on a rocky outcropping, Hunt surveyed the moonlit valley spread out below him. The mountains that ringed the valley were silhouettes in varying shades of indigo against the milky sky. A fair number of warm yellow pinpricks of light dotted the valley floor, more widely scattered on the slopes, and a few lights still moved slowly along the highway that bisected the valley. Only a few of the brightest stars gave them any competition.

His eyes, accustomed to nighttime reconnaissance, had no need of the night-vision goggles he carried in his backpack to make out the three men making their way steadily up the steep and rugged slope below him. They moved slowly and in utter silence as they closed in on their quarry, pausing every now and then to communicate with each other with hand gestures. They would be using infrared sensors, he thought, and would be well armed—with assault rifles at the very least.

He allowed himself a smile and a brief nod of approval. Then he laid his backpack aside and rose to his feet, holding his arms wide to each side.

Fifty yards below him, the three men halted, alert but not alarmed, forming a semicircle across his only reasonable route of escape. The middle one spoke in a voice not loud but heavy with authority.

"Sir, do you know you are trespassing on private property?"

"I do," Hunt said.

"Well, sir, I'm gonna need for you to come down from there and explain what you're doing."

"Of course. Sure. No problem."

"Backpack first, please. Toss it down—easy."

They hadn't asked him about weapons or whether he was alone, Hunt noted as he followed instructions, using one foot to nudge his backpack over the edge of the rocky outcropping. Which confirmed his assumption that they were equipped with both infrared sensors and night-vision glasses and already knew the answers.

"All right, sir, now keep your hands where we can see them and come on down. I would strongly advise you not to make any sudden moves."

Hunt chuckled. "Wouldn't dream of it."

He made his way down the steep slope through a jumble of boulders and brush, sliding on his backside a time or two since his hands weren't of much use to him, held wide, as they were, in a nonthreatening posture. Once clear of the rocks and on reasonably level ground, the voice of authority told him to stop right there, which he did. He stood relaxed and benign, while two of the men approached him.

The third went to retrieve his backpack. After confirming that it contained no weapons or explosives, he picked it up and came to join his comrades.

"I imagine you'll want to see my ID," Hunt said.

The trio's spokesman didn't seem all that impressed with his apparent willingness to cooperate. He pulled a tablet from somewhere on his person and said in his authoritative but oh-so-polite manner, "Sir, if you would place your hand, palm down, on the screen for me, please."

Again Hunt uttered a small grunt of approval. "Nice," he remarked as he complied with the *request*. IDs could be forged; fingerprints couldn't. "I'm impressed."

Still no response from the security guard, who was now busy tapping on his tablet screen. The other two guards remained silent but alert, weapons lowered but not put aside. After several tense minutes, the spokesman looked up from the screen and aimed an impenetrable gaze at Hunt.

"Evidently," he said in a voice like flint, "I am talking to a dead man."

Chapter 9

"I can explain," Hunt said.

"I'm looking forward to that, sir. Right now, I'm going to have to ask you to come with us."

"Sure, no problem." Hunt was feeling pretty good about what he'd seen so far of the security at Sam Malone's June Canyon Ranch.

On a rough dirt road at the base of the steepest slope, an electric ATV waited. Four passengers aboard made a tight fit, but the cart carried them all down the mountainside in near silence and with only a few truly alarming bumps and lurches. Another kilometer or so farther on, the ATV pulled up in front of what appeared to be an unpretentious rural residence. The three security guards got out and waited politely for Hunt to do the same.

Hunt allowed himself to be escorted into the house, where, in a modestly though comfortably furnished living room, he was invited to take a seat. Two of the guards remained standing, alert but at ease. The third laid aside Hunt's backpack and his own weapon and perched himself on the arm of the sofa, arms folded on his considerable chest.

After regarding Hunt in silence for a full minute, he said, "Well, sir, this is where you get your chance to explain how your fingerprints come to be an exact match to those of one Lieutenant Hunt Grainger, US Army Ranger, reported killed in action in Afghanistan three years ago."

Hunt gave a brief nod of acknowledgment. "I'm afraid I can't tell you that. Sorry, it's classified." The other man tensed almost imperceptibly. Hunt held up his hand. "What I can do is explain why I'm here, trespassing on private property, as you say. I can also give you the contact information of someone who will vouch for me. Will that do?"

"Start talking," the guard said, "and we'll see."

Yancy was a very light sleeper and accustomed to receiving various communications alerts at all hours of the day and night. The musical trill of an incoming text message woke her even from the desk across the room where she'd plugged her phone in to charge its batteries overnight. The time, given in large numbers on the main screen, registered first: 3:15 a.m. The message itself, from a number she didn't recognize, took longer. Two words, which for a moment her freshly awakened brain could make no sense of.

POOL. NOW.

She read them again: *Pool...now?* And knew a moment of clarity before her mind went blank with shock. How long she stood rooted to the spot while the room whirled around her she didn't know, but her first thought when she started thinking again was: *Impossible*.

Impossible in so many ways. Impossible that he could be here, in California, when she'd left him only a few days ago in Kabul, wearing the garb and full beard of an Afghan tribal elder. Impossible that he should think he could pick up where he'd left off three years before, popping into her life whenever he felt like it with no warning whatsoever, expecting she would welcome him with open arms. That she would drop everything at his beck and call, even in the middle of the night!

Impossible most all that she would. Still.

She stood for a few moments longer, waiting for her heart rate to return to normal, waiting for her hands to steady and her legs to grow firm and solid once more. The phone in her hand uttered its ripple of music again. She stared down at the lit screen.

Yankee?

She sucked in a full breath and huffed it out. *Don't be ridiculous. It isn't the same—of course it isn't. Whatever it was we had before, it's the past. All we have between us now is a child. He's come to see her, not me. He probably didn't want to disturb anyone else at this hour.*

Or...he has information about the bombing.

It took her several tries with stiff and not-quite-steady fingers, but she managed to text back: Coming.

She was digging through her suitcase for something to put on over her skimpy summer shift when exasperation hit her.

What is he doing? What am I thinking? Why on earth would he show up at the villa of a notoriously reclusive billionaire in the middle of the night to see his daughter when she and everyone else would be asleep? How did he get here? Where is security? Why would he expect—

Unless it was something important. Something that couldn't wait even the few hours until daylight. What could have happened? Something awful? Again?

She was a network war correspondent, after all; assuming the worst was a pretty safe bet in her line of work.

She couldn't find a robe—it was California, in the summertime, for God's sake—but did unearth a light beach cover-up that would have to do. She shrugged it on and tied it loosely at her side, then, with a glance at her sweetly snoring child, slipped out into the silent corridor. The stone tiles were cold on her bare feet as she half ran, half tiptoed down its shadowy length and into the kitchen. Warm yellow light from above the vast commercial stove lit her way across the breakfast dining area, the table already set up for the early-risers' breakfast.

The moon had set behind the high mountain to the west; the patio was dark, the pool area out of sight on the level below the low stone wall that enclosed the patio. The sliding glass door slid easily when Yancy tugged on it; she fully expected security alarms to sound.

No alarms went off. Outside, the world was silent. She could hear the beating of her own heart.

There were lights set into the stone wall, providing just enough illumination so she could navigate across the patio without crashing into umbrella tables and lounge chairs. Hugging her cover-up around her, she made her way down the wide stone steps that curved in a half circle to the pool deck. There, unlike the cool tile inside the house, the paving stones seemed to hold and give back the heat of the day. They felt warm beneath her bare feet.

Or maybe, she thought, they were only warm in contrast to the chill that had settled over her entire body.

What am I doing?

The pool deck seemed deserted, gently lit and surrounded by shadowy shapes of the granite boulders and native shrubs that would give the pool its unique and beautifully natural setting in the daylight.

I shouldn't be here.

"Hunt?" she called softly into the night, and one of the shadows separated itself from the rest and moved, soundless as a wraith, into the light. Yancy thought the earth was moving, then realized it was her own body rocking to the thumping of her heart.

Why? What is this? Why am I...what? Afraid? Nervous?

Excited?

Oh, no. Please, no.

She stood silently, not moving, determined not to speak first—although of course she already had, by calling his name.

He was still wearing the full beard, but that was all that remained of the Afghan elder. He was dressed in army-style fatigues, but in dark colors that made him all but invisible in darkness. His head was bare, his dark hair short, as always. His smile flashed, a fleeting reminder of the charm he had once employed to such devastating effect.

"Wasn't sure you'd come," he said.

Brilliant, Grainger.

He'd wondered what he'd say to her, how he'd explain his being here, where he had no good excuse for being. He'd accomplished his mission, done what he'd needed to do, which didn't require visiting either his daughter or her adoptive mother. He didn't know himself why he was here. So naturally that was the first thing she asked him.

"What are you doing here?"

She was wearing some sort of wrap that crisscrossed her body and tied at one side. It had long sleeves but came only to midthigh; her legs and feet were bare, leaving him to wonder if the rest of her was, too, under the wrap. Her hair was tousled, as it nearly always was, but this time there was the certain knowledge that she'd just come from her bed. Memory, physical and raw, slammed him in the gut. He tried again to summon the smile that had gotten him through some sticky moments in his life. "Seeing you, obviously."

"It's three in the morning."

"That never bothered you before."

In the long moment of silence that followed, he thought, *Don't go there, man. What the hell are you doing?*

It wasn't what he'd meant to say, not what he'd come for.

Wasn't it?

He waited out the silence, staying where he was, not smiling now. Finally she gave a small laugh with zero humor in it.

"This isn't a tent or a Quonset on a military base. It's the villa of a billionaire recluse who happens to be my grandfather. I fully expected a gazillion alarms to go off when I opened that sliding door. I don't know why they didn't, actually. Did you—"

He shook his head and moved toward her, one slow step at a time. "I didn't disarm it, if that's what you're asking. Didn't have to. Security here is designed to be invisible—and silent. But it's state-of-the-art and highly effective—trust me, I know." His smile went crooked.

"I gave it my best shot and didn't get within a quarter mile of this place."

"You did what? You mean you—"

"Checked out the security—yes." He was close to her now, an arm's length away. *Too close. Stay where you are, soldier.*

He moved closer. She didn't back away.

"Is that why you're here? To check out the security?" The snort she added was pure disbelief. He didn't answer, and after a moment, she said, "What about Afghanistan? Are you—" And her voice became thin and breathless. She looked almost fearful.

He shook his head, frowning as he gazed at her. Appraising. Wondering. *What if I touched her?* "No. I'm going back. Catching a ride out of Edwards Air Force Base later this morning."

She let out a breath he felt rather than heard. "You won't be seeing Laila?"

"It would only be for a few minutes. I don't think she'd understand. Just disappoint her again." *Don't touch her, you idiot.* He watched his hand lift and move and lightly touch her arm. "I just wanted to tell you—" he cleared his throat and pulled his hand back "—you're safe here. You and Laila."

"I never doubted that." She cleared her throat. "But thank you."

It was a whisper. And her eyes hadn't left his face.

She didn't know what could have happened to her voice. She hadn't meant to whisper; it had just come out that way. Her mind flashed on those moments in her Quonset, the first time he'd come to her, remembering she'd been powerless to resist. Remembering she hadn't wanted to.

He's too close, she thought. *Step away.*

She stayed where she was and thought, *I can't let him touch me again.*

Oh, how I want him to touch me again!

Where had this yearning come from? Seeing him again in Afghanistan after believing him dead all those years, she'd been able to resist the attraction she still felt for him. But this was different. What had changed?

Was it the way he'd held her, that day in the car, just after the bombing?

In the past their relationship—if it could even be called that—had been so simple. And unreal, in a way. A fantasy she'd never let herself examine too closely, knowing it could end in a heartbeat. And it had.

Seeing him again in Kabul, evidently back from the dead, had been a shock. Probably she'd been cocooned by the shock, her emotions numbed. Only her instinctive fear of losing her child had risen to the level of conscious thought. And there'd been the anger, too. Such contradictory feelings, the joy that he was alive mixed with the rage and sense of abandonment that came with realizing he hadn't died but had deliberately left her to believe he had.

But now both the shock and the anger had worn off; Hunt Grainger was alive, back in her life, and God help her, she couldn't get him out of her mind.

Worse, now she *remembered.*

Her body remembered. What his body felt like, heavy and solid on hers, hot and hard, pulsing with strength and need, slick with sweat. His mouth hungry, demanding, lips a satiny contrast with the roughness of beard, his tongue now a caress so exquisite it stopped her breath and brought tears to her eyes…and then all at once urgent, dominating, taking her beyond thought. His hands… Oh, God, his hands. Taking her to unbearable heights, then gentling her back to earth. His voice, a wordless croon that drowned all other sound. His scent, so often carrying reminders of the brutality he sought to scrub from his soul by immersing himself in her body.

They had been wonderful, those times. And terrible. And she'd thought she'd put them behind her forever.

But they were still with her, vividly, achingly real.

And after the bombing, he'd held her. Just held her.

And he was *here*.

"Yankee…" He breathed her name.

Don't, she wanted to say. She said nothing.

How had he come to be so close? She didn't recall him moving, but now if she tilted her head forward slightly it would almost…*almost*…rest on his chest. Oh, how she remembered resting her head on his chest, feeling it rise and fall with receding passion, hearing his heartbeat thump against her ear.

She felt a tug and release at the side of her waist. *Don't*, she knew she *should* say. Instead, she stood, not breathing, as her wrap fell open. Then she uttered a soft gasp when his hands slid inside to enfold her waist. The best she could summon by way of protest was to lift her own hands to lie flat against his chest.

Protest? If so, then how was it that, instead of pushing him away, her hands slipped around him at the same moment his came around her, and her face lifted as if of its own volition to meet the descent of his? How was it that his mouth found hers so unerringly and her lips were parted and waiting?

His beard, though expected, was a shock, the physical kind that raced through all the nerves in her body with shivers and tingles of sensation. A moan formed deep in her throat. She felt his hands push under her shift, flatten against her back, then move downward with the sureness of familiarity to cup her bottom inside her panties. Skin on skin. He pressed her hard against him and the moan in her throat became a growl. She opened her mouth to him and was instantly overwhelmed.

Oh, how I've missed this. How I've missed you!

She hadn't known how much. The screamed *no!* inside her head became a fading echo, drowned by the joyous, resounding *yes! Oh, yes.* She wanted to sob with the contradictions of anguish and elation, of grief and of bliss. How had she failed to realize that what she felt for him was so much more than a physical dalliance? Had she lied to herself, knowing to expect or hope for anything more was futile? And now he was here, holding her, kissing her, and she could no longer deny it. She wanted it to never end.

Except, of course, it would. This was Hunt, who never stayed for long.

She knew she should pull away. Instead, she leaned into him until her breasts pressed against his chest. She felt the hard seams and buttons and edges of his clothing through her thin shift and felt naked.

One of his arms moved higher on her back and his hand cupped her head, supporting it against the invasion of his mouth and tongue. She felt the warm, firm muscle of his neck against her palms, then the cool silkiness of his hair feathering through her fingers. She felt weightless, lost in a vortex of sensation and need. Her breath became a silent scream.

Then…somehow, her feet were once again touching earth. She sucked in air and felt the rapid thumping of a heartbeat against her ear. Felt strong arms holding her tightly, fingers pushing through her hair, hot breath against her temple.

"My God, Yankee." Hunt's voice was hoarse…guttural. "I've missed this. I've missed you."

She found that she, too, was capable of forming words. One word. "Yes."

He lifted his head and turned hers so he could look into her face. The patio lights would make hers visible to him, she knew, as it cast his into shadow. "Yes?" he murmured, and it was a question.

Somewhere off in the night a coyote gave its sharp, yipping bark, and the world crashed in on her like a breaking wave. The faintest of breezes came to cool the sweat on her throat. She shivered.

He felt her body tense and brought one hand up to cup the side of her face, his thumb sliding across her moistened lips. "Yankee…"

Her head moved, a quick, desperate shake. Her voice was hoarse. "No. I can't. We can't. Not here."

"We've always managed before. In worse circumstances than these. There's always the pool…" He kept his voice light, teasing, but his heartbeat had quickened with the realization that the moment had already slipped away.

She pulled herself free, and although he could feel the reluctance in her and knew if he wanted to he could change her mind, he let her go. She drew the sides of her wrap around her and held them in place with her folded arms. He thought she might be shivering and fought the urge to wrap her again in his arms.

When she spoke, her voice was steady but tense, as if it cost her to make it seem so. "It's not the same. You know it's not. What we had—it was a long time ago, Hunt. Things are different now."

"Because of Laila."

"Yes. And… Yes, because of Laila. I have a child to think about—"

"So do I," he said softly.

"—and she's my first priority," she said, as if he hadn't spoken.

"Well, mine, too," he said, batting it thoughtlessly back at her. In the moonlight he could see her unsmiling gaze.

"That's not true," she said gently. "You know it isn't."

He couldn't answer her. After a long silence, she turned away from him, still hugging her wrap around her. "Hunt, thank you for checking out the security, and for letting me know we're safe here. But you need to go now. I need to get back inside. If Laila wakes up and I'm not there... Besides, I'm getting cold."

He stood and watched her go, moving slowly at first, as if she didn't quite trust her legs, then running lightly up the curving stone steps and disappearing onto the upper deck. After a moment, he heard the scrape of the sliding door...open, then shut. He swore under his breath.

Grainger, you're an idiot.

He told himself that, and a good many other things even less complimentary, as he made his way down the brush and boulder-strewn hillside without the light of the vanished moon. He'd known it was a mistake, coming to see her. And he'd come anyway. The pull she had on him...

What *was* the hold she had on him? He'd always thought it was just lust, and sure, he desired her, hungered for her when he came off a mission, couldn't wait to bury himself in her for the comfort and release she gave him. But it wasn't any more than that. *Was it?*

These past three years he'd kept her in a box with the lid tightly shut, put away in the attic of his mind, fully expecting he'd open it when the mission was completed and find her waiting for him, all unchanged.

Stupid idea.

Even without Laila, she'd have changed—of course she would have. He knew that.

But there *was* Laila. *His child.* Yancy was his daughter's *mother.*

Was she right? Did that fact change *everything*? Did it change the way she felt about him? The way he felt about *her*?

The whole thing had him confused, and he didn't like the feeling. He couldn't wrap his head around it. Didn't know how he was supposed to feel. Didn't even know what he was feeling right *now*. Furious with himself, for sure. And probably some guilt. Okay, definitely guilt.

That's not true, she'd said. *You know it isn't.*

Well, dammit, of course she was right—his child had never been his first priority. His mission was, always had been. It had to be. Loyalty, dedication, single-mindedness—those qualities were what made him a success in his chosen profession. They were what kept him alive. The fact that he'd fathered a child—however unplanned and unexpected—was something he'd dealt with in the best way he knew how and a secret he kept buried deep in the protected place in his heart, along with the rest of his personal stuff. The stuff that had no place in the daily reality of a soldier's life. He didn't regret that—how could he? He'd provided for his child's safety, hadn't he? She was happy; she had a mother…

The trouble was, his secret child wasn't a secret anymore, and his feelings for her couldn't be ignored. The box he'd put her—and Yancy Malone—into for safekeeping was open, and it was a Pandora's box full of feelings and emotions that threatened to overwhelm him.

Now. At the worst possible time. He had a mission to complete.

There's always a mission.

Yes, but this was too important. It had to be his top priority right now. Dammit, it *had* to be. The great conference of Afghanistan's tribal leaders was less than a month away. He had only a couple of weeks, at best, to secure the vote that would unite the warring tribes once and for all against the Taliban. To form an alliance that would stand long after the US troops were gone.

It won't always be like this. When this is over...

But what then? Wouldn't there always be another mission? Another war? Could he change his life, become something—*someone*—else? Would he want to? He was a soldier; it was all he knew how to be.

An image flashed into his mind—or call it a specter, a recurring nightmare. Whatever it was, it had haunted him in his youth, though not for a long time. But it came to him now, along with the old familiar coldness in his belly, the wash of bleak despair in his soul. It was the view from the front porch of the farmhouse he'd grown up in: blue skies overhead, big trees shading a raggedy lawn, a rope swing stirring in the ever-present wind, and beyond that a dirt lane between fields of corn or wheat, a dirt lane that led, not to the paved road he knew lay just over the rise, but on and on and on toward the empty horizon and...nothing.

It was what had sent him running for his life as soon as he was able, away from the farm, the life his parents loved and had wanted for their only son, running in spite of the guilt that still haunted him for disappointing two of the people he loved most in the world. He'd hated doing that to them, but he'd felt he had no choice. He couldn't have stayed. It was that simple.

He shivered, thinking of those days, wondering why the nightmare should return just now to bathe him in cold sweat. The burden of guilt he'd carried for so many years had eased some when his sister had married a neighbor's son, a great guy with farming in his blood who'd been happy to step into the shoes Hunt had abdicated. And his mom and dad had been proud of the man he'd become; he knew that. So why now?

I have a child. Could that have something to do with it?

He didn't know.

And then there was Yancy.

He didn't even know how he felt about her. Sure, his body still ached and burned with wanting her. And leaving her had left him feeling torn and sore somewhere deep inside him that had nothing to do with sex denied. He knew the thought of returning to his house in Kabul made him feel lonely in a way it hadn't before.

Before she came back into my life.

And brought the fear with her.

Chapter 10

Yancy had always been an early riser. Add to that the fact that her body clock was still set to some distant time zone, and it wasn't surprising she did no more sleeping after Hunt's unexpected and upsetting visit. She alternated between wide-awake and semidreaming, and sometimes it was hard to tell the difference. In her dreams, Hunt returned and slipped into her bed, and she didn't turn him away. However, she couldn't respond to his lovemaking because she was terrified Laila, sleeping in the next bed, would wake up and find them together. In full wakefulness, she lay wretched and miserable and sick at heart, wishing she could find the off button for her brain.

Thankfully, Laila's body clock was set to the same time zone, so it was barely dawn before she was hopping out of bed, chipper as a sparrow and demanding to go to see if Sam had delivered the goats he'd promised her.

"Honey, he only promised last night," Yancy protested,

while knowing argument would be futile. "I don't think the goats will be here already this morning, do you?"

Laila tipped her head to one side and considered that for a moment, then said, "Yes, they will." She went hopping and skipping off to dig some clean clothes out of her suitcase.

Josie, the nice lady who fixed everybody breakfast, came out to the patio while Laila was finishing up the last bite of her French toast with fresh strawberries.

"Oh, good—you're finished just in time," Josie said, smiling a big wide smile. "Sage is waiting for you out in front."

"Does he have my goats?" Laila asked, licking some whipped cream and strawberry juice off her fingers.

"I think he might," said Josie, "but you'll have to go and see for yourself."

Laila gave her mother a "see, I told you" look and hopped down from her chair, then added generously, "You can come, too, Mom."

Outside, Laila found a white pickup truck parked beside the wide front steps. The motor was running, and Sage was sitting in the driver's seat with the window rolled down and one elbow hanging out. Freckles was in the back, so excited to see her he was wiggling all over. Laila went over to pet him and looked into the back of the pickup.

"I don't see any goats," she said accusingly to Sage.

Her mom said, "Laila!"

Sage said, "That's because they're down at my place. If you want to go and see them, you'd better hop in."

Laila caught her breath and looked at her mom. Mom nodded. Laila ran around to the other side of the pickup, and her mom was there to open the door for her. Laila climbed in, and her mom followed and shut the door. It was a little bit of a tight squeeze, but Laila was so excited she was barely sitting down anyway. She could feel her heart beating very fast. She couldn't believe she was going to have goats. Would they be her very own? she wondered.

She sat rigid on the seat beside her mom, stretching to see out of the front window of the pickup. Down the lane they went, past the tall trees, past the fence where the horses lived and where she'd met the very old man named Sam, who had told her he was her great-grandfather.

And he told Sage to get me some goats. That must mean they are mine, really truly mine. Mustn't it?

A little farther on they turned down another lane that led to a big barn and a little white house with a blue door and big trees in the front yard. Sage stopped the pickup beside the big open barn door, and the very beautiful lady with blond hair came out. She was smiling and holding something black and furry in her hands, tucked up under her chin.

"Oh, look, it's a kitten," Laila's mom said as she got out of the pickup. She went over to the blonde lady, whose name was Abby. Abby gave Mom the kitten, which she cradled under *her* chin, talking baby talk to it. "Listen— it's purring," she said to Laila. "Would you like to hold it?"

"Maybe later. Goats first," said Laila in a firm voice. She had a tight feeling in her chest because she was afraid the goats might not be real and she couldn't believe they were real until she saw them herself.

Sage laughed quietly and touched her shoulder. "This way."

Laila walked beside him into the barn, which was big and shadowy and quiet. Sage didn't say anything and neither did she as they walked together toward another big wide door at the far end. Sunlight was shining through the doorway, and it looked like a golden ladder leading clear up to the sky. She and Sage walked into the sunlight and then they were outside again in a dusty pen. Sage opened a gate on one side of the pen and held it for her so she could walk through into another, smaller pen. At first she didn't see anything, and her heart was thumping so loudly she couldn't hear anything, either. Then...

"Maaa!"

Her breath burst from her like air from a balloon. She looked up at Sage and he nodded. She looked back at the shadows beside the fence, and there was the most beautiful creature Laila had ever seen. She was shiny black with white spots, and her ears were long and hung down beside her head like a bonnet. She didn't have horns, and her nose was high and curved so that she seemed to be looking down at everyone.

"She looks like a queen," Laila whispered. She couldn't stop looking at the beautiful black-and-white goat.

"Yeah, I guess she does," Sage said. "Is that what you're going to name her?"

Laila jerked her eyes upward to stare at him. "Do I get to name her? Really?"

Sage shrugged. "She's your goat. So, you want to name her Queen?"

Laila shook her head. "No, her name is Mor. That means *mother* in my old language." She pointed. "See? She has babies. She's a Mor." She wanted to laugh but was afraid she would start to cry instead. She pressed both hands hard against her mouth as she watched two smaller goats step out of the shadows. They moved with dainty steps, like the gazelles she'd seen on the nature shows on television. They both had long ears like their mother, and one was all black and one was mostly white with black spots.

"I think they're shy," Laila whispered.

"Little bit scared," Sage agreed. "They just need time to get used to their new home. And you. What are you going to name the little ones?"

Laila studied the baby goats for a moment, then pointed at the black one. "That's Jasmine. And *that* one is Belle."

"Huh—good names," Sage said. "Any particular reason why those?"

Laila gave him the look she thought such ignorance deserved. "Because they're *girls*, right? And their mother is a *queen*, so…that means they are *princesses*." Sage just looked at her. She heaved a sigh. "Well, Jasmine and Belle are *princess* names, of course. Don't you know *anything*?"

"Laila!"

Her mom had her hands on her hips and a frown on her face. "Apologize to Sage for being rude. You know better than that."

"Sorry," said Laila.

"Well," said Sage, "I don't know much about princesses. You're right about that." He grinned at her and Laila grinned back.

"Ready for the grand tour?" he asked.

"Abby and Sage are going to show us around the rest of the ranch," Mom said.

"Can't I stay here with my goats? They have to get used to me. Sage said so."

Mom looked at Sage, and Sage shrugged. "Don't see why not. She'll be fine." Mom looked like she wasn't so sure about that, but she went off with Abby and Sage anyway.

After all the grown-ups went away it seemed very quiet in the pen. Mor stood on the other side of the pen and looked at Laila. Jasmine and Belle hid behind their mother and wouldn't come out. Laila wanted very much to pet them all, but she knew if she tried they would probably run away and be even more afraid of her. She stood very still and began to talk to them, telling them what a nice little girl she was and how much she loved goats and would never ever hurt them. Then she sang to them, a song in her old language she didn't know how she knew—she just did.

The goats went on looking at her from the other side of the pen.

"Oh, I wish I had some apples," Laila said out loud. "I bet you would come if I had something to feed you."

"Grain's better," said a crackly voice.

Laila gasped—and looked up. Way up. And there was Sam, looking at her over the top of the fence. She could see that he was sitting on a horse, the spotted one he called Old Paint.

"Well, what're you waiting for? Go get 'em some grain."

"I don't know where the grain is."

"In the barn, of course," said Sam.

"Yes, but—"

"In great big bags with pictures of cows and goats and sheep on 'em. You don't even need to know how to read to find 'em."

"I can read!" Laila informed him, beginning to feel a little angry. "I can read very well."

"Can you, now." Sam made a squeaky sound. She thought maybe he was laughing. "Girl, it doesn't do you any good to know how to read if you don't have a brain to figure out what it means. Go on, now—get your goats some grain. If you're gonna have animals, you better learn how to take care of 'em."

Laila was furious. And scared, because she didn't know how to do what Sam wanted her to do, but she was afraid if she asked one more question Sam would get mad at her. So she went stomping off to the barn, fists clenched at her sides, blinking to keep away the tears.

Inside the barn she stopped to let her eyes get used to the shadows, and out of nowhere a cat came and brushed against her legs. She bent down to pet the cat, and when she straightened up, she saw a pile of sacks over to one side, in front of the big stack of hay. One sack was sitting up on its end in front of the pile, and she could see it had pictures of cows and goats and sheep on it. It was even open. Almost as if someone had known she would need it and had left it for her on purpose.

She went over to the sack and put her hands in the grain. It felt moist. She picked up a handful and sniffed it. It smelled good.

She needed something to carry grain to Mor and her children. But what? She really didn't want to have to go back outside and ask Sam *again*. She could almost hear his crackly voice: *Girl, it doesn't do you any good to know how to read if you don't have a brain...*

She didn't want Sam to think she didn't have a brain. She wasn't sure why she cared what Sam thought, but she did.

And then she saw it. A bucket.

She carried the bucket over to the sack of grain and, using her two hands together, scooped grain into it. She spilled some even though she tried her best not to. When she thought it looked like enough grain to feed one big goat and two little ones, she dragged the bucket outside into the sunshine.

Sam was still sitting on his horse on the other side of the goats' pen. He didn't say anything when he saw Laila with the bucket, but he nodded, and for some reason that made her feel quite proud of herself. However, she didn't want Sam to know how pleased she was, so she poked her tongue into one side of her cheek to keep herself from smiling as she bumped her way through the gate with the bucket of grain.

Mor smelled the grain and came right over and stuck her head in the bucket. Laila managed to get one hand into the bucket to grab some grain, which she held out to Belle and Jasmine, cooing and calling to them in a soft voice. Jasmine came slowly and nibbled at the grain in Laila's hand. Laila giggled—she couldn't help it.

"Better get used to feeding those critters," Sam said. "That's your job from now on, you know. Every day, morning and night. No days off, either."

"I will," Laila promised. She felt quivery with happiness.

"Somethin' else. Now you've got your goats, you better be thinkin' about payin' for 'em."

Laila stared up at Sam. "P-p-pay for them? But... I don't have any money."

He snorted. "Girl, I don't want your money. I've already got more'n I know what to do with. Nope—the way it works is, I did something for you, gettin' you your goats. Now you got to do something for me."

"Like what?" Laila was beginning to have a bad feeling about this.

He made that squeaky sound again. "Well, now, there's no need to look like you just lost your last friend. It's nothing so terrible. All you got to do, if you want to keep those goats, is let me teach you how to ride a horse."

* * *

"Laila's going to be sorry she missed seeing the baby chickens," Yancy said, pausing at the gate to the goats' pen. "She's crazy about babies—of any kind."

"They'll still be here tomorrow," Abby said. "She's welcome to come see them anytime."

Sage had taken his pickup truck and gone back to the fields, leaving the two women to finish the tour of the old adobe ranch house and its orchards and animals. Yancy was becoming more and more intrigued by the tall, slender blonde woman who, in spite of her beauty and Sage's obvious adoration, seemed to consider herself an outsider—perhaps even an intruder. She'd mentioned she'd once been a dancer in New York City, and the reporter in Yancy sensed there was a good bit more to the story of how a big-city girl had found her way to a ranch in the California mountains.

She vowed to find out what that story was, but there would be plenty of time for that later. Now she nodded and smiled and said, "I'm sure she'll do that. I'm guessing sooner rather than later." She pushed open the gate, calling, "Laila?"

The occupants of the pen lifted their heads to gaze at her, still chewing industriously at whatever had been in the large white bucket at their feet.

"Laila?" She turned to Abby. "Where do you suppose she went?"

"I didn't see her in the barn. Maybe she went looking for us. She must have gone around one side of the house while we came around the other. I'll go see."

Yancy nodded as Abby disappeared into the shadows of the barn. It seemed pointless to follow in her footsteps, so, after a moment's indecision, Yancy climbed up onto the corral fence and shaded her eyes as she surveyed the empty pens and the pasture beyond. "Laila!" she called. And again. "Laila!"

Except for the placid chewing of the goats in the pen below, there was no sound. Uneasiness became fear that crawled down her spine like a trickle of icy water. Her mind flashed...

A crush of men, too close...too close. The heat and smell of their bodies. The distant sounds of traffic...a car horn beeping. The smell of dust.

She shook off the memory, telling herself it was ridiculous. Laila was safe here. Nobody had taken her. She was here somewhere. Of course she was.

She climbed down from the corral fence and hurried through the barn, calling her daughter's name as she went. Anger and fear fought a war within her, the tide flowing from one to the other and back again in an instant.

Laila, where are you? You are in so much trouble... Where could she be?

I'm going to kill her for going off without telling me!

She wouldn't do that! Something's happened to her— it's the only explanation.

She met Abby outside the barn.

"Couldn't find her anywhere around the house," the other woman said, breathing hard. "I called. Maybe she went to see the horses? Or to the creek?"

"Laila's terrified of horses." Yancy pressed one hand to her forehead, fighting panic. "She wouldn't go into the pasture for anything, not even to get to the creek."

"Could she have gone back to the villa?"

"I suppose she might have. You don't think she went with Sage?"

Abby shook her head. "He wouldn't take her without telling us. Wait—maybe he left a message on my phone..."

She fished it out of her pocket, glanced at it and made a face. "Damn. I keep forgetting there's no service here. Out at the end of the lane it's better."

She began walking down the lane and Yancy matched her stride for stride.

Where is she? She can't just vanish. Not here. Not here. We're safe here. Hunt said so.

Oh, God, where is she?

"No message," Abby said, sounding out of breath herself. She shaded her eyes with one hand and turned in a circle, clearly at a loss.

What do I do now? I don't dare fall apart.

Yancy felt a touch on her arm and struggled to bring Abby's face into focus. She found the other woman's eyes soft with compassion and concern.

"Listen—why don't you go back to the villa and see if she's there. I'll go make another circle through the barns and sheds. There's probably a million places she could be. Okay?"

Dumb with fear, Yancy could only nod.

She watched Abby run away from her, blond braid bouncing between her shoulder blades. Then she turned blindly to the smooth road that wound between copses of poplars and evergreens and beds of roses to her grandfather's villa. She walked with her head up and fists clenched tightly at her sides, barely aware of her surroundings, consumed by the terror that only parents could know. Realizing that until Laila she'd never really known fear.

How can that be, when I've stood on countless battlegrounds under fire from air and ground, reported from the midst of crowds bent on violence and mayhem, ridden various beasts along trails where one misstep meant a horrifying plunge to almost certain death? How could all that have left me cool and calm, while one missing eight-year-old child reduces me to mindless terror?

And the worst of it was she was alone in this. Utterly alone. She didn't remember much about losing her parents, but she did know she'd never felt alone. There had been her sister, Miranda, and her grandparents—her mother's parents, anyway. But now, as a single parent, she was on her own.

I shouldn't be, dammit!

In that instant, for an instant, she hated Hunt. Hated him for abandoning his child, for leaving his little girl in the care of someone ill equipped to take on the responsibility of a child.

Hated him for coming back from the dead only to vanish again.

Be honest—you hate him for leaving you.

Oh, yes, she did hate him for that. Not just for three years ago, but for this morning and all the other times he'd left her. Left her aching, sometimes with her heart still thumping and his sweat still drying on her skin.

Was it possible, she wondered, to hate someone and long for him at the same time?

Hunt, I need you, damn you!

And she had to face the fact that she was always going to need him, and he was never going to be there for her. Ever.

Laila wasn't at the villa. Yancy hadn't really believed she would be. Wrapped in her parent nightmare, now she was convinced her child was gone. Somehow or other, irrational and impossible as it seemed, someone had managed to swoop in and snatch Laila, leaving no trace.

She couldn't shake that memory of the crowd of bearded, turbaned men pushing in around her and Laila, the feeling of imminent danger, the suffocating surge of panic. *The Taliban?* Could they really reach so far? Was Hunt wrong and it was Laila they wanted after all? Or… did they want *her*, as Hunt believed, and merely meant to use her child as a way to get to her?

Either possibility was unthinkable.

Leaving the housekeeper, Josie, on the telephone spreading the word and rallying help, Yancy wandered out to the front of the villa. From the wide front steps she could see, straight ahead, the wide circular drive, the lane and the trees, the meadow beyond and the mountainside beyond that. To the left, the canyon dropped away to the valley floor, enveloped now in a summer heat haze. As she stood gazing at it all and seeing nothing, a sound penetrated her fear-dulled mind. A rhythmic sound. The clip-clop of a horse's hooves.

She shaded her eyes and stared across the drive to where the lane disappeared behind the trees. She saw nothing, but the clip-clops continued. And then, like a mirage slowly taking on substance, a horse and rider emerged from the trees into the deep shade. They came slowly on, stepping finally into bright sunlight. And Yancy could see now that it was not one rider, but two. One was an old man with shoulder-length white hair and a white beard. He wore a Western-style hat and sat straight in the saddle, the reins held in one hand. But it was the other rider, seated in front of the old man, that held Yancy's tear-shimmered gaze.

A child. A little girl. A little girl with dark hair.

She drew a trembling breath and held it, clamped it in with a hand across her mouth, while the pinto clip-clopped lazily up to the steps of the villa. It halted, bobbed its head, and a snort gusted from its nostrils. Almost in a trance, Yancy descended the steps.

"Howdy," the old man said, tipping the brim of his cowboy hat. "I'm your granddaddy Sam Malone. And I've got something here I think belongs to you."

Yancy held up her arms, and Laila, a determined smile pasted on her lips, released what appeared to be a death grip on the saddle horn. Sam Malone steadied the child with one hand while Yancy eased her daughter out of the saddle and lowered her feet to the ground.

"I wasn't scared, Mom," Laila whispered during the brief moments she was in Yancy's arms.

"She'll be ridin' with me every mornin'," Sam informed her. "Right after she gets done feedin' her goats. We have a deal—right, kid?"

"Right," said Laila, without much conviction.

"Seven o'clock, down at the old barn." Sam touched his hat brim and turned the pinto sharply. A few steps on, he halted and looked back, while the horse danced impatiently, hooves clattering on the pavers. "You ride, missy?" he asked Yancy.

"I do," she managed to reply. She added, "Eastern style, I'm afraid."

Her grandfather snorted. "Well, you're welcome to come along, if you want to." He and the pinto trotted on, unhurried, across the drive, down the lane and disappeared behind the trees.

Yancy's legs buckled and she sat down abruptly on the steps. A small hand came to pat her shoulder.

"It's okay, Mom," said Laila. "I wasn't scared. Sam was holding on to me really tight. He wouldn't let anything bad happen to me. He's my great-grandpa, you know."

The next morning Yancy was shaken awake at roughly six o'clock by Laila, who was already dressed and hopping with eagerness to eat her breakfast so she could feed her goats and go riding with Sam.

Stifling a groan, Yancy sent her off to the kitchen with her blessing, thus buying herself time for a shower.

Odd, she thought, how different it was, with no work schedules to keep, no phones to answer, no deadlines to meet. She'd spent most of her adult life keeping odd hours, getting up at all hours of the day or night, managing to look and sound presentable in front of a television camera often on little or no sleep and very few amenities. But after yesterday's upsetting morning, she'd felt as if she were sleepwalking through the rest of the day and then again had tossed and turned all night.

Not that it had been a difficult day. Far from it. She and Laila had driven the rented car around the valley, ending up in the river town of Kernville, where they'd had pizza for lunch and Laila had played on the swings in the riverside park and splashed in the river's frigid but gentle rapids. They'd wandered through some antiques shops and eaten ice cream sitting outside at a table with an umbrella, and Yancy had promised Laila they would return another day to go tubing on the river.

In the evening, after Laila had fed her goats under the relaxed supervision of Sage, he and Abby had again joined the rest of the family for dinner at the villa. They enjoyed another delicious meal prepared and served by Josie—as usual, she had emphatically refused all offers of help. And then the adults—Yancy, Rachel and J.J., Abby and Sage—had relaxed on the patio with glasses of wine or bottles of beer, talking quietly while Laila swam in the pool and baby Sean napped in J.J.'s lap.

The daytime winds had died and dusk had darkened slowly into peaceful night when Abby and Sage said good-night and went home to their little adobe. Rachel and J.J. went to sit on the edge of the pool, letting Sean kick and wriggle naked in the warm water like a little pink frog. Laila made the baby laugh by coming up in the water close to him and blowing a fountain of water onto his tummy.

When Rachel and J.J., too, said good-night and went indoors, Yancy coaxed Laila out of the pool with reminders of her new morning responsibilities and her early riding date with Sam. In their room, she checked the time on her cell phone and was shocked to discover it was after ten o'clock. She'd forgotten how short the nights were in late June.

After a brief shower and perfunctory teeth-brushing, Laila had fallen asleep almost instantly—and this morning had risen chipper as a bird. Yancy, on the other hand, now felt like a lump of cold oatmeal.

She didn't understand why she felt so flat. Briefly, she wondered if she might be depressed, although she didn't really know what that would feel like, never having had any experience with depression. At least, to the best of her recollection. True, her life had taken some unexpected turns, but that had never bothered her before. She'd always found the unexpected to be stimulating, in fact, and had relished the challenges it brought.

Could it—God forbid!—be because of *Hunt*?

And if it was, then what made his sudden reappearance and subsequent disappearance any different this time from all his other comings and goings over the years? He was Hunt Grainger, after all. It was just what he *did*.

A voice inside her whispered, *Yes, but this time maybe you expected more.*

A knot formed in her chest and a peppery rush stung her eyes. *Okay, maybe I did. Because of Laila. This time I thought…*

Impatient with herself, she brushed away the thought

and willed away the physical symptoms of her disappointment. She'd learned, after all, the only thing she could count on with Hunt was that he could not be counted on.

It was who he was. End of story.

Yancy and Laila walked down to the barn together, though neither said much. Each of them was lost in her own apprehensions, Yancy imagined, though she was pretty sure they weren't nervous for the same reasons. Laila would be worrying about the riding lesson, given her fear of horses. Yancy was more concerned about the instructor.

Sam Malone. What did one say to a grandfather barely remembered? A man known mostly for being unknown. A man notorious for his exploits and scandals, for his meteoric rise from mysterious beginnings to unimaginable wealth and power, and his equally rapid descent back into the shadows. A man who had never been interviewed, was seldom quoted and whose few appearances on film or camera predated the advent of color television. Based on her own brief experience with him, he was obviously a man of few words.

Although…there was that letter.

But this is not the time for regrets, and I can't change the past anyhow.

Those words echoed in her mind now. A shiver rippled through her, one that was more anticipation than fear. She wondered which part of her was looking forward more to the meeting with Sam Malone: the reporter on the brink of the story of a lifetime or the little girl yearning for her grandpa.

Sitting relaxed in the saddle on his favorite horse, Old Paint, Sam watched the two figures come walking down the lane toward the barn. The woman—his granddaughter, goldarn it—was slim and long-legged like her grandma, and the early-morning sun lit up the red in her hair like fire. The kid was wearing a ball cap today, he was glad to see—he'd have to find one for her mother, or she'd burn for sure in the California sun. She looked like a boy, the kid did, and for a second or two there, he could've sworn it was Kate and John Michael come to life again.

"Don't be a fool, old man," he said aloud, having reached the age where he didn't give a hoot whether anybody thought he was crazy. *He* knew he wasn't, which was what mattered.

He took his handkerchief out of a hip pocket and blew his nose to get rid of the sting that had slipped up on him unexpected. Then he slipped back into the shadows behind the corral fence while Sage went out to meet the two visitors. Sage had stuck around this morning to saddle the horses and help the kid with her goat chores, since he was of the opinion she was too small to stand up to a hungry animal taller than she was. Sam's opinion was that the kid needed to learn to stand firm and show the critter who was boss, but he'd been overruled.

Well, hell, when it came to the ranch, Sage was the boss and did a damn fine job of it. Good thing, too, since it would all be his, one day. Probably not too far off, either. Not even Sam Malone could figure on living forever.

From the Memoirs of Sierra Sam Malone:

> *I remember that day like it was yesterday, though it was one I'd give my fortune to forget.*
> *We'd gone out riding that morning, Kate and I,*

in the mountains of West Virginia near to where I was born. I'd taken a place there after the twins were born so Kate could be close to the grand-babies across the way in Virginia. My own kinfolk were all long dead and gone by then, and Califor-nia had been my home for so long I didn't have any particular feeling left for the place, or it for me. But Janey's folks were in Virginia, not too far from Washington, where John Michael worked, and that was where the little girls stayed when their parents were off on another one of their mis-sions to save the world.

I wasn't against them doing that, you under-stand, but I'd been around long enough to know it was a losing battle they were fighting.

I guess they had it in their blood, those two, though John's had come from his mother's side, for sure, not mine. They'd found one another whilst they were down there somewhere in South Amer-ica, working in that thing Kennedy started—the Peace Corps, I guess they call it. Janey was from a family of do-gooders a lot like Kate's except for being better off moneywise, and the two of them matched up as well as any two people could. It didn't seem like they'd ever find time to settle down and raise some kids, the way they were always off in some godforsaken part of the world trying to save somebody else's, but then here came the twins. Kate was in grandma heaven.

For a while, then, it looked like John Michael and Janey were through with gallivanting all over the globe and were going to be content with work-ing in DC and raising those two little girls.

Then came that famine over in Ethiopia, and,

*well, they just had to go. Wasn't anything any-
body could do to change their minds. They left
the twins with Janey's folks there in Virginia, and
off they went.*

*We came riding up to the stables that day, like
always, and from a ways off I could see Gladys
and Willard, the couple that looked after the place
for me, standing outside waiting for us. I got a bad
feeling in my gut, but I didn't say anything, and I
didn't look at Kate in case I'd see my own fears
looking back at me.*

*Closer we got, I could see Willard holding his
hat in both hands, and Gladys had her hands
wrapped up in her apron and tears running down
her face.*

*Beside me, Kate started to whimper even be-
fore Willard got the words out of his mouth. "Mr.
Malone, sir, I'm sorry. The plane..."*

Kate whispered, "No. No. No..."

Gladys covered her face with her apron.

*"It went down, sir. They're gone. They're both
gone."*

*Kate slid off her horse and crumpled on the
ground like a broken doll. I sat in the saddle like
I was made of stone. Willard, he went over to Kate
and tried to help her up. She turned her face up to
me, and I still see her face in my memory, clear as
I saw it then. I knew what she needed from me, but
I couldn't give it to her. God help me. I turned my
horse around and headed back up into the West
Virginia hills.*

*I don't recall much about the next few days. I
know when I came down from the hills, Kate had
gone to Janey's folks to be with the little girls. Me,*

I ordered up my airplane and had my pilot fly me home to California, home to these mountains that gave me their name.

Chapter 11

"You favor her, you know," the old man said.

Yancy threw him a questioning look over one shoulder. She was sitting on a rock beside the little creek, watching Laila try to catch pollywogs in her hands while the horses drank and nibbled on the grass that grew green along the creek banks. Sam hadn't dismounted; Yancy thought it was probably because he'd need some help getting off the horse and back on again.

"Your grandma, I mean." His eyes weren't on her, but focused somewhere on the rocky hillside beyond the creek.

"Really?" She got up, brushing at the seat of her pants, and climbed the gentle slope to where he sat on his pinto horse, leaning on the saddle horn. "I don't remember her very well, but I wouldn't have thought so, from the pictures I've seen."

He made a gesture, brushing that aside. "Not your

looks, exactly—guess I'd have to say you've got your mama's features and coloring. Something about you, though. Brings her to mind—my Katie. She was tall like you, and leggy—had the look of a Thoroughbred. She was a classy dame, your grandma."

She didn't know how to respond to that, so she smiled. He laughed, a sound like a rusty gate hinge.

"Your nature, now—that adventurin' streak—you got that from me. Kate, she was a homebody. But me... I had that yearn to wander, you know. Always did. And I handed it down to you through your daddy—well, and your mama, she had it, too, I guess. They were two of a kind. So you got it in your blood, girl. Both sides. No use denying it. Yep..." He heaved a sigh.

Yancy closed her mouth, which she'd opened in bemusement, both at his words and the fact that he'd strung so many of them together at one time. But the sadness in his face stopped the questions she might have asked, and after a moment, he added, "She blamed me, you know— your grandma—for what happened to your folks. Them goin' off like that...the plane crash that killed 'em."

"Oh, she couldn't—" She was shaking her head, poised to argue, but his gaze came back to her, no longer unfocused but fierce as a hawk's.

"Yes, she could, and she was right. And I blamed me, too. It was me passed that adventurin' spirit to our boy, and that's a fact. That's who he was. Can't change who you are." He waved a hand to where Laila squatted at the water's edge. "Her daddy—seems like he's got it in his blood, too."

She uttered a laugh, denying the quickening of her heartbeat. "How can you know that? You've never—" She stopped, because he was laughing again.

"Oh, I know, missy. I know. And nobody—not you or

me or that little girl down there—is ever gonna change him. Best you remember that." He gave the pinto's reins a tug, making her dance restlessly. "Time we was headin' back to the barn. Storm's coming." He quieted his horse, then looked down at her and winked. "And I'm an old man, you know. Time for my nap."

After the ride, Laila wanted to stay to play with the kittens in the barn, and Abby said she would bring her home in time for lunch. With the rest of the day stretching ahead of her and nothing she could think of to do to fill it, Yancy thought of calling her sister. They hadn't really talked since Yancy had returned from Afghanistan. However, she'd forgotten there was no cell phone service at either the barn or the adobe, so she fired off a text instead. She was almost back to the villa when she heard the chirp of a voice-mail notification.

Hey, big sister, got your text. Call me.

She thumbed Callback and listened to the rings while she walked. She was thinking it was going to go to voice mail when her sister picked up, sounding out of breath.

"Yancy? Hey."

A smile came to her automatically, along with a quivering breath. "So, what's this 'big sister' stuff? I'm all of five minutes older than you are." It was an old routine, comforting as a hug.

"Five minutes, five years—what's the difference? Older is older. So, how is it, there on the farm?"

"It's a ranch, not a farm."

"What's the difference?"

Yancy laughed. "To tell you the truth, I'm not quite sure."

"Okay, so what's he like, our grandpa Sam?"

"That's kind of hard to put into words. You really should come meet him yourself. You are planning to, aren't you?" She closed her eyes for a second, hoping Miranda wouldn't hear the plea in her voice. *I miss you, Randy. I wish you were here.*

She shouldn't have worried—as usual, Miranda was too caught up in her own problems to notice anyone else's.

"Uh…well, I can't right now… I have some stuff going on here. Kind of hard to get away. But I will, I promise, as soon as I can."

Unlike her sister, Yancy was tuned to the nuances of speech and tone, with a talent for hearing what wasn't being said in addition to what was. She kept her voice casual, the question light. "Yeah? What's going on?"

"Oh, you know. Just…stuff. Um, the gallery's keeping me pretty busy right now."

It didn't take a twin sister's intuition or the skills of an experienced interviewer to hear the evasion. Little pulses of alarm began to beat in some far-off region of her consciousness, but she didn't push it. It was probably nothing; Randy was a bit of a drama queen.

And so fiercely independent she probably wouldn't tell her "big sister" even if it *was* something.

They chatted about nothing for a few more minutes, and Yancy disconnected feeling even more alone than before the call.

She told herself she should have known better than to expect much from Randy. She and her sister had been able to share and talk about anything when they were kids, especially after the deaths of their parents. It had been just the two of them against the world then. But their lives had taken such different paths, and as adults they'd seemed to have little in common. They seldom talked anymore, and when they did, it seemed as though they had nothing much to say.

Yancy stood in the smooth dirt road, frowning at the phone in her hand. What had she expected? Or hoped for?

Maybe something to drown out the words that were playing over and over in her mind like a song that refused to go away—what did they call it? A brain worm?

You got it in your blood, girl. No use denying it.

Can't change who you are.

Her daddy, he's got it in his blood.

Nobody—not you or me or that little girl down there—is ever gonna change him.

Best you remember that.

It was only what she'd been telling herself all along, wasn't it? She didn't understand why she should now feel weighed down by those words.

Weighed down. Yes, that was how she felt. Heavy. Burdened. As though every step took more effort than it should. As if she were slogging through deep sand. Was this, she wondered, what it felt like to be depressed?

As if in support of her mood, the world suddenly darkened and thunder rumbled. She looked up at the sky, surprised to see clouds piling up over the mountains to the north and east. Surprised that rain ever happened here in this semidesert in the summertime. Although she did remember, now, that the entire southwestern part of the country was prone to monsoon rains. And the flash floods that sometimes came with them.

A gust of wind ruffled the grass in the pasture next to the road, carrying with it the smell of thunderstorms and lifting Yancy's spirits a little in anticipation of what was to come. She'd always loved thunderstorms. They brought back memories of growing up in the Southeast and of sitting on her grandparents' front porch with Miranda, arms wrapped around her pulled-up knees, watching the raindrops dance on the cement walk. She hurried on, breathing in great gulps of the rain smell, waiting for the plopping sound of the first big raindrops.

To her disappointment, the rain didn't come, and Josie told her that was the way it usually was.

"My grandfather used to say, 'All signs of rain fail in a dry time,'" she said with a shrug, then smiled. "But it's better it doesn't rain right now. I think Sage has hay down in the field. Rain isn't good for hay, you know."

Yancy nodded and went off to her room to shower before lunch, restlessness coiling inside her like a spring being wound and wound, tighter and tighter.

Standing under the cooling spray, she gave herself what amounted to both a stern scolding and a pep talk. Depression, she told herself, was not productive. *Of course* she felt restless and even bored—she was totally unaccustomed to inactivity. No—more than inactivity, she hated the feeling of being cut off from everything. Out of the loop. Isolated. She hadn't been in the field since becoming Laila's foster and then adoptive parent, but at least in WNN's Washington bureau she'd had access to all the news, every hour of every day. Here she was limited to the network broadcasts and frustrated by the knowledge that there was so much more going on that the public would never see.

The way she felt, she told herself, had nothing to do with Hunt Grainger and his sudden and seemingly miraculous reappearance in her life. Nothing whatsoever. She would never allow herself to count on him, and she would do her best not to allow Laila to do so, either. She'd been happy with her career and her daughter—and occasional and casual male company, perhaps—and there was no reason for that to change.

With her eyes closed against the stinging shower spray, an image flashed into her mind. It came with the explosive suddenness of summer lightning.

The warm, firm muscle of his neck against her palms... the cool silkiness of his hair tangling in her fingers... his hand cupping the side of her face, his thumb sliding across her moistened lips. His voice...a whisper. "Yankee."

She had no defense against it. She sucked in a breath at the pain. Furiously, she turned off the water, reached for a towel and scrubbed her head with it as if she could somehow scrub the images from her mind.

Surprisingly, for the most part she was able to keep the images and thoughts of Hunt at bay. During the daytime, at least. Most of the time. As long as she kept busy and in the company of others. Mornings began early, since Laila was expected to report to Sage's barn by barely past the crack of dawn. Yancy had no problem with the early call: network newspeople were rarely allowed a leisurely sleep-in, and war correspondents sometimes had a hard time finding time to sleep at all.

After a hurried breakfast with Josie hovering and sometimes sitting down with them to sip her cup of coffee, there was the walk down to the barn. Then there were the horses to groom and saddle while Laila fed her goats and coaxed them into letting her pet them, all this under the watchful eye of Sam Malone. Yancy didn't know how the old man managed it, but he was always already up on his pinto horse, the one he called Old Paint, before she and Laila arrived. She had to assume it was Sage who brought the horses in from the meadow and got Sam's horse saddled for him, and probably it was also Sage who helped him mount up.

There wasn't a lot of talking during the ride, but each day Sam took them farther up the canyon, to where the meadow narrowed down to nothing and the climb into the timber began. Times like that, Hunt and Afghanistan seemed very far away.

After the ride, there was lunch, which usually included Rachel and the baby, as well as J.J. and Josie, and sometimes Abby and Sage, although Sage was often busy in the fields, and when he was absent, Abby seemed to stay away, as well. The dynamics of those relationships— Abby and Sage, Rachel and J.J.—interested her greatly and were welcome distractions from the complexities of her own.

In the afternoons she was kept busy finding activities to keep Laila occupied. The local middle school, Josie had told her, had summer-school classes in various arts and crafts, as well as swimming lessons for all ages, from babies to adults. Laila objected to swimming lessons, insisting she already knew how to swim, but Yancy convinced her she would have fun and maybe meet some new friends. Which she did, of course, and then there were playdates and sleepovers to plan.

Yes, the days were full.

So were the nights. Full of thoughts she couldn't keep out of her head. Full of images that played in full and living color on the backs of her eyelids. Full of memories that made her body grow hot and her pulses throb, that made her ache in places she wanted to feel nothing at all.

In the daytime she lived on June Canyon Ranch, in the southern Sierra Nevadas of California, USA. In the night, she was back in Afghanistan. With Hunt. She remembered it all, from the first time she'd laid eyes on him, when he'd appeared like a superhero out of the smoke and chaos of battle to rescue her and carry her to safety. To the last time. When he'd come *here* and kissed her by the pool, and she'd known she should push him away but instead had pressed against him, hungry for the taste of him, the softness of his beard on her skin, the roughness of his hands, holding her tightly to feel his own hunger and desire.

God help me. I still want him. How insane is that?

The really crazy thing was that she found herself remembering things she hadn't even known she'd noticed at the time. Like the dimple in one cheek when he smiled, the dimple that was camouflaged most of the time by beard stubble and, more lately, by the full beard. Like the way his voice became a growl in the darkness, so soft it was almost a purr, and the way it stirred goose bumps when he breathed words against her skin.

Finally one night, restless and frustrated beyond bearing and afraid of disturbing Laila, who was breathing softly and sweetly in the other bed, she got up and put on the beach cover-up she'd worn to meet Hunt at the pool. Then she went silently into the courtyard.

Though the courtyard was lit at intervals along the verandas, the night was dark and humid, with clouds covering the stars. Faint rumbles of thunder came from far away over the Sierras to the north, and flickers of lightning cast the bell tower in intermittent silhouette. She might not have noticed the faint glow in the tower window if her attention hadn't been drawn there by the lightning. At first she thought the glow was a reflection of the lightning, but how could that be when the lightning was behind the tower? And when the lightning was gone and darkness returned, the glow remained.

Sam spends most of his time in the high country, these summer days. Or the tower.

She remembered Sage's words. That would be Sam's room, of course, though how the old man managed to get up there she couldn't imagine. Unless there was an elevator. Of course, there must be an elevator.

Her curiosity roused, she crossed the courtyard to the heavy iron-studded wooden door at the far end. This was the door to the chapel, she'd learned during her initial tour of the villa, and was never locked. It opened silently for her now, then closed her into darkness so heavy it felt like a cool cloth over her face. She wondered whether there was a light switch but didn't look for one. She would have hated to turn it on even if she'd found it. A candle seemed more appropriate, she thought. Or a lantern.

Having neither, her cell phone would do—she'd carried it with her into the courtyard out of long habit. She thumbed it on and, in its dim silvery glow, made her way down the center aisle of the chapel to the altar, which was pulled out from the wall to reveal an open doorway. Stepping through the doorway, she found a spiral wrought-iron staircase leading to the bell tower. There was a metal track mounted on the stone wall of the tower. So, not an elevator, but a chairlift. And since the chair was nowhere in sight, that must mean Sam was up there in his room now. With the light on. So there was a good chance he was still up.

The cell phone's glow faded to black while Yancy stood wondering whether she should take a chance on maybe finding her elusive grandfather awake. Maybe, like her, he was finding sleep elusive, as well. Since that day at the creek, she hadn't had a chance to exchange more than a few words with him. What little talking he did during their daily riding lesson was to give instructions and an occasional grunt of encouragement to Laila. She'd been hungry for more information about the parents she'd lost so young and the grandmother she didn't remember.

She was a classy dame, your grandma.

She blamed me, you know—your grandma—for what happened to your folks. Them goin' off like that...the plane crash that killed 'em.

Her stomach knotted and her chest tightened, but she drew in a resolute breath and began to climb the stairs. She'd knock—softly—she told herself. If there was no answer, she would simply go away.

She had barely set her foot on the landing when a raspy voice called out, "That you, Josie?"

With hammering heart she cleared her throat and replied, "No, Gr—uh, Sam, it's me. Yancy."

There was a sound somewhere between a cough and a snort, and then he said, "Well, you might as well come in."

The room was small and square; clearly it had once housed bells, the openings now fitted with windows on three sides. It was warm, with an electric fan the only source of cooling. The only light came from an old-fashioned gooseneck lamp that stood on a battered wooden desk. Sam Malone was sitting at the desk, in a straight-backed wooden chair, although he'd hitched himself around to watch her, one forearm resting on the pile of papers on the desktop. The pen he'd evidently just put down lay on the papers near his hand. The only other furnishings in the room were a rocking chair, a chest of drawers and a single-size bed, neatly made and covered with a faded patchwork quilt. A row of hooks on the wall to the right of the door held an assortment of clothing and hats, with several pairs of boots lined up neatly below them. The only adornment on the walls, in the space not taken up by windows, were photographs, mostly black-and-white.

So simple a room for one of the world's richest men, she thought. Almost monastic. And then she thought, no, except for the electricity, what it reminded her of more than anything was a little room in a log cabin, maybe somewhere in the Ozarks. Or the Appalachians.

That's where his roots are—and mine, too.

He was waiting, in the patient way of the very old, for her to speak.

"I saw your light was on." She nodded toward the bed. "So you don't sleep at night, either?"

He made the creaky sound that was his laughter. "Not much. Old as I am, don't like to waste what time I've got left sleeping."

She strolled slowly toward him where he sat at the desk, tugging the short beach cover-up down as far as it would go. "I'm sorry to interrupt you. I can see you were writing. If you'd like for me to go—"

The gnarled hand that lay on the desktop jerked, and he turned his head to look at it for a moment before lifting it and nudging the stack of papers with it. "Nah—you just as well stay. It's for you, anyway."

"For me?"

"My memoirs—guess you could call it that." He gave the papers another nudge, this time in her direction. "Figured you might be interested in knowing something about where you came from. About your grandma."

"My grandmother?" Yancy frowned. "You mean—"

"Your grandma Kate. I don't suppose you remember her much."

"I do remember her. But not very well. We didn't see her very often after..." She drew a shaky breath and picked up the handwritten pages. "I remember she was a little scary. We only called her 'Grandmother.' Never 'Grandma.'"

His laughter came again, and he rubbed the back of one hand across his nose. "Yeah, she could be a little bit scary, Kate could. Tough as nails, too. But just on the outside. Like I said, you remind me of her, some." He waved a hand toward the rocking chair. "Go on—sit. It'll be slow goin', to read my handwriting, I reckon. Alex, he gets the pages typed up for me, but those I hadn't got around to giving him yet. Take your time. And don't be alarmed if I doze off for a spell. I'm pretty sure I'm not goin' to be dying just yet."

While the old man was chuckling to himself in his wheezy cackle, Yancy lowered herself into the rocker and began to read. After the first couple of lines she looked up. "This is about—"

Sam Malone nodded, and his blue eyes dimmed. "Your daddy—yep. The night he was born."

From the Memoirs of Sierra Sam Malone:

Katie did have a mind of her own, and guts, too, which came as no surprise to me considering the way she laid out her partnership proposal to me.

We made a deal that night, and I had every intention of holding up my end of the bargain. She held up her end, too, giving me all the respectability I could ask for, even if I did decide early on that politics was not for me. For my part I paid off her family's debts and saved their home, and a draftier pile of bricks and timber I hope I never have to see the inside of in my lifetime. But there was the second thing Katherine had asked me for, and that turned out to be a lot harder to supply than the first.

Though it wasn't for lack of trying. And I will not go into the details of that, which was just between Katie and me and that's where I mean to leave it.

For a while it looked like maybe motherhood wasn't going to happen for her. Katherine wasn't a young woman when we married, and the two miscarriages that followed were just two more strikes against her. But the third time was the charm, and if there was ever a happier woman to be in the family way, I can't imagine it. I was glad, too, and not just for her, though I had grown fond of Katherine. Maybe I even loved her, in my own miserable way. No, I was thinking I might not be opposed to another shot at being a father myself, even if I didn't deserve it, not after the way I'd squandered my first two chances.

Somewhere along the line, Kate got it in her head she wanted to do this new thing called "natural childbirth." Said it was the way it was meant to be, something beautiful, not with all the drugs and the mom being put to sleep and whatnot. Well, now, I could have told her I'd been present during the birthin' of my first son, which was about as natural as it could be, and there wasn't much about it that was beautiful, as far as I was concerned. Just a lot more screamin' and hollerin' and mess than I could stand to witness and I had no desire to go through all that again. My second child, my daughter, she was born when I wasn't even in the same state, and that was entirely fine with me. But I didn't say anything, just let Katie go ahead with her plans, and all the exercises and breathing they made her do to get prepared for the blessed event, while I made my own plans to be nowhere in the vicinity when the big day came.

Which was the way it happened, for me, anyway. As far as Katie's plans went...

I was out in California to watch the testing of a new engine I'd been planning to sell to Uncle Sam for the rockets they were about to send up to orbit the earth, when I got a telephone call from my housekeeper. Said that they'd had to take Kate to the hospital in an ambulance. That there'd been complications and they'd had to do an emergency C-section, and that my son was fine, and Kate was okay, but there wouldn't be any more babies for her. Ever.

It ended there. Yancy turned the last sheet of paper over, looking for more, then carefully placed it on top of the others. After a moment, she looked up to find the old man watching her, his eyes still faded and sad. She cleared her throat and said, "That must have been hard. For her, I mean."

Sam nodded. "I expect it was, though I wasn't there to see it. She was a proud woman, Katie was, and by the time I got there she had herself in hand, and if it hurt her she never let it show." He shook his head slowly. "She even forgave me, you know. For not being there for her. That time and a thousand times more. Then..." His voice faded as he gazed at something only he could see. Yancy had begun to wonder if he would continue, when he straightened, placed his hands on his knees and lifted his head to look at her, eyes now bright and sharp as ever. "It was the day your mama and daddy died. She couldn't forgive me for that."

"But," Yancy protested, "that wasn't your fault."

He shook his head. "No, but she needed me then. And when she needed me the most, I let her down. I'd let her down before, but I guess that was just one time too many."

Thunder was still rumbling, though way off in the distance now, when Yancy crossed the shadowy courtyard to return to her room. It made a bass accompaniment to the echoes of Sam's voice that were playing over and over in her mind.

I let her down...one time too many.

But not me. *Hunt didn't let* me *down*, the voice of reason in her head insisted. How could he, when she'd expected nothing from him? She'd accepted him on his terms, hadn't she?

It was Laila he'd let down. Of course it was. So why did Hunt's abandonment weigh so heavily on her own heart?

Because Laila was her child, and it hurt to see her disappointed; that was why. That was all it was.

At the door to the room she shared with Laila, she paused, listening to the ominous grumbles of the distant storm. The restlessness was still with her, along with a feeling of vague disquiet. She knew she wouldn't be able to sleep, that her wakefulness might disturb Laila, so once again she turned away from her room and this time made her way silently along the veranda to the double French doors that opened into the living room.

She'd decided early on that the living room was one of her favorite places in the villa. In spite of its size it was a cozy room, with clusters of comfortable sofas and chairs at opposite ends of the long space, one gathered around the huge fireplace, the other in front of an equally huge flat-panel television set mounted on the wall. There was a game table in one corner, shelves filled with books on either side of both fireplace and TV, and chairs with reading lamps set apart from the communal areas for quiet and privacy. Two of the reading lamps had been left on, turned low.

She was much too restless for reading, so she picked up the TV remote and thumbed it on. Standing in front of the giant screen, she muted it and began to surf through the late-night offerings. None of the movies on the basic cable channels interested her; nor did sports commentary and rehashing of old contests. Twenty-four-hour news channels would be nothing but commentary, too, most likely, but she clicked onto WNN, her own network, because she missed it and wanted to feel a sense of familiarity. Of home. Of the world she'd been a part of for so long. Of friends. Of familiar faces.

But the face that filled the screen, though familiar, was not a friend's. It was there for only an instant before it vanished, replaced by stock footage of men in Afghan costumes and rumbling vehicles and mud-brick buildings, and the banner across the top that flashed, BREAKING NEWS!

Icy cold clutched at her. Her hand shook so that it was long seconds before she could find the button to turn on the sound.

"...the crash of a US Navy helicopter that was returning to the capital city following a meeting of Afghan tribal elders. Arman, whose name ironically means 'hope,' had worked tirelessly behind the scenes for years to bring about the coalition of Afghan tribes that many believe will provide the basis for a united Afghanistan. The historic agreement reached during yesterday's meeting is

thought to be this war-ravaged country's best hope for stability in the wake of the withdrawal of US troops."

The face that had turned her to stone reappeared on the screen. The face of a man wearing the headdress of an Afghan tribal elder. A dark face half-hidden by a full dark beard. But there was no hiding the eyes that blazed out of that darkness. Eyes like golden flame.

"Arman had often been spoken of as a possible future president of Afghanistan, but had resisted all efforts to draw him into national politics. He preferred to work in the background, convincing the often contentious factions to unite for the good of all. Sadly, he didn't live to see his work bear fruit. Arman Haziz—dead in a helicopter crash. The world has lost one of its most dedicated fighters for peace. He will be sorely missed. Back to you in Washington..."

The screen switched to in-studio commentators and voices droned on. The remote control slipped unnoticed from Yancy's hand and clattered onto the hardwood floor.

Chapter 12

She had no idea how long she stood before the TV screen, paralyzed with shock. She heard nothing but a humming sound inside her own head, saw nothing but unrecognizable shapes, splotches of light and dark arranged in random patterns. It was only when the splotches became darkness and the sound in her head a deafening whine that she realized she had forgotten to breathe and was on the verge of fainting.

She'd never fainted in her life and fought against it now with all her strength and will. Somehow, she was sitting down, then leaning forward with her head between her knees. She concentrated on breathing slowly in…then out. In…then out. Slowly the darkness receded, the whine diminished. She began to feel her own body again, clammy and shaking. Nausea clutched at her and she fought that, too.

No. No. No.

It was the only coherent thought in her head.

No. Not again. It's not true.

Slowly she rose and made her way to the double French doors, opened them and stepped out into the warm muggy night.

It shouldn't hit her this hard. It wasn't the first time she'd thought him dead. It had never affected her like this before.

But this… This was different. She'd seen him only… When? A few weeks ago. She'd been in his arms, kissed him, felt the vibrant warmth of his neck with her hands, measured his pulse with her palms. He had a mission to complete, he'd told her, and then he would return. She'd been afraid of what his returning might mean for her, for Laila. Now it seemed he wouldn't be returning, not ever.

Killed…in a helicopter crash.

What was she supposed to do with that?

She found herself once more before the doors to her own room, one hand gripping the door handle. She leaned her forehead against the cool glass and closed her eyes.

How am I going to tell Laila? What am I going to tell her? That her beloved Akaa Hunt isn't going to come to see her ever again? Do I tell her he wasn't her uncle, that he was really her father? When do I tell her that? Now? Years from now? How old is old enough to understand?

She opened the door and stepped into the room, listening for the deep, even breathing of a sleeping child. The room was shadowed, not fully dark. She stood for a while, gazing down at her daughter, sleeping as she usually did, on her side with one hand under her cheek, the other clutching to her chest a corner of the sheet that covered her to just below her arms. Sleeping soundly. Peacefully. Happily.

Not now, she thought. *I don't have to tell her now. Or even tomorrow. It can wait until...when?*

When she's ready. No—when I'm ready.

I will never be ready.

Silently she untied the sash of her beach cover-up and let it slip to the floor. She lay down on the rumpled bed she'd left—oh, a lifetime ago—and, staring up into the shadows, waited for the pain.

She woke up, surprised to realize she'd actually slept. How long she'd slept she didn't know, but she had the feeling the day was well under way. Laila's bed was empty and unmade, and her nightgown lay in a pile on the floor. The baseball cap she always wore when riding with Sam wasn't on the desk where she usually left it, so she'd be long gone, off to the barn to feed her goats and spend the morning with Sam. Strange, Yancy thought, that a little girl and a very old man had become such good friends.

All of that flashed through her mind in a second or two. And for those brief moments, she forgot.

Memory returned in a flood, like a cold ocean wave, making her gasp. For a few moments she only wanted to roll over, curl herself into a ball and stay there.

Why did it hurt so much? She didn't remember so much pain, pain that was physical, like the worst stomachache she'd ever known, but in her chest and throat and face, too. Why this time? Why now?

Because things have changed? Because now there's Laila?

And from the deepest reaches of her mind came a whisper. *No. Because you've changed. Because—*

No. She slammed the lid on that thought before it could even form.

She had to get up. She had to put on her mask and

face everyone as if nothing had happened. Because if she didn't, everyone would want to know what was wrong and she would have to lie, and nobody would buy her lie, and sooner or later Laila would know something was wrong, and then she would have to tell her. She wasn't ready for that. Not yet.

But, to her relief, there was no one in the kitchen when she went out, freshly showered and dressed. No one to smile for, no one from whom to hide the fact that she felt as though she'd been dragged out of the wreckage of a collapsed building. Breakfast had been laid out for her, who knew how long before, but she couldn't have choked down a bite if her life had depended on it. Even the thought of coffee made her throat close. She left the silent, empty house without knowing or caring where everyone had gone off to and walked down the long drive, past the rose gardens, the poplar trees, the horse pasture and pines. Down the lane to the big old barn she went, trying not to break into a run. If she started to run she was afraid she might not be able to stop.

Winnie, the pretty chestnut mare she'd been given to ride, was waiting for her in one of the small holding corrals. The mare whickered a greeting to her, but this morning Yancy had no treats, no soft words to give her. In silence she led the mare into the barn, brushed and saddled her, then lifted herself into the unfamiliar Western-style saddle and in minutes was riding out across the meadow, heading for the distant mountains where the thunderheads were already building, mounds and billows of gray and white against a sky of vivid blue. Once again she had to use all her willpower to hold the mare to a sedate trot, when she wanted nothing more than to let her have her head, let her run flat out until there was nowhere else to run.

She followed the meadow until it narrowed down to nothing, then the trail that followed the creek until its course became too steep and rocky and the trail angled away to wind up through the foothills to the high country. Sam had a cabin somewhere up there, she knew, but since she didn't know the way or how far it was, she stopped there beside the creek and dismounted. Winnie was a seasoned working cow horse and trained to stand when her reins were dropped to the ground, so Yancy felt safe in leaving her there in the shade of some pines, where there was water to drink and a few blades of grass on the creek bank to nibble on. The air was warm and smelled of sunbaked pine needles. The nearby creek made happy chuckling sounds as it trickled over rapids and little falls. In a patch of sunshine thickly carpeted with pine needles, Yancy dropped to her knees, then doubled up with her head in her hands, with her face almost touching the warm earth, and let the sobs come.

The thunderclouds no longer resembled piled-up mounds of meringue when Yancy rode back down through the meadow, but had lowered and spread out in a ceiling of ominous gray that blocked out the sun. Knowing an open meadow was no place to be during a thunderstorm, she allowed Winnie, who was also eager to get back to the barn, to quicken her gait to a gallop.

After her sleepless night and recent bout of weeping, she was exhausted and headachy, drained but calm. There would be no more tears, she promised herself. Hunt Grainger would take up no more of her emotional energy. She would save that for the support and comfort her daughter was going to need—and the strength she herself was going to need when she had to break the news to Laila that her beloved Akaa Hunt was gone. And not coming back. She didn't know, yet, how she was going to do that. She hoped she would know when the right time came.

In the dim and quiet barn she unsaddled and brushed the chestnut mare while the kittens came to climb her pant legs and cry for attention and food. As she turned the mare out to pasture, she noticed that both Sam's and Laila's horses had been turned out, as well. She felt pangs of guilt about leaving her child to the care of others for the afternoon, until she remembered this was the day Laila would go with Josie to the Native American Center.

Two days a week during the summer, Josie taught a children's class there in Pakanapul, the language of the Tubatulabal, and had invited Laila to go along. There would be other children around her age, Josie had said, but Laila had been enjoying the classes themselves as much as the chance to play. Like most bilingual children, she picked up languages easily and had been going around happily practicing the names of the farm animals and the birds and trees and mountains she saw all around her and singing the native songs she'd learned. Sage was even going to make her a flute, she'd told Yancy proudly. And teach her to play it, too.

So Laila was happy and occupied for the afternoon. *Maybe I'll take a nap*, Yancy thought. *Maybe if I sleep I won't have to think. Maybe if I take a nap I'll be able to smile and face everyone at dinner. Maybe.*

She paused to unhook a kitten from her jeans and cuddled it under her chin. But for only a moment, because she could feel the ache building in her throat again, and she'd vowed there would be no more of that.

No more. I'm done.

Sam's words whispered in her mind.

"One time too many..."

And besides, thunder was beginning to rumble, sounding much closer than it had on previous afternoons. As she left the barn a gust of wind tugged at her hair and sent a small flurry of dust across the yard in front of her. Any minute now, surely, the clouds would open up. The drought-stricken earth seemed to hold its breath.

She started walking down the lane, heading back to the villa. And paused when she saw a car parked along the lane, just past Sage's gate. It was a black SUV, not one she'd seen before. A visitor, maybe? Another family member she hadn't met yet? Or someone lost and in need of directions?

Yes, that was probably it, she thought, because as she came closer, the driver's-side door opened as someone prepared to get out of the car. At just that moment a stronger gust of wind rocked her and blew stinging dust into her eyes, and she turned her head and put one hand up to hold her hair back from her face. When she turned again to look at the SUV, the driver had emerged and was standing beside the car, waiting for her to approach.

She had no warning. No premonition. For a moment, as she watched the man come around the rear of the car and start toward her, she didn't recognize him. A tall man, powerfully built, clean shaven, with dark hair a little too long for a military cut, wearing jeans and a black T-shirt.

She halted, not aware that she did.

He moved forward, smiling, and said her name, although she didn't hear it. She heard nothing but a strange wild humming in her head. He came closer, until he was standing right in front of her, and all she could see were his eyes. Golden even in the stormy twilight.

She didn't know she was going to do it. She'd never struck another person in her life, except for self-defense classes. She didn't know she *had* done it, until she felt the sting of it on her palm, felt the jolt of it all the way to her shoulder. The force of the blow rocked her backward, and she stumbled a little before she regained her balance. For a moment she stared at him, seeing her own shock mirrored in his face, seeing his hand come up to touch the place where she'd hit him. Then she turned and ran for the barn as if all the hounds of hell were nipping at her heels.

In planning for a mission, it had always been Hunt's practice to consider every imaginable scenario, in order to avoid unpleasant surprises. Now as he rubbed his stinging jaw, it occurred to him that women might be considerably less predictable than the Taliban.

Hopscotching his way on military flights across the Middle East, Europe and the United States, he'd had plenty of time to think about what he would say to Yancy when he saw her again and to try to imagine what her response might be. But he could honestly say having her clock him in the jaw was one scenario he hadn't foreseen.

Damn but the woman did pack a wallop.

He stood for a long moment, considering his next move and watching the woman in question hightailing it down the lane in the direction of the big old barn. Obviously, his handling of the situation up to now had left a lot to be desired and, he realized now, probably hadn't involved a whole lot of clear thinking.

What *had* he been thinking? That he would show up in the dark of night, climb into her bed stinking of sweat and blood and guns and expect her to open her arms and her body to him, the way she had always done before?

Good God, he hoped he wasn't that stupid. That unfeeling. Obviously, seeing him had come as something of a shock to her. To put it mildly. Right now, good sense suggested he ought to get back in his rented SUV and continue on up to the villa, give her some time to cool off. But his gut was telling him— Well, hell, he didn't know what it was telling him, except he needed to go after her. Right now.

Plus, he was no expert on local weather conditions, but it looked to him like the sky was about to open up, and whatever he was going to do, he'd better do it fast.

The first big raindrops hit him in the face as he was jogging down the lane. He increased his pace and was glad to see the barn door was standing wide open, which meant she hadn't barred it against him. That seemed to him like a good sign.

Dark as it was outside with the thunderstorm about to hit, inside the barn it was even darker. He stood just inside the door for a few moments to let his eyes adjust to the gloom, then called softly, "Yankee?"

She didn't reply, but some mewing sounds drew his eyes to a tall stack of hay bales, unevenly stepped back like a crumbling pyramid. Yancy was sitting on a ledge a few feet above the level of his head, her lap, shoulders and arms full of... Kittens?

She seemed calm enough, so he ventured closer to the stack. When he did, all but the kitten she was holding in her hands scampered up to a higher ledge from which vantage point they observed him cautiously, a row of little triangular heads with great big eyes peering down over the edge of the bale.

"You want to tell me what that was about?" Rubbing his jaw between thumb and forefinger, he gave his head a rueful shake. "You know, you've got a pretty good right cross, for a girl."

She made a sound, halfway between a laugh and a snort, but didn't say anything, just went on cuddling the kitten under her chin.

He climbed onto the haystack and settled himself on the ledge one level below hers, and he was instantly surrounded by smells he hadn't smelled in a very long time. Hay and dust and bird droppings, old leather and animal sweat. Smells that filled his soul with nameless dread.

He pulled up one leg and turned sideways so he could see her. He let out a breath. "I guess you saw the news."

"Yes. A helicopter crash." Her voice was matter-of-fact. Cool and steady. "They said you were dead."

He gave a soft huff of laughter. "It's hardly the first time you thought I died. You said so yourself. It was why—"

Her eyes met his, but in the dusky light he couldn't read their expression. He really wished he could, because her voice told him nothing.

"You know, this time I believed it. I'm not sure why, but I did. I truly *believed* it." She straightened and reached out to put the kitten on the ledge with the others.

Without knowing he was going to, he lifted one arm and intercepted the kitten, bringing it down to his own chest. It squirmed and squalled in momentary panic and dug its claws into the front of his shirt. Though it had been years since he'd last held a kitten, his hands seemed to remember just how to reassure it, how to stroke and cuddle it. In a very few seconds the kitten had settled down and was snuggled against him, purring like a buzz saw. He gazed down at it, conscious of a strange stirring in his chest.

"I couldn't tell you," he said, watching the kitten curl itself more comfortably into the nest of his hands. "The plan for my extraction had to be top secret. You must know that. If my identity had ever leaked, everything I'd worked for all those years would be for nothing."

She dusted her hands, then rubbed her palms on her thighs. "I do know. Oh, I do. I understand." There was the tiniest break in her voice before she caught a quick breath and went on, once again sounding cool and oh so calm. "It was the mission. It always has been and always will be." She stood up, her feet on the bale he was sitting on, and brushed at her backside.

"You've always known that," he said quietly. There was a coldness deep down in his belly. "Yankee. Come on. It's the way it's always been with us."

She nodded. "Yes. That's true. You can't help it. It's who you are."

A crash of thunder shook the barn. Hunt placed the kitten on the ledge Yancy had just vacated, and it scurried to join its siblings and disappear with them into the cracks and crevices of the haystack.

He reached for Yancy's wrist and gently tugged, pulling her down to sit beside him. He took her hand and held it because he couldn't think of anything to say. Her hand was cold, in contrast to the warmth he felt all down his side even though she wasn't touching him, and all he wanted to do was remedy that, pull her into his arms and kiss her until she forgot to be hurt and angry with him and responded with the passion he remembered. Wasn't that the way it had always been between them?

He didn't know how, now, to fix things with only words.

She was right: things were different between them now. In ways he couldn't—or didn't want to—name. But he knew it, and the knowledge made him feel lost. He, who was known for his cool head in the most desperate of situations, now felt close to panic.

"Yankee—" he began, without knowing where to go next.

She sniffed in a breath as she straightened up and pulled her hand from his. She used both of her hands to wipe her cheeks, then lifted her head and shook it, making her hair fall back and lick her shoulders like flames. It occurred to him that he'd never seen her hair so long. On assignment in war zones she'd always kept it shorter. It had looked tousled and windblown. As if she'd combed it with her fingers. Or just gotten out of bed.

Outside the barn the rain made a rushing sound, and it was hard to hear her when she finally spoke.

"I can't do this anymore, Hunt."

His body went still; his mind shut out all distractions and focused with laser-like intensity on the moment, the way it did when he was moving through dangerous enemy territory. Quietly, carefully, he said, "Do what?"

"This. The not knowing. You know. Wondering whether you're alive or dead. Believing—" She caught her breath and whispered, "Thinking I would never see you again. The…fear. I don't want to feel that fear anymore. I can't."

Ah.

Listening to her words, he thought he probably should have felt alarm or a sense of impending doom. Instead, he felt a spark ignite somewhere inside him and grow steadily until it filled his chest with… He didn't know what, exactly. Awareness. Hope. Triumph?

"Don't want to feel…what? The fear?" He was almost whispering, too, now.

She shrugged and turned her head away from him. He put his hands on her shoulders and forced her to face him. But her eyes were closed, her face pale in the deep gloom.

"So…does this mean you care?" Which he knew was an asinine thing to say, even before he said it.

She jerked out of his grasp. "Of course I care. Don't be ridiculous. You're Laila's father. She'd be devastated if her Akaa Hunt—"

"No. Don't do that. Don't make this about Laila. This is *you* I'm talking about." Having said such a stupid thing once, he figured he had nothing to lose, so he said it again. "Do you? Care what happens to me?"

"That…is an incredibly *stupid* question." She bit out the words, her voice bumping as she slid off the bale to the next one down, then the next.

He followed her down. "Maybe. Yeah, it is. But I still want an answer."

Having reached the floor of the barn, she stood up, brushing at the seat of her jeans, then stalked toward the barn's wide-open door. Her movements were jerky with anger. He assumed it was anger.

The rain was a silvery curtain across the doorway.

"Come on, Yancy. Don't go out there. You'll be soaked in a heartbeat."

He was right, of course. She halted, close enough to the downpour to feel its spray, its dampness, its chill. She felt his warmth come close behind her.

She didn't want him there. She *didn't*. She shouldn't.

It took all her will and strength not to lean toward his heat, not to turn into his arms and feel them come around her, strong and protecting as steel. To lay her head against his chest and feel his heartbeat thumping in her ear. Oh, *God*, how she longed to hear that sound.

"Of course I care." She cleared her throat. Shook her head. "But it doesn't matter."

"What do you mean, 'it doesn't matter'?" The words were murmured, a warm breath very close to her ear.

She shivered but shrugged away his hand when he would have touched her. "We've been through this before, Hunt. Things are different now. You know they are."

"Because of Laila."

"*Yes*, because of Laila. The way things were back then, that can't happen now. You must see that. Whatever was between us—" She halted, shaking her head.

Oh, she wasn't explaining it well! She, who made her living with words, couldn't seem to find the right ones now to make him understand.

Understand what? How could she, when she didn't understand herself?

"What *was* it between us?" There was a rasp in his voice now. It seemed to come from deep in his chest, like a tiger purring.

She shook her head, unable to answer. He took her arms and turned her to face him, giving her a little shake so that she had to look at him. And she did, as a matter of pride if nothing else.

Oh, but looking into his face was a mistake, as she'd known it would be. *Ah, those eyes, those golden eyes.*

The huge knot inside her chest burst, spilling warmth all down through her body, into her belly and thighs, sending it pulsing through her blood, into every part of her. Her cheeks felt hot, her breasts tender, her legs weak.

"What was it, Yankee? Tell me."

Don't tell him. You can't tell him. Now or ever. It will only make things worse.

"Sex," she said, summoning every ounce of strength she had just to keep her voice steady.

He let a breath out slowly. "Just sex? That's all?"

She looked away and made a gesture, casual and dismissive. "Maybe not *all*. You needed someone. I understood that. And...I guess I was there."

"And that's it? You really think I didn't care whose bed I hopped into?" There was an angry edge to his voice.

She snapped her gaze back to him. "I'm not saying that. I just meant that I was what you needed then. You had all this...this pent-up adrenaline, maybe. And maybe you needed to forget what you'd just seen. And done."

He snorted. "When you say it like that, I sound like a selfish son of a bitch, don't I? Was it really so one-sided?" He slid his hands up her arms and over her shoulders to curve around the sides of her neck. "Was there really nothing in it for you?"

It took all her willpower to keep from closing her eyes. But willpower couldn't stop her reflexive swallow, couldn't keep him from feeling it, from hearing it. His eyes burned into hers. Tension seemed to hum in the air between them.

"Was it all one-sided, Yankee?"

"No," she whispered. "Of course it wasn't."

"You always seemed to welcome me when I came to you. Was I wrong about that?"

Aching and miserable, she shook her head. "No. You weren't wrong."

"Okay, so you know why I wanted you, or at least you think you do. My question is, why did you want me?"

It struck her then that there was something in his voice. Something in his face. Was it…*vulnerability*? Her heart wanted—yearned—to respond to it, to go into his arms, thoughtlessly, joyously, heedlessly, the way she'd always done before.

Before Laila. Oh, so long ago!

But her body remembered. *Oh, God, yes.*

She had closed her eyes. Now she opened them and pulled away from him, putting up her hands to hold her hair back from her face. Her hands felt cool against her hot cheeks. "What does it matter now? That was the past. This is *now*. I have to figure out what to do."

"What to do about—"

"About *you*, Hunt." He tried to inject another exclamation, but she spoke over it, rapidly, her voice rising dangerously, on the edge of control. "We were happy, Laila and I. We *were*. Then you came back from the dead, and everything turned upside down. Then you were dead again. And now you're alive, and you're *here*. I'm still not sure what you want or what you expect or how you're going to fit into our lives. Never mind what we did or didn't mean to each other back *then*, it's what happens next I'm concerned about. So tell me, Hunt. What is *next*? What do you want?"

"What do I *want*?"

He folded his arms across his chest, making her aware—suddenly, vividly—of the way his muscles bulged, in his arms and beneath the formfitting black knit shirt. Making her remember that he'd seemed to her, the first time she'd laid eyes on him, like some sort of superhuman being, part man, part machine.

It was only later she'd learned how human he really was.

His voice went soft. "Well, for starters, I want to see my daughter."

My daughter!

Fighting for calm against the cold rise of panic inside her chest, she said evenly, "Yes, of course. And she will be thrilled to see you. And after that, what?"

"What do you mean, *what*?" Although his folded-arms stance hadn't changed, it somehow seemed defensive now.

"I mean, what happens after you've seen her? Are you planning on staying a few hours? A few days? A week? Then you'll leave again for...? How long this time? A few weeks? A few months? A few *years*? I can't let you do that to her, Hunt. Not again. Not this time. She's not five years old anymore. She's old enough to ask questions. To want answers. She wants to know about her daddy. What do I tell her? Do you know how many times I've had to lie to her about her daddy? Do you know how hard it is—" Her voice broke at last, and she turned blindly toward the door, needing to escape the tension, needing to put distance between herself and its source, needing to regain control of her emotions.

The rain had stopped. The sun had come out, and steam was rising from the gravelly dirt driveway. The storm's coolness was yielding once more to the late-afternoon heat. She could have walked out of the barn, down the lane, back to the villa.

She didn't. What would be the point? He would only follow her, and she certainly wasn't going to outrun him. The thought was so ludicrous it almost—*almost*—made her smile. No, he was here, and she was going to have to deal with him. Sometime.

Once again, she felt him come behind her, felt his heat, his size, his strength. Overwhelming, almost. She drew her defenses around her like armor.

Which he pierced with a whisper. "Yancy, I'm sorry. I truly am."

Chapter 13

She didn't reply.

Her shoulders looked tense, implacable. But her hair, the ends curling just above them, looked soft and slightly damp. He longed to touch it and her neck beneath. He knew how her neck would feel in his hand—warm, vibrant, strong, but slender and strangely vulnerable, too. The urge was so strong he actually lifted his hand, then curled his fingers into his palm to resist it.

"I guess we have a lot to talk about," he said.

"Yes." She took a deep breath. "But not now. Please? I need—" She gave a small, liquid-sounding laugh. "I'm still getting used to the idea that you aren't dead. I'd like to at least take a shower before we—"

His resolve shattered. He put his hand on her shoulder and gently turned her, and after a moment's resistance, she came into his arms while he wrapped them around her and held her close. Her arms came around his waist and her head lay against his chest. He felt her tremble just slightly and rested his cheek on the top of her head, while something grew heavy inside his chest.

What do you want?

The question terrified him as nothing he'd faced during combat missions had ever done. Maybe because he didn't know the answer? Or maybe he did know, and it was the answer that terrified him.

Images, feelings, memories…they whirled through his mind like the leaves he used to rake up from the front yard of the house he'd grown up in, picked up and scattered and swirled by an autumn dust devil.

Yancy's body, warm and musky with sleep, her voice murmuring a question, then laughter smothered against his neck…

Big brown eyes, going shiny with recognition when he'd see her somewhere in the daylight, then softening with secret knowledge…

Her voice, husky and soft, with her usual greeting, "Hello again, soldier."

A little girl with tear tracks in the dust on her cheeks, sleeping with her head on the flank of a growling mother dog…

A little hand clutching his as though her life depended on it, frightened eyes lifted up to his…

The same little girl lifting her arms to Yancy, lamplight turning her nightmare tears to gold…

Or leaping with baby goats in a farmer's field, laughing as she called out, "Mom, did you see me?"

Then…wind chimes on his mother's porch…the smell of hay and barns and kittens, and his father's tobacco…

The endless prairie sky, the hills wavy with grain or dotted with cattle, the distant horizons and the restlessness in his soul that felt like an itch he couldn't scratch…

The sadness in his parents' eyes when he'd said goodbye.

All of those memories and a hundred more swamped his thoughts as he stood in the sunlit doorway of another barn with a woman in his arms. A woman he felt he'd known for half his life yet didn't know at all.

Yancy.

What do I want?

He wanted the woman, Yancy, the way he'd always wanted her. Ready for him when he needed her, demanding nothing for herself. Didn't he? And yet the thought made him feel strangely bereft.

He wanted the child, Laila. *His* child. Wanted her needing him, looking to him for safety and protection. Didn't he? And yet the thought made his insides quiver with fear.

He couldn't have one without the other. He knew that. And yet the circumstances for both of them had changed so drastically. He couldn't have them the way he once had, without cost, without commitment. And commitment was the way of life he'd once run from as if his soul's survival depended on it.

Wasn't it?

The way he saw it, he couldn't have Yancy and Laila in his life without sacrificing the freedom he'd given up so much for already. The freedom he needed the way he needed air to breathe. How could he reconcile those two and be happy?

It seemed impossible.

It was then that she lifted her head and turned her face to his, and without thought he closed his eyes and lowered his mouth to find hers unerringly. Found her lips cool and moist and tasting slightly of tears. He'd never known her to cry before. Never.

Something lurched dangerously inside his chest, and

it seemed as if his world tilted on its axis. He tightened his arms around her and took what she offered, took her mouth like a lifeline, while everything in him cried out in denial.

No! I didn't want this. I didn't come here for this.

Didn't want...what, Grainger? It's only sex, after all.

She'd said it. *Sex.* That was all it was. It always had been. Whenever he'd needed her, wanted her, she'd been there, ready and willing to accommodate him. Even the last time he'd come here, only a few weeks ago, when he'd had her in his arms and known he could have taken her with very little effort, that was what it had been about: *sex.* Physical desire. Lust, pure and simple. Uncomplicated.

Of course it was.

There was something like desperation in the way he took her mouth, in the thundering hunger that all but overwhelmed him. He knew she must have felt it, too, from the way she opened to him, from the little whimpers of desire that came from her mouth into his, the tremors in her body, all the things he remembered of her responses to him. His body ached with the need to be inside her. It was such a familiar feeling, and somewhere in the instinctive part of his mind were cries of joyful recognition.

Yes! Oh, yes, I've missed this! I've needed this! I want this!

Touch her—yes, there! Make the barriers go away. Make her hot and wet and ready for you!

His hands moved, without guidance from his clamoring thoughts, it seemed. They moved upward over her back, flattened across her shoulder blades, curved over the rounds of her shoulders and gripped hard, with an effort that made his muscles quiver and the voices in his head scream in protest.

No! What are you doing? Don't stop, you idiot! You want this!

No. He didn't.

The realization left him chilled and a little sick. This wasn't what he wanted. At least, not *all* he wanted. He'd never been good at self-delusion, and this new awareness wasn't something he could hide from. His feelings for Yancy Malone had changed. He didn't know what to call it, what he felt for her, but it was more than just sex. That much he knew. What he didn't know was what he was going to do about it.

Especially since for her, apparently, it was just sex. She'd told him so.

He laid his hand over her cheek and ear and pushed his fingers into her soft, damp hair. He held her head against his chest while he lifted his head and stared up into the old barn's cobwebby shadows. For one of the few—perhaps the only—times in his life, Hunt Grainger had no idea what he was going to do.

What was it she felt, with her head laid against his beating heart, her own heart hammering in her throat? Pain, yes. Pain in her chest that made tears seep between her lashes and her breath shudder. Relief? She felt she *should* be relieved that he'd pulled back—pulled them both back— from the brink. But what she felt instead was something like grief. Grief, because what she wanted so badly she knew she could never have.

She loved him. She couldn't deny it any longer. She knew that Laila loved him, too, on some instinctive level, without even knowing he was the father she so desperately wanted.

But Hunt was Hunt, and neither she nor Laila would ever be enough to hold him. He would always have other priorities. He could never be counted on.

Sam had said it.

Can't change who you are.

Nobody—not you or me or that little girl down there—is ever gonna change him. Best you remember that.

Oh, but how good it felt to be wrapped snugly in his arms, his heart thumping in her ear and his hand holding her head nestled there against his chest. *How I've wanted this. How good this feels.*

He'd held her like this before. Just like this, gently, almost...tenderly. Without urgency or passion. Just... held her. Right after the bombing of the WNN offices in Kabul. Had anyone else ever held her like this? Her mother or father, maybe, when she was very small, but if so, she didn't remember it.

The pain inside became an ache that threatened to undo her, a longing so vast it would swamp her pride and common sense, all her defenses, like so many rowboats in a hurricane. If she didn't pull back now. She had to stop this. Now.

Somehow, she found the strength to lift her head and take a step back, and her whole body quivered in protest. His hands slipped down along her arms and she drew her hands free and used them to finger-comb her hair back from her cheeks. Her hot cheeks, which she hoped weren't flaming brightly enough to be noticeable in the barn's dim light.

"Laila will be home any minute," she said. "I should—"

"Of course," he said. "My car—"

"You'll want to come up to the villa, I guess. Meet—"

"Yes. Sure. Are you—" His grin was crooked. "It seemed like you were heading that way, when I—"

"Yes. I am. I was, uh—"

"Can I give you a lift?"

The whole conversation, spoken in breathless fragments, seemed ludicrous in the context of what had just happened, the circumstances, the emotions simmering just beneath the surface. For her, at least. And probably for him, too. Yes, almost certainly for him, too. He was *here*, after all, barely hours after his own faked death on the other side of the world. That had to mean something.

She didn't doubt Laila was important to him. Of course she was. She was his *child*. Right now, she might even be the most important thing.

And I? Am I important to him?

Do I want to be?

The answer to that, she told herself, was *no!* Bad enough she loved him. If he loved her, that would only make things worse. Because it wouldn't change anything. He would still have his job, his duty, his next mission, all of which would always be a higher priority for him than she was, or even his child. He could never be counted on. He would always let her down. Let *Laila* down.

No, she didn't want to love Hunt Grainger. She didn't want Laila to love him, either. But she did. They both did. And that was enough to have to deal with. More than enough.

She didn't want to get into a car with him. She didn't want to be close to him, not there or anywhere. More than anything she wanted to walk back to the villa, walk slowly, breathing in air that had no trace of him in it. She wanted to be far away from him so her mind might have time to clear and her emotions settle.

"Might as well," she said, then glanced at him. "I

didn't mean that the way it sounds. I just mean, I probably should go with you, to introduce you to everyone."

Introduce him? As what? Who do I tell them he is?

Sam knew already, in the mysterious way he had of seeming to know everything about everyone. But would he have shared that knowledge with anyone else? Josie, for example. Or Sage? It didn't seem likely he'd have told anyone else, but the important thing was that *Laila* didn't know. And for the time being, it should stay that way. Of course, at some point it would become necessary to tell Laila her beloved Akaa Hunt was actually her father. When the time came, who would tell her? Would it be Hunt, or would that impossible task fall on Yancy—her mother? Or would they tell her together, she and Hunt?

The thought made her feel sick to her stomach.

Somehow, they were walking down the lane, the ground still wet, puddles soaking rapidly into the parched earth. Far away in the north, thunder grumbled. In a few more minutes the sun would slip behind the mountain to the west. Evenings were long in June Canyon.

They walked without speaking, then both spoke at once.

"You said—"

"She'll be—"

Yancy gave a short laugh and said, "You first."

His laugh was an echo of hers. "You said Laila was going to be home soon. I was just wondering where she is."

"She went with Josie to the Native American Center. She's learning the language of the Tubatulabal people. She seems to have a gift for languages."

"Ah." His smile tilted sideways. "I guess she gets that from me."

She glanced at him and felt a heaviness come unexpectedly to settle in her chest. She thought how much smaller he seemed to her now, though not in a way that diminished him. Not at all. She thought it might be just that, without his military armor or Afghan robes, he had lost that air of authority, that arrogance—or perhaps it was only supreme self-confidence. Without it he no longer seemed invincible.

She wondered whether she was glad about that or sorry.

As they reached the end of the lane where Hunt had left his car, Yancy could hear the growl of a four-wheel-drive engine. A moment later, Josie's SUV appeared at the top of the wash like a whale sounding. It sorted itself out and came on toward them, and Yancy watched it with an inexplicable sense of dread. Though she didn't look at him, the tension in the man beside her seemed almost audible, like a hum just beyond hearing.

Josie pulled her SUV in behind Hunt's car and stopped. For a moment, silence hung in the air, dense as humidity. Then Hunt was moving toward the SUV, moving slowly, with his arms hanging loose at his sides. Through a humming in her ears, Yancy heard him say something. The passenger door opened and Laila slid out, her sandals reaching for the ground. She stood motionless, frowning, hanging on to the door for support almost, Yancy thought, like a shy child clinging to her mother's skirts.

Of course, she thought. *She doesn't recognize him. She's never seen him without a beard.*

Hunt spoke again. And it was as if a floodlight had been switched on in Laila's face, transforming it in an instant from suspicion to sheer joy. She hurled herself at Hunt and was swept up into his arms.

Yancy put her hand over her mouth, knowing how easily the laughter forming in her throat could become a sob. Her chest was heavy with pain. *Oh, God,* she thought, *he's going to break her heart. And I can't do anything to stop it.*

Hunt had set Laila down, and she was hopping excitedly around him, still clinging to his hand while she chattered about how she knew he would come, and he must come and see her goats, and guess what? She can ride a horse now because Grandpa Sam taught her, and there are kittens in the barn, and he must come and see them, too.

Yancy stood hugging herself, watching the two of them go off together, one pulling the other along like a tugboat towing an ocean liner. Neither one looked back.

"Would you like a ride to the house?" Josie asked, leaning across to call through the open passenger's-side window.

Yancy nodded. She took a deep breath and climbed into the SUV. Neither she nor Josie spoke on the way to the villa, while Yancy sat very still and willed the tears lurking behind her eyes not to fall.

Laila had never been so happy. She could hardly believe Akaa Hunt was really *here.* At Grandpa Sam's house!

At first she could hardly believe it was really him, though, because he didn't have his beard. When she asked him why, he told her it was because he was in America now, and in America most men didn't have beards. Which Laila didn't think was true, because she'd seen plenty of men who had beards. Lots of the cowboys on Grandpa Sam's ranch did.

But that didn't matter, because he was *here.*

He was even going to stay over and sleep here. She knew that because she'd heard Josie invite him, and he had said yes. His room was right across the courtyard from hers and Mom's room. When she thought about that, her stomach felt fluttery, which she thought was mostly happiness. But maybe a little bit of scared, too, because—well, because Akaa Hunt would leave again, like he always did. Why did he always have to leave?

If Akaa Hunt would only stay, Laila thought, everything would be perfect. She could live here with Mom and Akaa Hunt, and the goats and kittens and horses and chickens, and Sam and Josie, and Rachel's baby, and everybody. It would be so…perfect. She would be happy *forever*.

"Honey, are you through brushing your teeth?" Mom called.

"Yes, I'm coming," Laila said. She rinsed her toothbrush and stood it up in the cup on the counter beside the sink, then splashed some water on her face and scrubbed it with the towel so that most of the dirt came off. She wiped her hands on her T-shirt nightgown and went into the bedroom. Mom had already turned down the bedclothes and was waiting for her. She took a flying leap and landed in the nice cool sheets, then wiggled down under the light blanket Mom pulled up to her chin.

Mom leaned down to kiss her good-night on the forehead, like she always did, and Laila put her arms around Mom's neck and hugged her tightly. She'd already gotten a big hug from Akaa Hunt when she'd said good-night to everyone, but she closed her eyes and just for a moment thought about what it would be like if Akaa Hunt was there, too, standing right beside Mom. She opened her eyes and looked into Mom's eyes and thought they seemed a little bit sad. And she thought maybe, just maybe, if Akaa Hunt stayed forever, it would be perfect for Mom, too.

Maybe... Oh, I wish. I wish...

"Did you say your prayers?" Mom asked.

Laila nodded.

Wishes were the same as prayers, weren't they?

Yancy was finding it impossible to sleep, which came as no surprise to her at all. It was a warm night—no surprise there, either—and more humid than nights usually were in that valley so close to the Mojave Desert. The moonlight revealed that Laila had thrown off even the sheet and was sleeping on her back with her arms outflung rather than curled on her side as she usually did. Yancy's throat tightened as she remembered the joy on that little girl's face when she'd heard Josie invite Hunt to stay at the villa. And the smile that stayed on her face even into sleep.

It's all so simple, Yancy thought. *For a child.* She loved her "uncle" Hunt, and he was here, and for now that was all that mattered.

She sat on the edge of her bed and raked her fingers through her sweat-damp hair, then rose and walked to the French doors that opened onto the courtyard. They were closed now, of course, since it was so warm outside and the air-conditioning was going full blast. Silently she opened the door and was about to step out onto the veranda when she remembered she was wearing only a flimsy nightgown that was little more than a shift. She shrugged into the light cover-up she'd worn the night she'd gone to meet Hunt by the pool and stepped into a pair of sandals, since the paths in the courtyard, though flagstone, were sometimes strewn with leaves and flower debris. She slipped quietly into the moonlit night.

The air, soft with humidity, reminded her of Virginia's summer nights—without the racket of cicadas and the whip-poor-will that used to sing its little heart out in the woods behind her grandparents' house. Here there was only a faint rustling of leaves stirred by the hint of a breeze and a dog barking far down in the valley somewhere.

And something else, something more felt than heard.

She stood still and waited, and after a moment, a shadow separated itself from the veranda across the courtyard and moved into the moonlight.

"You couldn't sleep, either." It wasn't a question, spoken so softly it was almost indistinguishable from the night sounds. Almost.

Yancy laughed as softly and pulled the cover-up around her, hugging it across her waist as she walked to him with slow, careful steps. Her legs felt oddly unreliable. "It's the humidity," she said. "I'd forgotten how sticky it feels. At night. Especially."

"Yes," he said. "Care to walk with me? There's more of a breeze, I think—" his head moved, pointing "—out there."

"Sure." She drew in a silent breath. "We can go through the living room, the front door. The doors aren't alarmed."

"I know. Remember?"

There was a hint of a smile in his voice, and she could almost see his grin—cocky, confident, charming. She hugged herself more tightly and led the way to the set of French doors that opened into the living room, where a reading lamp had been left on, the same one that had been burning the night she'd heard the news broadcast about the death of an Afghan tribal leader. Only a few days ago. So much had happened, it seemed much longer.

In silence they walked through the room and entryway, through the heavy front doors and down the flagstone steps, across the circle drive and down the lane. The moonlight was bright enough to cast their shadows onto the paved road before them. And Hunt was right—

there was more of a breeze here. It came down out of the canyon to the north, carrying with it the smell of pine and just a hint of rain. Yancy felt oddly exposed in that bright moonlight, with the breeze lifting her hair and brushing the hem of her cover-up against the backs of her legs. She was glad when they reached the trees and were once more in shadows.

He walked so silently, she thought. She was so intensely aware of him it seemed as though she could hear his heart beating, hear the swish of the blood through his veins. Feel the energy shimmering from his body like heat waves on a summer afternoon. Tuned to him as she was, when he broke the silence it felt like a thunderclap, a percussion in her ears, even though he spoke in barely a murmur.

"For what it's worth, I did miss you, you know." She jerked her head toward him and he laughed softly, as if he could see the look on her face. "Okay, not every minute of every day, obviously." They walked on a few paces in silence. "But I thought of you." He stopped walking and made a sound that wasn't quite a laugh. "More often than I wanted to, actually."

She'd stopped walking, too. She didn't look at him and was pretty sure he wasn't looking at her, and for uncounted seconds they stood there, side by side in silence in the moonlight. Around them the night sang with tension.

She thought again how much her perception of him had changed, how he seemed to her now… And once again she struggled to find a way to define the difference. Because it was a contradiction, somehow, that he could seem both less invincible and yet every bit as powerful, less superhero and yet even more masculine. More—oh, much more—*real*.

A shiver coursed through her.

Hunt felt it—of course he would—and turned slightly

toward her. He touched her arm. "Are you cold? Do you want—"

She shook her head. Her body felt stiff, clumsy, and seemed to rock with the force of her heartbeats. She lifted one hand to touch his shirtfront, and his hand closed around her elbow and drew her closer, while the other hand came to cup the side of her face. She flattened her palm against his chest, spread her fingers and felt the warmth of his body through the fabric as her other hand rose to lie along his jaw, feeling the rasp of a day's growth of beard. All this seemed to happen in slow motion while her mind raced in circles like a panic-stricken rabbit.

I shouldn't do this. It will only make things worse.
But I want this! I've wanted this for so long!

His head came between hers and the moonlight. With her eyes closed, she felt the warm brush of his lips on her forehead. Tears burned the backs of her eyelids.

I have to be sensible. I have Laila to think of now. Her needs come first.

But what about me? What about what I want? What I need?

Oh, how she hated for him to know her vulnerability, but she couldn't stop herself from trembling. His lips moved from her forehead to hover over her mouth, then paused, held motionless there by his hand on her face and her hand on his. She drew a small sip of air that was more like a whimper or a sigh.

Oh, God, I need this. I need him. I need.

He took her mouth gently at first, but it was as if a dam burst inside her, drowning all rational thought, all sensible resolve. So clearly she remembered the very first time he'd kissed her, when the need had been so strong and fierce in him and the kiss had been like wildfire through tinder. She had opened herself to him without question then, given to him without reservation.

Had she loved him even then?

Who knew? Did it even matter?

And now it seemed the need was in her. She needed him desperately, maybe the more so for knowing there was no future for them, not a happy one, anyway, just a future of brief visits and long absences, and a little girl with longing in her eyes.

Yes, he knew the need was hers, and this time, as she had done for him so long ago, it was he who answered without holding anything back.

He wasn't sure what made it different from when he'd kissed her earlier today, in the barn, and he'd been the one to pull them both back from the brink. Maybe it was just about sex, like she'd said, but right now that didn't seem to matter to him all that much. Maybe it was just as simple a thing as that he was one hell of a hungry man who'd been without a woman for way too long. And maybe it was as complicated as the feelings he had for her that he didn't understand, mostly because he didn't want to. Or then again, maybe he was beginning to think that, much as he wanted more, sex was all there was ever going to be between them, and if that was the way it had to be, then so be it.

None of that was conscious thought in the moment that he hesitated with his mouth just a breath away from hers and her palm measured his heartbeat. He'd meant to be gentle, to start off slowly, keep some semblance of control over the situation. But then he heard the soft sound she made just before he kissed her and felt the same twisting pain in his chest as earlier when he'd tasted her tears. It took away his breath. Feeling like a drowning man surfacing for one last gasp of air, he drove his fingers into her hair and held her head cradled in his palm, turning her face up to his. He felt her mouth open to him and let go of every reservation, every lifeline, every rational thought. He let it all go.

It *was* a little like drowning. And it was a little like peace.

He came to himself sometime later—he had no idea how much later—realizing they were standing in the middle of a tree-lined lane deep in moon shadow, holding on to each other like survivors of some great cataclysm. He'd been through bombings and shellings and firefights and couldn't remember ever feeling quite like this. *Shaky. Dazed.*

They both spoke at once, the same word, the same inarticulate question.

"What—"

They both broke off without finishing, laughing a little.

What the hell was that?

What are we going to do about this?

"I don't—" Once again they said it together.

"You first," Hunt growled.

After a pause, she tipped back her head and looked at him, catching the moon's reflection in her eyes. "I don't feel like walking anymore."

"Funny," he said. "That's what I was going to say."

"You were not." Her voice was bumpy; she felt quivery with a strange mixture of laughter, excitement and something very much like fear. She tried to remember what it had felt like the first time she'd ever been with a man—no, a boy, really—but she couldn't, it had been so long ago. But she thought—she remembered—it must have felt something like this.

"Okay, then I wish I'd said it." He kissed her again,

his tongue doing things to her mouth that made her body remember with every sense and cell what it had felt like to have him inside her. Her head swam and her legs grew weak. He tore his mouth from hers at last and pulled her closer, one hand pressing her lower back, bringing her tightly against the heat and hardness of his body. His lips moved on her forehead. "I know one thing, though. We can't go on standing here like this."

"No." She said it on a breath of shaken laughter.

When had her hands come to be inside his shirt, roving hungrily over hills and valleys of rock-hard muscle, finding ridges and dimples of old scars, once so familiar, now rediscovered with an ache in her throat that felt strangely like homecoming?

Words came tumbling, whispered, breathless.

"Where can we—"

"Not the house."

"No—the barn?"

"Too far. I don't think I can—"

"What's this place?" He was looking past her at the long white stucco building with the red-tile roof she'd walked past so many times on her way to and from the barn.

She turned to look. "I don't know. A garage, I think."

They left the road and walked together, his arm around her shoulders, hers around his waist, feeling their way through the tree shadows, crunching awkwardly through a drift of dry leaves and pine needles.

From a window in his room high in the bell tower, Sam watched the two dark figures meld into one and a few moments later turn from the road to disappear behind the garage. He curled his arthritic old fingers into a fist and thumped the windowsill twice in sadness and frustration.

"Damn kids," he muttered. "Got no sense. I tried to tell her it wasn't ever gonna work. Not the way they are, too durn much like me. Don't have a prayer."

We made it work, didn't we, Sam?

The whisper came from the room behind him, maybe only the wind stirring through the curtains. Maybe not. He heard those voices more and more often these days, but it didn't trouble him much.

"Aw, Katie," he answered with a sigh. *You married me for a child—you know you did.*

Yes. And they have a child between them already. It's not a bad reason to marry.

Ah, Katie. But when trouble came it wasn't enough, was it? We'd have needed love to weather that storm.

Oh, Sam. There was love. Don't you know that?

He waited for more, but the whispers were silent.

The moon's shadows blurred and wavered before his eyes, and after a moment, he turned from the window. The tears didn't bother him much, either; they came easily, these days.

Chapter 14

Once free of the trees, their feet found better purchase on a graveled drive that lay broad and silver in the moonlight, running along the length of the building on the side that faced away from the paved lane, paralleling the barbed-wire horse-pasture fence. On that side of the building there were five wide garage-type doors.

Hunt gave a low whistle. "A five-car garage. What do you suppose is in it?"

"Knowing Sam, it could be anything." Her voice came raggedly with her uneven breaths.

"Shall we see?"

"If it's not locked."

"It won't be." He was already guiding her toward the regular-sized door closest to the end of the building. "I told you what the security for this place is like... There. See?" He pushed the door open into a well of darkness.

"No windows," Hunt said. "But there's probably a light switch—"

"No! No lights." She felt vulnerable, on the verge of panic.

She heard the whisper of fabric and then he said, "How about this?" A pale light from the cell phone in his hand turned the blackness to shadows. For a few moments they both stood in silent awe.

Then Hunt gave a low laugh and said, "Wow."

"Sometimes," Yancy whispered, "I forget just how rich Sam is. When you meet him you'll understand why."

They walked down the row of automobiles, some shrouded in car covers, others in a layer of dust.

"Oh, my God," Yancy said, "is that a Gullwing?"

"A Mercedes 300 SL? Yep, it is. And…" Hunt picked up the edge of one of the covers and laughed softly. "How would you feel about making out in a Rolls?"

"Intimidated. A Chevy is probably more my speed."

"Yeah, me too. And there's one of those here, too. Looks like a '57 convertible."

He looked at her, his golden eyes silvery in the cell phone's dim glow. She looked back at him, breath held, her lower lip caught between her teeth.

After a moment, she heard him exhale, as if he'd been holding his breath, too. "Have you ever?"

"Have I ever…made out in a car?" She shook her head and laughed, feeling a little wistful. "I was the good twin, you know. My sister, Miranda, on the other hand…"

After a long pause he said, "Have we lost the moment?" His voice sounded regretful.

Her insides fluttered. "No, but maybe…lightened it a little?"

Gruffly he said, "I don't know that I want it lightened. Do you?" He thumbed off the phone and darkness enveloped them in warmth and intimacy. She felt his hand on the nape of her neck, gently massaging. Then his breath on her forehead and the soft brush of his lips, with just the hint of beard stubble. Her breath caught, and a shiver she couldn't control rippled through her.

"You're shaking," he said, turning his head to lay his cheek against her forehead. For some reason her shivers made his chest feel tight. An ache began to build in his throat. He wrapped his arms around her, as much for himself as for her.

"I don't know why," she said. "I seem to be—"

"Nervous?" His voice was raspy, like the purr of a lion. "It's not like we haven't done this before."

"It's been a long time, Hunt." She stirred in his arms, tilting her face to his; he could feel her warm breath in the darkness. "It feels—"

"Strange?" It did for him. As if he was someone he didn't know. Or someone he'd once known and had all but forgotten.

She shook her head. "Different. Just…different."

Different. Because maybe, after all, it's not just…sex?

He didn't say it, because he really didn't want to discuss it anymore. But it stayed in his mind, and for some reason it became important to him to prove her wrong about that.

But if not just sex, then what?

He didn't know what to call the feelings inside him, but he knew those feelings were what made his hands gentle when he took her face between them and his mouth tender when he lowered it to hers. She made a soft sound when she opened to him, and that sound only made the feelings more intense, almost to the point of pain. He allowed the kiss to deepen, but slowly, oh so slowly, and heard her whimper and felt her arms come around his waist. Her head now rested in his palm, her hair so soft and slightly damp, and his other hand slipped under it to cradle the warm, moist nape of her neck. His muscles quivered with the strain of self-control.

She felt the tremor deep in his body, something she'd never ever imagined she would feel in this man. This was *Hunt Grainger*, the man who had seemed invincible, not quite human. *Superhuman.* And she had made him *tremble*? The thought might have given her a sense of power, but instead it was tenderness that filled her, taking her breath, bringing tears to her eyes.

Oh, God, I don't want to love him. But I do.

With his fingers tangled in her hair, he pulled her head back, separating his mouth from hers, then coming back for another sip, then another, and finally, with a deep sigh, letting his lips touch her forehead instead. "I want to make love with you," he murmured, the sound deep in his throat.

She nodded and whispered something that was not quite words.

"Do you understand?" he said. "Not sex. I want to make *love* to you."

Out of the turbulence inside her she could think of only one word. "Yes."

He caught her small sip of air with his mouth, the kiss so gentle, so all-consuming and yet so tender she wanted to weep. Shaken, she pulled her hands from around him and gripped his wrists, tearing her mouth from his. She buried her face in the hollow beneath his chin and felt his arms close tightly around her.

"Not here," he growled. "Not in the backseat of a car."

He turned from her then, keeping one arm around her to hold her close to his body. She felt his muscles gather and tense, heard the swish of fabric and felt the air move, cooling her hot cheeks. "Hold this," he said, and she felt the shape of his cell phone in her hand. She thumbed it on and held it while he gathered the cover he'd pulled from the Chevy into a bundle under his arm. He looked down at her, his eyes gleaming in the silver light. "I want to love you. Make love to you. And I want plenty of room to do that. Okay?"

She nodded and wondered whether her legs would carry her to whatever place he had in mind. Her insides seemed to have melted, and pulses drummed their urgent demands deep and low in her body. But with his arm supporting her, she walked with him, out of the garage and across the graveled lane.

The moon was in the west now, and soon it would set behind the mountain. But for now there was enough light to guide Hunt to the barbed-wire fence. He tossed the car cover over, then held the wires spread so Yancy could crawl through easily before ducking through himself.

He didn't think about what he was doing or whether or not he should. Now his mind was focused entirely on her and what he wanted.

Now. Just now.

Quickly she helped him spread the cover over the thick meadow grass. He knelt on the billowy softness and held up a hand to take hers and guide her down beside him. She knelt facing him, her hands going to the tie at the side of the cover-up thing she was wearing. She pulled on the tie and he took the two halves of the cover-up and pushed them over her shoulders. As it slid to the ground, she picked up the bottom edge of her nightshift and drew it up and over her head, leaving her naked except for a very small triangle of fabric. Her body was pale in the moonlight and so beautiful his breath caught in his throat. As she hooked her thumbs in the sides of the underpants, he moved his hands over her shoulders and down her arms, so that it was both their hands that pulled them off.

She leaned into him then, and his hands slid around to cup her buttocks as he lowered his mouth to the side of her neck. Her breath became a sigh. He could barely breathe at all, his heart was hammering so hard. It was becoming hard to remember why he'd wanted to take her here, outside in the open air where he would love her slowly and there was room to savor every moment. His own clothing felt like a prison, walls of fabric keeping him from the exquisite sensations of her body touching his, skin on skin. He growled in frustration.

"I want—" she whispered.

He replied, "I know," then lowered her gently to the soft bed he'd made for her on the meadow grass.

He watched her belly move in and out with her breathing as he quickly disposed of his shirt and then his shoes, and finally shucked off his jeans and briefs. Her eyes were dark as they followed his every movement, and when he was naked, she lifted her arms to guide him down, not onto her but to lie beside her. He raised himself on one elbow and gazed into her eyes for a long moment while his hand stroked across the gentle concavity of her stomach to the soft mound below. Her eyes drifted closed, and she shifted her legs to allow him access to the sweet, hot places between them.

When he lowered his mouth to one breast, she felt his body quiver—from the strain, she thought, of holding himself back. And when she tangled her fingers in his hair and arched into his mouth, she was trembling, too.

When his fingers found her most tender places, the sensation was so sharp she gasped and would have closed her legs, but his hand kept her open to him. She whimpered and curled herself toward him, and he raised his head and tucked her face into the hollow of his neck while he murmured comforting things into her damp hair. His hand gently housed her softness in warmth and reassurance, and she could feel her pulse beating against the pressure of his fingers as they slowly pushed inside her.

The pressure inside her became unbearable. It seemed to be everywhere—in her belly and chest, in her breasts and throat, in the part of her that pulsed against his hand. She lifted her face to him, seeking blindly, and his mouth came down to fill hers, his tongue keeping the rhythm of his fingers as they slid deep inside her, then partly out again, stroking, teasing, driving her to the edge of sanity. She couldn't stand it another second. Didn't want it to end.

She sobbed…something, she didn't know what, and he answered, "Shh…" as his weight moved over her, as his knees shoved hers aside, as the hot, hard part of him replaced his fingers and pushed deep inside her. He pushed deep and then stopped and held both of them still. Held them still while her body adjusted itself around him and her breathing became less frantic. He whispered, "Hush… softly now," against her forehead, until the panic that had threatened to overwhelm her dissolved into sighs of pleasure.

He kissed her eyelids, her nose, her cheeks, her mouth with such tenderness her throat ached and tears slipped beneath her eyelashes. He took the tears in his mouth, then carried them to hers. And then…slowly began to move inside her. So slowly…

She arched upward, her breathing quickening. And once again he gentled her down. Time after time he slowed and gentled her when she wanted more. Brought her back when she thought she surely couldn't stand the exquisite agony another moment, when she raked her fingers down his back and gripped his buttocks and writhed against his strength, whimpering, pleading...

She barely knew when he quickened his thrusts, only that the pressure inside her was building beyond even his ability to control it, that she was certain she would come apart and fly into a million pieces and there was nothing she could do to stop it. And then she did come apart, and it was his arms and strength and weight and the deep growl of his voice that held her together, that held her while the cataclysms rocked her. Then held her while his own cataclysm claimed him and his body became rigid as steel, then liquid heat she felt deep inside. And finally, human flesh and blood once again, flesh that was slick with sweat beneath her hands, warm breath that gusted into her damp hair, a pulse that pounded against her own thumping heart. She wrapped her arms around him and held him tightly, trembling and aching, not knowing whether the sounds that shook her were laughter or sobs.

She only knew she didn't want to let him go. Knowing that this might be the last time she would ever hold him like this.

He wasn't sure how long it was before he remembered how heavy he must be and tried to lift his weight off her. She held on to him a moment longer before letting her arms slip away from him, and he felt her body shudder as if in protest. Braced on his elbows, he took her face between his hands and kissed her and tasted tears.

"Yankee?" he whispered. "What's wrong? Why are you—" He couldn't believe how shaken he felt.

She gave her head one quick shake and tried to turn her face away. He refused to let her evade him, and at last she drew in a breath and whispered, "I'm not. I don't know—it's just—it's been so long. I didn't think—"

"I know," he said on a long exhalation. "I know. I'm sorry."

He was sorry. Sorry for all the times he'd come to her and taken the comfort she gave so freely and hadn't thought to wonder why it was he'd felt such a need for her—and for her alone. Sorry for all the times he'd left her without telling her what he felt for her in his heart. Sorry he hadn't known himself what it was he felt, until now. Sorry for the years he'd thought about her and let himself believe that thinking was enough.

He turned on his side and wrapped her in his arms, and she laid her head on his chest and snuggled as closely against him as it was possible to get. He felt a shiver ripple through her although it wasn't cold, even though their bodies were damp with sweat. The air was warm and moist, and thunder rumbled somewhere not far off.

And he thought about the summers of his childhood in Nebraska.

He thought about summers that turned into autumns rich with the colors and smells of harvest, and county fairs, and pumpkin carving, and much too soon into long cold winters. Then spring with the trees blooming and grass growing and new babies of every kind and the threat of tornadoes that lasted into another long hot summer. The rolling of the seasons, endlessly, one after the other, ever changing, always the same. And the rhythm of the days, with animals that had to be fed and the cows milked and the ground tilled and the crops planted. Day after day, never changing. Like a carousel, he thought, going round and round, up and down, up and down.

"Yankee," he whispered, wondering if she was asleep, "are you happy?"

She lifted her head and rested her chin on his chest. "Happy?"

"Yeah. Living here, I mean."

She turned her head to lay her cheek once more on his chest, and it seemed a long time before she replied so softly he had to strain to hear her. "It's where I have to be, right now."

"I know. But are you *happy*?"

Thunder rumbled, louder and closer now. Her hand moved on his chest, fingers stroking through the hair, then following it downward over his belly. His body stirred.

"Have you been happy," he insisted, "working in the newsroom, away from the action?" Her hand continued its journey, and he laughed a little, then growled, "Tell me the truth. And, dammit, quit trying to distract me."

She laughed a little, too, then drew a shuddering breath. "It's hard to admit it, you know. I love Laila more than life, but—" Her voice thickened, then became a whisper. "If you knew how guilty I feel. That it's not enough, I mean. That she's not enough. But—oh, God, Hunt, I miss it so much. I do. I can't help it. But I know—"

He caught her hand and rolled her under him, pressing her wrist to the cloth covering the grass while he cut off the words with his mouth. The anguish in her voice was an ache in his own throat, a tightness in his chest. There was no gentleness in him this time as he kissed her, plunging his tongue hungrily into her mouth. And the thunder boomed and crashed around them as if the heavens understood his need to obliterate thought.

She answered his need the way she always had, wrapping her arms and legs around him, lifting her head to meet the demands of his tongue, angling her body to fit his so that their joining was quick and sharp and deep. She gave a shuddering gasp that might have stopped him, or at least returned him to a measure of control, if he hadn't felt her nails raking his back and buttocks, if her body hadn't met the urgency in his with a wantonness of its own. If the violence of the storm hadn't fed the passion in his soul and drowned out all voices of reason.

It was over quickly, as a storm of such intensity must be. She arched and cried out even as his own climax took him to the edges of sanity, then brought him back exhausted, drained and awash in remorse. He felt her body quaking beneath him and was certain he must have hurt her, something he'd never done and would never forgive himself for if he had. It was all he could do to bring himself to open his eyes and look down into her face.

And she was laughing. Breathless with laughter, the aftermath of passion, with sheer joy. He began to laugh, too, with relief, with thanksgiving. And yes, with joy.

At that moment the heavens opened up and the rain came down in sheets. In a moment water was cascading from his forehead, from the end of his nose, onto her face. He tried to wipe it away, but it was futile.

"Let's get out of this before we drown!" he shouted, and she nodded. But it was a moment longer before he could bring himself to withdraw from her, first kissing her again, slowly and deeply, lingering there as long as he could because separating from her felt so much like pain. As if she'd become a part of him he was having to tear away.

But, of course, he had to end it even though he felt that hollowness in his chest he couldn't put a name to.

They were on their hands and knees, scrambling to find their clothing, their shoes, gathering everything into the car cover, into one big awkward bundle. Dashing blindly through the rain, making it through the barbed-wire fence without serious injury, splashing through puddles in the packed sand and gravel driveway, to take shelter at last in the garage. Laughing and gasping while they sorted sodden clothes and tried without much success to dry themselves with the equally sopping-wet car cover, shivering and talking in breathless bursts.

"Oh, my God, I can't believe we did that!"

"I know—what are we, *twelve*?"

"I don't think I was this crazy when I was twelve…"

"I know I wasn't. I'd have been in so much trouble…"

"Aren't we now?"

"I don't know—what time is it? They get up really early—"

"Oh, hell, we can't go in the front—"

"Looking like—"

"Drowned cats!"

It was the laughing and shivering and craziness, Yancy thought, that got her through the aftermath of what had just happened. For a while, at least, she didn't have to face the realization that those moments with Hunt, making love on a makeshift bed beneath a stormy sky, were probably all they would ever have. Later she'd wonder how she was going to find the strength to say goodbye to him and mean it, when every part of her was aching with wanting him, needing him.

Loving him.

"You're shivering," Hunt said, and for a few more moments she allowed herself to be wrapped in his arms and to soak in the warmth and comfort and strength of his body.

Later she'd wonder how she was going to find the strength to hide her own grief when the time came to help Laila deal with hers. Later she'd find a way to ignore the voices in her head that even now were urging, begging, pleading with her reasoning self to find a way, somehow, to let Hunt be a part of their lives, for however long or for as much as he was able. Because it was what *she* wanted.

Later, much later, she would find a quiet place and maybe, just maybe, allow herself to cry.

For now, she would laugh in spite of the pain in her heart, and if there were tears...well, they'd just seem to be a few more raindrops, and no one—certainly not Hunt—would notice.

"Seriously," Hunt said, resting his chin on her head as he took a settling breath, "any bright ideas how we handle this? I think the rain has slowed down, but no matter how you slice it, we are busted."

"Hmm. Maybe not." She pulled away, wiping her cheeks with her hands, and turned before she could give in to the yearning to kiss him one more time. *Just once more. But it would only make it hurt worse, wouldn't it?* "There's an outside door to the chapel—a big heavy one like the front door. It's probably not locked."

"Sounds like a plan," Hunt said. "Help me spread this cover out so it'll dry. Then let's make a run for it."

With some streaks of pink-tinged sky showing off to the southeast, it was light enough to see their way when they left the garage. A light mist speckled their faces as they dashed from under the dripping trees that lined the drive and across thick grass to the chapel. The flagstone circle drive that was the approach to the villa's front door didn't extend to the chapel doors, which weren't used very often. Here, a single flagstone and concrete step surrounded by lawn approached the massive double doors, and sprigs of Bermuda grass had found their way between the pavers. The doors weren't locked, but creaked and groaned when Hunt pulled them open, like a grumpy giant awakened from a long nap. As they stood on the step peering into the chapel, the rising sun found an opening in the clouds, making the darkness inside seem almost impenetrable.

"Close your eyes for a few seconds," Hunt said. "It'll help your night vision."

Yancy followed his suggestion and when she opened her eyes was able to make out shapes well enough to guide him to the side aisle and, from there, feeling their way along the wall, to the door that led to the courtyard. With her hand on the latch, she let out a breath of relief at having avoided the humiliation of getting caught sneaking into the house half-dressed, like a couple of delinquent teenagers.

She started violently, her heart jumping half out of her chest as a cracked and rusty voice came from the deep shadows only a few feet away.

"Kind of early for a walk in the rain, ain't it?"

Chapter 15

Hunt's conditioning kept him from jumping out of his skin, but he felt Yancy's violent start. "Sam Malone, I presume?" he said as he squeezed her hand in reassurance.

From the shadows came a scratchy sound he was pretty sure was laughter. "You got good nerves, son—I'll say that for you. You can let go of my granddaughter's hand now. She needs to get some dry clothes on before she catches her death. And the little girl's gonna be waking up pretty soon. Best she doesn't find her mama gone."

"Couldn't agree more," Hunt said and was turning once again for the door, Yancy tucked into the curve of his arm. He could feel her body quivering.

"Not you, son," the old man said. "You can stay awhile. Got some things to say to you."

Uh-oh. Seriously? Hunt thought. He felt Yancy's hesitation and murmured, "It's okay. You go on."

He stayed where he was until he heard the door latch behind her. His night vision was excellent, and he could see Sam Malone sitting in a pew on the side aisle near the door. He went to lean against the wall beside him and folded his arms on his chest. "Okay, sir, I'm listening."

Sam gave his scratchy laugh. "No need to 'sir' me, son. I'm not your CO and this ain't the army." There was a long pause, which Hunt patiently waited out. Then the old man gave a gusty sigh. "Ah, hell, I never was one for words."

"Not true," Hunt said. "I read that letter you sent to Yancy. Seems to me like you do a pretty good job of saying what you need to."

Sam snorted. "That's writing. You can think on what you want to write. Change it if it doesn't sound right. Speaking's different. Never could figure out how to tell a woman how I felt about her. Maybe why I couldn't make any of my marriages work—well, one reason, anyway." There was another pause. Sam shifted restlessly on the hard pew. "You say you read my letter, so you know how I ruined things with all three of my wives and my children, too. That's the thing I regret the most in my life, you know, and it's been a long life and I've done a whole lot to regret. But that's the biggest. That I never knew my kids. Oh, yeah, I did see my son grow up—that's Yancy's daddy, you know—but I wasn't home enough for him to know who I was, hardly. And then he was gone, and it was too late. Too damn late." His voice cracked and faded away. He cleared his throat and went on.

"Oh, I thought what I was doing was important, making a lot of money. Money I didn't need, since I already had more'n I knew what to do with. What it mostly was, though, was I had this… I guess they call it the wanderlust. It was what made me hop on that freight train way back when I wasn't much more than a fool kid, though I told myself it was because I was hungry and needed a job. It was the Great Depression, you know. No, I just never took well to stayin' in one place, doin' the same things over and over. Thought I needed adventuring to be happy, and maybe I did, back then. Took me a while longer to learn what was important and what wasn't."

This time the pause was so long Hunt thought maybe he was through. But then the old voice took on strength. "You understand what I'm sayin' to you, son?"

Hunt straightened up and cleared his throat. "Yes, I believe I do," he said. He wanted to say more, but it seemed he wasn't any better than Sam Malone when it came to talking about what he was feeling.

Maybe because he wasn't sure himself what that was. Which was something that seemed to be happening to him a lot lately. He frowned into the shadows, trying to home in on just what he was feeling at the moment.

Scared. Again.

Surprisingly, not resentful.

He felt chilled, and not because of his wet clothes. This cold was deep down inside.

"She's like you," he surprised himself by saying.

The old man's head moved, nodding in agreement. "She is. But she'll do what she thinks needs to be done—for the little girl, you know." He gave a gusty sigh. "Women are better at making those kinds of sacrifices than we are. Shamed to say it, but it's true."

He shifted around, going about the task of getting to his feet. Hunt thought better of trying to help him.

"Well, you go on now. I expect you're just as wet as she was. Sage'll be by here shortly to get me…take me down and get me up in the saddle. I like to be ready for the kid, you know, when she comes down for her ride."

Once again, Hunt surprised himself by holding out his hand. The old man's was large and callused, his grip strong. "Thank you," he said and just did manage to stop himself from adding *sir*.

He left the chapel and was halfway across the courtyard before he realized his heart was pounding and his body vibrating with unspent adrenaline, his mind racing, replaying the words and scenes and thoughts of the past day. And he realized it was the way he'd often felt right before a mission when he was preparing himself mentally and physically for events that might change his life forever.

Yancy had always done some of her best thinking in the shower. This morning, though, all the cascade of warm water drumming on her head did was foster a ridiculous urge to cry. She couldn't seem to find a way to get her mind past the pain. Pain that was everywhere—in her throat and her chest. Even the muscles in her face hurt. Her stomach was in knots. All she wanted to do was find a corner somewhere, curl up in it and weep.

But she wasn't a crier, never had been. And Laila was an uncommonly perceptive child and would be sure to notice.

And how would I explain?

How do I explain this to myself? How do I explain that, even though I love Hunt and even though I think he loves me and I know he loves Laila, and even though he is her father, in spite of all those things, I have to tell him...

Tell him...what? Oh, God, what do I tell him?

When Yancy finally emerged from the bathroom in a cloud of steam, dressed in shorts and T-shirt, hair towel-dried and finger-combed, she found Laila up and chipper as a sparrow, all but dancing in her eagerness to see Akaa Hunt.

"Do you think Akaa Hunt will come riding with me and Sam—"

"Sam and *me*," Yancy corrected automatically.

"—and I want to show him my goats and how I'm not afraid of horses anymore—well, not as much as I used to be. Do you think Akaa Hunt knows how to ride a horse? Because if he doesn't, I could teach him. Or Sam could. Mom, I can't find my shoes! Do you think Akaa Hunt is awake yet? Can I go and see? If I knock really quietly—"

"No, you absolutely may not wake him up," Yancy said firmly, while her insides fluttered and her head grew light at the thought of facing him again. So soon after... *Oh, God, not yet. I'm not ready!* "He's probably tired after such a long trip yesterday. Go on out to the kitchen and eat your breakfast. When Akaa Hunt wakes up, and *after* he has his breakfast, I'm sure he'll want to see your goats, and maybe he'll go for a ride with you, too."

Oh, yes, please, let him go for a ride with her. Please let me have more time.

"O-kaay," Laila said with a heartrending sigh. "But you better tell him to come with me, Mom." Having retrieved her shoes from underneath the bed, she shoved her feet into them and clumped her way to the door. *"Promise,"* she threw over her shoulder as she opened the door and went out.

Yancy winced as the door slammed behind her daughter.

She couldn't bear the thought of breakfast, or even coffee, but crawling into bed and pulling the covers over her head seemed like a cowardly option. Feeling as if she was moving through molasses, she tugged the bed-clothes into some sort of order, then went out to the veranda. Though it was already warm and muggy, the sun hadn't yet reached that side of the courtyard, so she settled onto a chaise longue and lay back with a sigh. *I'll only close my eyes for a few minutes*, she told herself.

Just a few minutes.

Hunt emerged from his room, having showered and put on dry clothes, feeling cloaked in the same mantle of calm with which he usually faced a difficult mission. He felt focused. He felt ready.

He stood for a few minutes on the veranda, thinking about his next move. Coffee first? Breakfast? He didn't feel like eating. He usually didn't, before a mission, but normally forced himself to eat anyway, knowing he would need the energy. But this being more of an emotional battle than a physical one, that probably didn't apply.

The sun was hot already, and he was about to retreat into the cool of the house, when he saw Yancy. She was lying on a chaise longue on the veranda. His heart gave an odd little kick, then settled down to a slow, heavy beat as he crossed the courtyard, moving as silently as he knew how.

When he got closer to her, he saw that her eyes were closed. Sleeping? Not too surprising, he thought, considering the night just past. Instead of moving on, he stood for a few minutes, just looking at her.

She was incredibly beautiful.

Well, hell, he'd always thought she was. But it occurred to him now that it had been a long time since he'd thought about that at all. When had she become just...Yankee? Not a pair of brown eyes that inexplicably matched almost exactly hair that was indisputably auburn. Not a wide and generous mouth that curved upward at the corners, or a pair of legs that were long and slender, and a body that...

well. At some point she'd stopped being any of those things. Now to him she was simply *Yancy*.

He drew a long breath, disconcerted to find that it wasn't quite steady, and went to join her, intentionally making his footsteps audible.

She stirred and opened her eyes. Looked up at him, not smiling. "Hi," she said, her voice husky.

"We need to talk," he said.

We need to talk? You just orchestrated a complex treaty among factions that had been killing each other for hundreds of years, and that's the best you could come up with?

"Yes," she said.

She took the hand he offered to help her up, but when he would have brought her on into his arms, she slipped past him and stepped off the veranda, into the courtyard. He followed her, though every nerve and muscle in his body screamed in protest at not being able to hold her. It would have been so much better, he thought, if he could just hold her.

"Yancy," he said. She stopped, her back still turned to him. He took in a breath. "I think we should get married." Then he counted her silence in his own heartbeats.

She turned with a soft gust of laughter. "What did Sam say to you? Tell you to do right by me? Threaten you with a shotgun?"

He tried his best to smile back at her. "Nothing like that. No, he...just talked about his own life. His regrets..." He drew a breath, and the tightness in his chest made it painful. "Uh...and priorities. *You* know. And I think—" She was shaking her head. He put up a hand to stop whatever it was she wanted to say. "No—let me say this. I think— Dammit." He thrust his fingers through his hair and tried to laugh. "He told me he—Sam did—

that he never could tell the women in his life how he felt about them. I get that. I really do. But I'm trying to—I *need* to do better than that. So… I'm just gonna say it. Yankee, I think— No, I *know*. I love you. I really do. I think I always have. And—" She made a small wounded sound and whispered something he couldn't quite hear and chose to ignore. "And maybe you love me, too? And there's Laila. So… I think we should just…get married. Don't you?"

Laila had finished feeding and brushing Mor and Jasmine and Belle, and Akaa Hunt still hadn't come. Sam was already on his horse, Old Paint, and he was waiting for Laila to finish her chores so they could go for their ride. Sweet Pea, Laila's horse, was all saddled up and ready to go, too.

But Laila was disappointed that Akaa Hunt hadn't come. She had really wanted him to come and ride with her, and every minute that went by and he still hadn't come made her feel sadder and grouchier. And maybe a little bit scared, too.

She didn't *think* Akaa Hunt would leave without saying goodbye. But…what if he had?

"I don't want to go riding today," she told Sam. "I'm going to go and see Akaa Hunt."

She ran almost all the way back to the villa. When she saw that Akaa Hunt's car was still there in the driveway, she stopped beside the fountain to catch her breath. Happiness flooded back into her chest, making her feel warm inside. He hadn't left after all! He was probably eating breakfast. So maybe there was still time for him to come for a ride with her and Sam.

Smiling, she skipped around to the side gate and scampered up the steps and across the patio to the kitchen.

Nobody was there, not even Josie. Laila could hear her singing and the vacuum cleaner going in a different room somewhere. Akaa Hunt must be in his room, she thought. Surely it wasn't too early *now* to wake him up.

She ran through the dining room, across the entryway and then the living room, pausing only long enough there to call out "hi" to Josie. In the corridor, she stopped running. She walked sedately to the door of Akaa Hunt's room and knocked. Quietly. She waited. Then she knocked again, loudly this time.

No one answered. She thought about opening the door and just walking in, but she knew that wouldn't be polite. Anyway, Mom would probably know where Akaa Hunt was.

So back through the house she went, around to the other corridor and down to the door to the room she and Mom shared. This time she didn't have to knock. She opened the door and went in. Across the room, through the closed French doors, she could see Mom and Akaa Hunt. They were in the courtyard, talking.

No. They were arguing.

Laila's heart began to beat very fast. Her stomach felt cold inside. She crept across the room, right up to the glass door, and now she could see Mom's face. She looked almost like she was crying.

She knew she shouldn't. But she had to hear what Mom and Akaa Hunt were saying to each other. *She had to.* So, very, very quietly she pushed on the handle and opened the door. Just a little bit.

She heard Mom say, "Oh, Hunt, I can't marry you."

Laila made a sound—she couldn't help it. She clamped her hand over her mouth to keep the sound inside.

"Do you love me?" Akaa Hunt said.

"That doesn't—"

"Do...you...love...me."

"Yes! Oh, yes, I do love you..."

It seemed to Laila that was a very happy thing. But why was Mom crying? And why did Laila feel so scared and sad?

"What I said in the barn—that hasn't changed," Mom said. "I can't let you do this anymore, Hunt—not to me and certainly not to Laila. Never knowing when you're coming, when you're going, whether you're alive or dead—"

"What if I stopped all that? The coming and going, the dangerous missions. What if I quit Special Ops? What if I quit the army? Got out of the service altogether?"

Mom was shaking her head. "Oh, Hunt." She laughed a little, even though she was still crying. "What would you do? Work in an office? Here, on this farm?"

"I don't think those are the only options—"

"You'd be miserable away from the action—you know you would. That wouldn't be good for either of us or for a marriage, and certainly not for Laila."

"What about you?" Akaa Hunt's voice had gotten louder, and he sounded kind of angry. "You miss being where the action is. You told me that. So, you can do it but you think I can't?"

"I didn't say you can't. I said you'd be unhappy."

"And you're not?"

"It's what I need to do right now. It's where I need to be. Laila needs a parent that's going to be—"

"She needs *both* her parents," Akaa Hunt shouted. "Dammit, Yancy, she's my *daughter*. When are you planning on telling her? When she's..."

Laila didn't hear any more. There was a noise inside

her head, like the wind blowing. And it was saying the same thing, over and over:

She's my daughter...my daughter...my daughter...

Now she could hear that Mom was saying something.

"When she's ready, Hunt. We'll tell her when she's ready."

"And who decides that? You?"

"I'm her mother, and I know her better than you do, so...yes. But...when the time comes, we can tell her together."

Akaa Hunt—no, but she couldn't remember the word for *father* in her old language—turned away from Mom. His face looked angry and upset. Mom touched him on his arm. Mom's face looked— But it hurt Laila to see her mother's face, so she closed her eyes as tightly as she could.

"Hunt, I do love you. I have loved you for such a long time. I will always love you. But for right now... I think it would be best for all of us if you go."

No!

She wanted to run into the courtyard and scream at them. *No, no, you can't go! Please don't go!*

She wanted to run away. Far, far away, where nobody, especially not Mom or Akaa—not *Hunt!*—could find her.

I hate them! I hate them. How could Mom lie to me? How could they lie to me? Why is Mom making him leave?

She was trembling. But she had to get away before they saw her. They mustn't know she'd heard.

She backed up until she felt the bedroom door against her back. She opened it and closed it as quietly as she could. She ran down the hallway and through the kitchen, not stopping even when Josie called to her. She knocked over a chair as she ran across the patio and didn't stop to pick it up. The dogs came and wanted to play with her as she ran down the driveway, but she ignored them and turned blindly toward the meadow. She crawled on her stomach under the barbed-wire fence and didn't even care that the grass was wet and she was all muddy now. Across the meadow she ran, with the dogs bounding along beside her, thinking it was all a lot of fun.

She had a terrible pain in her side, but she didn't stop until she came to the creek. It was the place she'd been to before with Mom and Sam, the place where she liked to wade in the shallow water and look for pollywogs. But today she didn't want to stop there. She splashed across the creek to the other side, where there was a rock she liked to sit on sometimes and dangle her feet in the water. She climbed up on the rock and pulled up her knees and wrapped her arms around them and rested her forehead on them.

She wanted to cry. Oh, how she wished she could cry. But she was too angry to cry. All she could do was rock herself back and forth and wish she could just disappear. Like magic. And they would all wonder what had happened to her. They would be sorry.

After a while, she noticed that her bottom was wet. The water in the creek was all the way covering the rock!

She had a bad feeling. A very bad feeling.

She stood up on the rock and looked across the creek, and it seemed like it was much farther away than it was supposed to be. The dogs were over on the other side, and they were running back and forth, splashing in the water on the edges of the bank and barking.

Laila got down on her stomach on the rock and lowered her feet into the water, but it was much deeper than before and running very fast. It pulled on her, and the rocks under her feet were slippery. Before she could even catch her breath or cry out, she wasn't standing up anymore. Instead, she was being carried away by the water, and she couldn't stand up, no matter how hard she tried.

Laila had never been so scared in her life.

The trees and bushes that were supposed to be on the edges of the creek were right in the water, and they were going by very, very fast.

Somehow, she managed to grab on to a tree branch, and she wrapped her arms around it and held on as tightly as she could. She could still hear the dogs barking. She breathed hard for a few minutes until she could catch her breath, and then she began to yell as loud as she could.

It didn't surprise Sam much that the kid didn't want to ride with him this morning. He guessed she was disappointed her daddy had let her down. Well, hell, wasn't that what daddies did—let their children down?

He was in a pretty black mood himself, to tell the truth, and when he felt like that, the high country was where he wanted to be. So instead of unsaddling Old Paint and turning him out to pasture, he turned him toward the north and gave him his head.

About the time he was running out of meadow, he noticed how black the clouds were, up there in the mountains, and he could hear the thunder rumbling off in the distance. And something else, too. Much closer by, he could hear the creak running high and fast.

Sam hadn't gotten to be as old as he was by being a fool, and he knew darn well the high country wasn't any place to be during a thunderstorm. So he turned his horse around and headed back to the barn.

He was about to let himself into the corral when he heard the dogs barking down by the creek. Really going at it, too. He'd never heard them make such a ruckus. Even that old hound dog of J.J.'s was sounding off. That was pretty unusual, so Sam figured maybe he ought to go and see what all the fuss was about.

When he got close to the creek, he could hear the sound of water running in flood. And something else. Something that made his old heart quiver inside his chest.

The little girl was hollering. Hollering for her mama and her daddy.

It wasn't often Sam would ride a horse at full gallop across a muddy meadow, with footing that wasn't sure. Not too long ago he'd done it because somebody he loved was in terrible danger, and he did it again now. With a wild yell he kicked his heels into the pinto horse's sides and rode across that field like the hounds of hell were nipping at his behind.

When he got to the creek, the dogs were running back and forth along the edge of the water, whining and whimpering and carrying on. He couldn't see the kid at first, but he could hear her, and that was all he needed. He untied the roping lariat he kept tied to his saddle— not that he'd used one in more years than he could even remember—and bailed out of the saddle. Old Paint was a cow pony, and he knew what he had to do. When Sam dropped the reins to the ground, the horse stood like he was tied. Sam hobbled to the creek bank, unreeling the rope as he went, and the horse kept some tension on it, just like there was a bucking calf on the end of it instead of a crippled-up old man.

The creek was in flood, and the little girl was out there in the middle of it. He could see her a ways down, hanging on to a tree branch for dear life. Sam stepped into the water and let it take his legs out from under him and carry him downstream, while he held on to the rope and reeled it out, and the horse kept taking up the slack. When he got to where the kid was, his old heart was a-pounding like a freight train, and he thought, *Oh, Lord, don't let me die now!*

The little girl had quit hollering, and when he got to her she latched on to his neck, like to choke him, and he could feel her shaking.

"Hush up—I got you," he told her. "Just hang on now."

And then he lost the rope.

Silently cussing old age and arthritic fingers, he watched the end of it riding the current like a snake. He wasn't nearly strong enough to risk trying to grab for it, and anyway his hands were stiff from the cold water and he probably wouldn't be able to tie it. So he did the only thing he could. He wrapped one arm around the tree branch and the other around the kid, and he started praying.

Yancy stood on the curving front steps and hugged herself as she watched the taillights of Hunt's rented SUV wink on before it made the turn at the bottom of the driveway. She wouldn't cry. She'd promised herself she wouldn't. But every part of her body *hurt*.

She kept hearing the last thing he'd said to her, her spirits reeling drunkenly between hope and despair.

I'm going right now because it's what you say you want. But I'm not leaving this valley without talking to my daughter. This isn't over.

And her reply, forced past the unbearable ache in her throat: *I do love you. I will always love you.*

His reply had been silence and a look in his lion's eyes that she feared would haunt her for the rest of her life.

For a moment, panic overtook her and she found herself running down the steps, running after the disappearing SUV. But of course she couldn't possibly catch up with it, which she realized once the reasoning part of her brain caught up with her adrenaline-charged reflexes. And even if she did, what could she possibly say? She'd done what she had to do, said what she had to say, and nothing would change that. She slowed to a stop in the middle of the paved lane, in almost the exact spot where she and Hunt had stopped in the early-morning darkness and turned into each other's arms, pulled by forces neither of them could resist.

Grief replaced panic. She doubled over, arms across her waist to keep the sobs from bursting forth, gasping for breath. But for only a moment. Then she straightened resolutely, grimacing with pain, and turned toward the meadow, retracing the path they'd taken, first to the garage, then to the barbed-wire fence. Fighting the pain, holding back the tears, she gazed out across the meadow, where the early-morning rain and today's sunshine had restored the grass and erased all traces of the place where they'd made love on the car-cover bed.

With her senses dulled by pain and her thoughts turned inward to her own grief, it was a few minutes before she became aware that the horses, usually placidly grazing, had gathered closely together and were staring intently toward the distant creek. Holding her breath, she could hear a dog's frantic barking. And then a sound that sent a shiver through her body, a sound she'd heard long ago when she was growing up in rural Virginia: the full-throated baying of a hound in full cry.

She was climbing through the fence to investigate whatever it was that had the dogs so agitated when she heard the drumming of hoofbeats. The hoofbeats of a horse in full gallop. She straightened up and looked across the meadow. And caught her breath, frozen in place by the shocking sight of a pinto horse racing flat out toward the creek, and her grandfather, Sam Malone, crouched like a jockey over the horse's neck, his white hair blowing back in the wind.

Galvanized by a nameless fear, Yancy began to run. Her mind was blank; she ran on pure instinct. *Something's wrong. Very, very wrong.*

She was barely aware of her feet touching the ground, completely unaware of her pounding heart and bursting lungs. But as fast as she ran, she lost sight of Sam long before she reached the creek. The dogs had gone quiet, but as she came nearer to the creek she could hear the sound of rushing water. When she topped the gentle rise before the slope down to the creek, she could see the pinto, standing on what had once been the bank of the gently trickling stream, now ankle deep in swiftly running water. A rope, tied to the saddle, trailed off down the stream like a fisherman's line.

For a few terrible moments she couldn't see Sam. Then she did see him. And terror slammed into her, so hard she staggered. Terror unlike anything she'd ever known.

Oh, God—Laila.

She wasn't aware of moving, but somehow she was in the water, holding on to the rope with all her strength, half walking, half swimming, mostly just carried like a piece of flotsam on the flood.

It was colder than she'd expected.

She thought she called out. Maybe it was only inside her head. *Hold on, Laila! Hold on—Mommy's coming. Hold on, Sam. Oh, please, hold on…*

Hunt rested his forearms on the steering wheel and gazed through the windshield at the road ahead. Or rather, where the road was supposed to be. The ravine he'd come across the day before, with its shallow trickle of water at the bottom, was now filled halfway to the top with a raging brown torrent. He swore aloud, but the noise of the water drowned the words. Which was just as well, he reflected, and he'd better get used to editing out the kind of language he wouldn't want his daughter to hear.

My daughter. Laila.

Yancy.

He'd transitioned through so many stages of anger—yes, and grief, too—since his confrontation with her in the courtyard, he wasn't even sure where he was anymore. Blind fury, helpless frustration, shock, disbelief, cold steely rage, stomach-clenching fear. He'd careened from one to the other and back again so wildly his head was spinning. It wasn't a situation in which he was accustomed to finding himself, and he didn't like it. Most of all he didn't like feeling vulnerable.

Dammit, he *hurt*.

All he'd wanted to do was get as far away from the source of his pain as he possibly could, just so he could figure out what to do. So he could *think*.

And now this. Incredibly, he was stuck here. Stranded. No way he was going anywhere until the water went down, and maybe not even then, since the road would undoubtedly be washed out.

Well, hell, he couldn't very well sit in his vehicle waiting for that to happen. He swore again, silently this time. As much as he hated the thought of facing Yancy right now, it would seem he didn't have much choice. He was going to have to turn the damn car around and go back to Sam Malone's villa.

He was going to have to try to explain to his daughter why Akaa Hunt was running out on her again.

Damn Yancy. Damn her.

Because what hurt most of all was knowing she was right. Not about everything—he still believed Laila needed to know who her father was, and now rather than later. But the kind of job he had wasn't going to give a little girl much of a dad. And he couldn't imagine any other job he'd be happy doing. So it seemed he was going to be choosing between his own happiness and his child's.

Which, it occurred to him, was exactly what *she'd* done. Yancy had chosen her daughter's well-being over her own happiness. Why couldn't he?

Dammit, why couldn't I?

He threw the rented SUV into Reverse, then did a tight U-turn, bumping and jouncing over boulders and through brush until he was back on the road and heading for Sam Malone's villa. At the T intersection he made a hard left onto the paved lane that ran along the barbed-wire fence.

Memories came, unbidden and unwelcome, clenching his belly, tightening his groin, making something lurch inside his chest. *Dammit, Yancy...* He found himself slowing down, his head turning almost of its own volition as he gazed out across the meadow where not more than twelve hours ago he'd made love to her on a car cover over thick meadow grass. He swallowed several times and closed his eyes briefly, trying to dispel the images that insisted on filling his mind. When he opened them again the images still lingered, so it was a moment or two before he realized what he was seeing in reality.

Yancy, way off on the far side of the meadow, running toward the creek. Running very fast. Running hard.

Hunt hadn't survived as many Special Ops missions as he had without the ability to sense when something was off. When something didn't look, sound, smell, *feel* right. Natural instincts or training—didn't matter which, but it had saved his life and the lives of his team more than once. Right now, it had him piling out of the SUV and shinnying under the barbed-wire fence faster than his mind could form rational thought. Then he shot from a crouch like a sprinter from the starting blocks.

He'd lost sight of Yancy, but the only place she could have gone was into the trees that lined the creek. What the hell was she thinking? If the branch of the creek that crossed the road was flooding, it was pretty certain this one would be, too. What could she be doing—

The answer came to him like the kick from an RPG launcher. And if he'd thought he was running as fast as he was capable of running, he found out he was wrong.

Chapter 16

Yancy was cold. Colder than she could remember ever being in her life before. The cold was all through her, deep inside and even in her bones. Her muscles were cramping, and her fingers had lost all feeling. But as cold as she was, what scared her more was that the thin little body in her arms felt even colder.

She'd managed to get the rope wrapped around herself and Sam with Laila sandwiched between them. Laila had her arms around Sam's neck in a stranglehold, and her face was buried against his chest, tucked under his beard. Sam's eyes were closed. She could feel them both breathing, but they had stopped shivering except for an occasional convulsive shudder.

She knew she didn't have the strength to pull them all to safety, and she didn't know how much longer she could hold on to the tree branch. If she let go of the branch, she wasn't sure she would be able to keep their heads above the churning water. Sam's pinto cow horse was keeping the rope pulled taut, but he was trained to keep a roped calf from struggling, not to pull people out of a flooding creek. Without someone to give him commands, he would undoubtedly keep doing what he was doing.

She had to do something. But what? Pray? She was pretty sure she was already doing that. What she needed was a miracle.

"Whoa, boy." Hunt laid a reassuring hand on the horse's sweat-soaked neck. He'd never been much of a cowboy himself, but he'd been to enough rodeos to know a well-trained roping horse when he saw one.

Farther down the creek he could see Yancy and Sam, with Laila between them, clinging to a half-drowned tree. Knowing they were safe for the moment, he took the time to kick out of his shoes and tuck his watch and phone inside them before stepping off the bank and into the swiftly moving current. When his feet could no longer brace against the pull of the water, he let it take him, following the rope line downstream.

"You came," Yancy said when he reached her. He got behind her and wrapped his arms around her. She laid her head back against his shoulder, but for only a moment, and he couldn't be sure, but it seemed to him she was laughing. "I...asked for—and you came."

"Shh—don't talk. Let's get you out of this. Can you keep your head above water?" She answered with a quick, emphatic nod. "Theirs, too?"

"Yeah. I just couldn't—"

"I know. Just keep everybody's head above water. I'm going to work us over to the bank."

She nodded. But he had to pry her cold fingers off the tree branch.

It was easier and took less time than he'd expected, but with the horse backing up, keeping the rope taut, in a matter of minutes they were all safely on the creek bank. Yancy was shivering violently in spite of the warm humid air. She got to her feet and reached for Laila, but the kid hung on to the old man's neck like a cocklebur. Hunt reeled the horse in and untied the blanket roll from the back of the saddle.

"Can you stand?" he asked Sam as he draped the blanket over his shoulders. The old man nodded, and Hunt pulled the blanket snugly around both him and Laila, then helped him to his feet. When he swayed, Hunt scooped the two of them up and lifted them onto the horse's back.

"They're both hypothermic," he said quietly to Yancy. "Probably in shock."

"We should call 911," she said through chattering teeth. "They should go to a hospital."

Hunt snorted. "There's no cell service down here. And if there was, there's flooding in that wash the road crosses. It would take a chopper to get through. I think if we get them back to the house, get them warmed up—"

"No need talkin' to me like I'm not here," came a cracking voice from on top of the horse. "The kid and me, we'll be just fine. This ain't the worst off I've been in my life, not by a long shot."

Yancy looked at Hunt, and for a moment it seemed as if she was going to laugh again. Then all at once her face crumpled. He pulled her against him and held her while her body shook with sobs. After a moment, he lowered his face to her wet hair and took slow deep breaths until the ache in his throat eased.

"We really have to get these guys back to the house," he said as he reluctantly peeled his arms from around her.

She nodded, and then she did laugh, just a little, as

she pulled away from him. "I think Sam's way ahead of us on that."

They both watched the pinto's tail swish as he ambled away across the meadow, with Sam sitting tall in the saddle, one arm around Laila, the other hand on the reins.

Hunt cleared his throat. "Talk later?"

She nodded. He put his arm around her shoulders and they walked together, following Sam's horse back to the barn.

Yancy was still in a daze an hour or so later—she'd lost all track of time. She was sitting on the patio, on the steps that led down to the pool deck, soaking up the afternoon's heat radiating from the flagstones. Even now a shiver would grip her from time to time. When it came, Hunt would tighten his arm around her and hold her close until it passed. He hadn't left her side since he'd pulled her out of the creek, even helping her out of her wet clothes and into a pair of sweatpants and pullover he'd managed to find somewhere. Sam and Laila had been similarly cared for by Josie and were now sitting in one of the patio chairs, Laila on Sam's lap, the two of them cocooned in a down comforter in spite of the summer heat. Laila seemed to have fallen asleep with her head resting on Sam's chest, while Josie, J.J., Rachel, Sage and Abby hovered nearby.

Yancy leaned her head against Hunt's shoulder and closed her eyes. She drew a long breath and felt his warmth and his scent come deep inside her. What a strange and wonderful feeling it was, to feel so much a part of someone. To feel so safe, so protected. So loved.

To think how near she'd come to throwing this away.

"Hunt," she whispered, "I'm so sorry." He didn't reply, and she felt his lips press against the top of her head.

Tears, never far from the surface now, filled her eyes again. "I'm an idiot."

"No. Well, maybe a little." She felt his chest move with a soft laugh that became an exhalation. "But you weren't wrong. Not about everything, anyway."

She pulled away so she could look at him, wiping tears from her cheeks. He reached for her hands and held them in both of his. His eyes closed briefly, then opened and burned into hers.

"But the thing is, I almost lost you today. You and Laila both. And I know one thing. Whatever else I do with my life from now on, the only thing I care about is that I want you in it. You and my daughter. And I'm willing to do whatever it takes to make that happen. If it means getting out of the military, getting a job somewhere—"

"Oh, Hunt." She smiled at him through her tears. "You would be miserable. You know you would."

He shook his head, and there was an endearingly stubborn set to his mouth. She laid a finger against his lips to stop the protest she knew was coming.

"I've been thinking about…well, us, too. And you were right—I haven't been happy stuck behind a desk. Quite frankly, I've been bored to death, not to mention I think I've been depressed. And I'm never depressed. And here's the thing. My parents weren't a stay-at-home domestic couple. They worked together, traveled all over the world on behalf of human rights."

"Yes," Hunt said quietly, "and they died together, didn't they? And I know that's left you with some scars."

"Yes. But I think the odds of something like that happening again are pretty slim, don't you?" She drew their clasped hands to her lips and held them there for a moment, fighting for control. She drew an unsteady breath and whispered, "But even if it did, I would rather die with you than live without—"

She couldn't finish. Hunt pulled her against him and wrapped his arms around her. "We'll figure something out," he said in a broken voice.

They were silent for several minutes. Then Hunt cleared his throat and rested his chin on her head. "You know," he said, in a voice that seemed to vibrate through her body, like the purr of a big cat, "my particular skill set, not to mention I have…ahem, some knowledge of the languages and customs of the part of the world where that outfit you work with—what's it called?"

"INCBRO." She sat up slowly, a buzz of excitement beginning deep inside her chest. "Yes. You do know it's working to stop the practice of child marriage. And you know so much about parts of the world where it's still practiced. Oh, Hunt. You would be incredibly valuable to INCBRO. Do you really think—"

"That we could work together? Yeah, I do. But what about—" He nodded toward the two people sitting a little ways off, still wrapped in the comforter.

Yancy felt her chest constrict, a small squeezing around her heart. "She's so angry with us right now," she whispered. "I think she must have heard us talking. She hasn't spoken to either of us since— Hunt, she won't even look at me."

He drew her back against him, crossed his arms over her chest and brought his cheek next to hers. "We'll talk to her—together." His voice was gruff and strangely thickened. "You know, I have a feeling she's going to forgive us." He laughed softly, then drew a breath. "No, I meant, what happens to Laila when we're off saving the world?"

As if she had heard her name mentioned, Laila stirred and stretched, then emerged from the comforter like a blossom unfolding. She looked around as if discovering for the first time where she was, then smiled and turned to snuggle against Sam once more.

"I think that's been taken care of," Yancy whispered.

They both watched as the little girl sat up, patted the old man's bearded cheek, then turned to the gathering of family members and announced, "Sam is okay now. He isn't going to die."

There was a ripple of laughter. Then Sam said in a voice both strong and fierce, "Damn right, I'm not—not until I've met my last granddaughter!"

Epilogue

Los Angeles, California

"Hello, Miranda. Do you like my present? It's beautiful, isn't it? I hope you like it. And the next one will be even better. Soon you're going to understand how much I love you. And when you do..."

Miranda dropped the phone and pressed shaking hands to her lips. *"No,"* she whispered. *"No, no, no, not again."*

A wave of sickness bent her double, and she gulped in great breaths to keep from throwing up. This couldn't go on. She had to do something.

The sickness passed and cold took its place. Cold resolve. She straightened and drew one more breath, this one to strengthen and sustain her. Then she reached for the letter she'd left lying on her bed. *"My Dear Miranda,"* it began.

"First off, my name is Sam Malone, though for some reason many have preferred to call me by the nickname Sierra, and I happen to be your grandfather."

There was another letter with that one. It was from a law firm. Her hands were steady as she picked up her phone and carefully thumbed in the firm's number.

* * * * *

Don't miss the previous books in the
SCANDALS OF SIERRA MALONE *series*
by Kathleen Creighton

THE SHERIFF'S WITNESS
THE PRETENDER

Available now from Harlequin Romantic Suspense!

ROMANTIC suspense

Available November 8, 2016

#1919 RUNAWAY COLTON
The Coltons of Texas • by Karen Whiddon
After Piper Colton is framed for her adoptive father's murder, she takes off in an effort to clear her name. Her brother sends bounty hunter Cord Maxwell after her. Their unexpected attraction leads them to strike a dangerous bargain that has them both walking a fine line between truth and deception.

#1920 OPERATION SOLDIER NEXT DOOR
Cutter's Code • by Justine Davis
Former soldier Tate McLaughlin just wants to be left alone and find peace, but Lacey Steele is detemined to bring him into the community fold. When a series of accidents escalates, Tate digs deep into forgotten memories of his time overseas to find the culprit and keep Lacey safe.

#1921 THE BODYGUARD'S BRIDE-TO-BE
Man on a Mission • by Amelia Autin
Tahra Edwards saved a schoolyard full of children from a bomb and lost all memory of the past eighteen months of her life—including Captain Marek Zale, who claims to be her fiancé. Now Marek must save Tahra from the ruthless terrorist organization that wants to silence her.

#1922 MORE THAN A LAWMAN
Honor Bound • by Anna J. Stewart
When she's targeted by a serial killer, Eden St. Claire turns to her brother's best friend, police detective Cole Delaney, for protection. Cole spent years fighting his feelings for Eden, and this time, with her life on the line and a ticking clock, he must convince Eden he wants far more than friendship.

REQUEST YOUR FREE BOOKS!
2 FREE NOVELS PLUS 2 FREE GIFTS!

ROMANTIC suspense

Sparked by danger, fueled by passion

YES! Please send me 2 FREE Harlequin® Romantic Suspense novels and my 2 FREE gifts (gifts are worth about $10). After receiving them, if I don't wish to receive any more books, I can return the shipping statement marked "cancel." If I don't cancel, I will receive 4 brand-new novels every month and be billed just $4.74 per book in the U.S. or $5.49 per book in Canada. That's a savings of at least 12% off the cover price! It's quite a bargain! Shipping and handling is just 50¢ per book in the U.S. and 75¢ per book in Canada.* I understand that accepting the 2 free books and gifts places me under no obligation to buy anything. I can always return a shipment and cancel at any time. Even if I never buy another book, the two free books and gifts are mine to keep forever.

240/340 HDN GH3P

Name   (PLEASE PRINT)

Address   Apt. #

City   State/Prov.   Zip/Postal Code

Signature (if under 18, a parent or guardian must sign)

Mail to the **Reader Service:**
IN U.S.A.: P.O. Box 1867, Buffalo, NY 14240-1867
IN CANADA: P.O. Box 609, Fort Erie, Ontario L2A 5X3

Want to try two free books from another line?
Call 1-800-873-8635 or visit www.ReaderService.com.

* Terms and prices subject to change without notice. Prices do not include applicable taxes. Sales tax applicable in N.Y. Canadian residents will be charged applicable taxes. Offer not valid in Quebec. This offer is limited to one order per household. Not valid for current subscribers to Harlequin Romantic Suspense books. All orders subject to credit approval. Credit or debit balances in a customer's account(s) may be offset by any other outstanding balance owed by or to the customer. Please allow 4 to 6 weeks for delivery. Offer available while quantities last.

Your Privacy—The Reader Service is committed to protecting your privacy. Our Privacy Policy is available online at www.ReaderService.com or upon request from the Reader Service.

We make a portion of our mailing list available to reputable third parties that offer products we believe may interest you. If you prefer that we not exchange your name with third parties, or if you wish to clarify or modify your communication preferences, please visit us at www.ReaderService.com/consumerschoice or write to us at Reader Service Preference Service, P.O. Box 9062, Buffalo, NY 14240-9062. Include your complete name and address.

Whatever Piper's intention, her words coaxed a reluctant
smile from him. "It's the truth," Cord insisted, merely
because he wanted to see what she'd do next. "I never lie."

"Never?"

"Never."

She circled him, keeping several feet between them.

"That must make life difficult for you sometimes."

Thoroughly entertained, he acknowledged her comment
with a nod.

"Do you like me?" No coquettishness in either her
voice or her expression, just simple curiosity.

"Yes. Actually, I'm beginning to," he amended, still
smiling. "Why do you want to know?"

She shrugged. "Just testing to see if you really won't
lie. Are you attracted to me?"

A jolt went through him. "Are you flirting?"

Though she colored, she didn't look away. "Maybe.
Maybe not. I'm trying to find out where we stand with
each other. I also noticed you didn't answer the question."

He laughed; he couldn't help it. "I'd have to be dead not to find you attractive," he told her. "But don't worry, I won't let it get in the way of the job I have to do. Or finding Renee. Both are too important to me."

Color still high, she finally smiled back. "Fair enough. Now how about we call it a night and regroup in the morning."

Though it was still early, he nodded. "Okay. Good night."

She sighed. "I'm probably going to regret this, but…"

Before he could ask what she meant, she crossed the space between them, grabbed him and pulled him down for a kiss. Her mouth moved across his, nothing tentative about it. A wave of lust swamped him. Damn if it wasn't the most erotic kiss he'd ever shared.

Standing stock-still, he let her nibble and explore, until he couldn't take it any longer. Finally, he seized control, needing to claim her. He tasted her, skimmed his fingers over her soft, soft skin, outlining her lush curves. He couldn't get enough, craving more, breathing her in until the force of his arousal told him he needed to break it off right now or they'd be in trouble.

He'd be in trouble, he amended silently. Despite the fact that he physically shook with desire, he stepped back, trying to slow his heartbeat and the way he inhaled short gasps of air. Drowning—that's what this had been like. Drowning in her.

Don't miss
RUNAWAY COLTON by Karen Whiddon,
available November 2016 wherever
Harlequin® Romantic Suspense
books and ebooks are sold.

www.Harlequin.com

Turn your love of reading into rewards you'll love with
Harlequin My Rewards

THE WORLD IS BETTER WITH *Romance*

Harlequin has everything from contemporary, passionate and heartwarming to suspenseful and inspirational stories.

Whatever your mood,
we have a romance just for you!

Connect with us to find your next great read,
special offers and more.

f /HarlequinBooks

🐦 @HarlequinBooks

www.HarlequinBlog.com

www.Harlequin.com/Newsletters

H HARLEQUIN®

A *Romance* FOR EVERY MOOD™

www.Harlequin.com

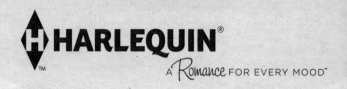
HARLEQUIN®

A Romance FOR EVERY MOOD™

Love the Harlequin book you just read?

Your opinion matters.

Review this book on your favorite book site, review site, blog or your own social media properties and share your opinion with other readers!

Be sure to connect with us at:
Harlequin.com/Newsletters
Facebook.com/HarlequinBooks
Twitter.com/HarlequinBooks